MDC CS

DISCARD

RALPH COMPTON:
THE BLOODY TRAIL

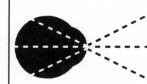

This Large Print Book carries the
Seal of Approval of N.A.V.H.

RALPH COMPTON: THE BLOODY TRAIL

A RALPH COMPTON NOVEL

MARCUS GALLOWAY

THORNDIKE PRESS

A part of Gale, Cengage Learning

GALE
CENGAGE Learning™

Detroit • New York • San Francisco • New Haven, Conn • Waterville, Maine • London

GALE
CENGAGE Learning™

Thorndike Press® Large Print Western.
The text of this Large Print edition is unabridged.
Other aspects of the book may vary from the original edition.
Set in 16 pt. Plantin.
Printed on permanent paper.

LIBRARY OF CONGRESS CATALOGING-IN-PUBLICATION DATA

Galloway, Marcus.
   The bloody trail : a Ralph Compton novel / by Marcus
Galloway.
    p. cm.
   At head of title: Ralph Compton.
   ISBN-13: 978-1-4104-0531-9 (alk. paper)
   ISBN-10: 1-4104-0531-1 (alk. paper)
   1. Wagon trains — Fiction. 2. Bounty hunters — Fiction. 3.
Fugitives from justice — Fiction. 4. Large type books. I.
Compton, Ralph. II. Title. III. Title: Ralph Compton, The bloody
trail.
PS3607.A4196B57 2008
813'.6—dc22   2007046701

Published in 2008 by arrangement with NAL Signet, a member of
Penguin Group (USA) Inc.

THE IMMORTAL COWBOY

This is respectfully dedicated to the "American Cowboy." His was the saga sparked by the turmoil that followed the Civil War, and the passing of more than a century has by no means diminished the flame.

True, the old days and the old ways are but treasured memories, and the old trails have grown dim with the ravages of time, but the spirit of the cowboy lives on.

In my travels — to Texas, Oklahoma, Kansas, Nebraska, Colorado, Wyoming, New Mexico, and Arizona — I always find something that reminds me of the Old West. While I am walking these plains and mountains for the first time, there is this feeling that a part of me is eternal, that I have known these old trails before. I believe it is the undying spirit of the frontier calling, allowing me, through the mind's eye, to step back into time. What is the appeal of the Old West of the American frontier?

It has been epitomized by some as the dark and bloody period in American history. Its heroes — Crockett, Bowie, Hickok, Earp — have been reviled and criticized. Yet the Old West lives on, larger than life.

It has become a symbol of freedom, when there was always another mountain to climb and another river to cross; when a dispute between two men was settled not with expensive lawyers, but with fists, knives, or guns. Barbaric? Maybe. But some things never change. When the cowboy rode into the pages of American history, he left behind a legacy that lives within the hearts of us all.

— Ralph Compton

CHAPTER 1

Martha's Ferry, Wyoming 1878

When Jeremiah Correy stepped up to the bank of the Sweetwater River, it was his first step onto a trail of blood that led straight into a storm of lead. But, like any other deer caught in a hunter's sights, Jeremiah didn't know about the approaching storm, so he smiled and enjoyed his last bit of clear sky.

The pier in Martha's Ferry wasn't much to look at, but it served its function well enough. Warped wooden planks were stacked two and three high in places after holes were patched up or breaks were repaired along the four feet it extended into the Sweetwater River. As water lapped against these planks, it thumped against the empty barrels underneath the pier that kept sections of it from going under. As Jeremiah stepped onto the pier, he felt the boards creak and bend under his boots.

Jeremiah stood just over six feet tall. His

lean frame was solid, with a slight hint of a paunch around his midsection. The black hair under his hat had been freshly cut, but the stubble on his face was growing out. Thick, callused hands hung at his sides and friendly eyes glanced down at the pier before looking around at the few other people that were nearby.

None of the faces were familiar to Jeremiah and only one of them acknowledged him with an open-mouthed scowl.

"You mind steppin' aside?" the scowling man asked.

Jeremiah grinned and took half a step to the side, which brought him within an inch of slipping into the river. "Both of us probably shouldn't be on this," he said with a chuckle. "It feels like it's gonna give us a bath any second."

The other man wasn't amused. "Pier's been here more'n twelve years. It ain't goin' nowhere."

Although Jeremiah thought of ways to pass off his comment as a joke, he gave up on winning the other man over. Instead, he simply nodded and walked back onto dry land. From there, Jeremiah could see where a few posts had been sunk into the ground, but could also find plenty of cracks in that weathered lumber.

"You waitin' for the three o'clock?"

Jumping at the sound of the other voice, Jeremiah straightened up and turned to look over his shoulder. "Yes, I am. Is the boat still meant to arrive at three?"

"That's why it's called the three o'clock," replied a squat man with enough thick layers of muscle under his skin to make him look like a tree trunk. "Wait over there with the rest."

"Oh. Sure. Sorry about the . . ."

But the squat man was already moving along. He carried a barrel on one shoulder and had a few lengths of rope looped around his arm. Walking along that short length of rickety planks, he and the scowling man transferred enough crates, barrels and sacks to fill up the entire right side of the pier as well as a good portion of the nearby bank. Now that Jeremiah was no longer in their way, those two men continued moving past one another like ants building an impossibly tall pile of dirt.

Jeremiah stood with his arms crossed while rocking on his heels. There was space on the bench behind him, but he was the only one who seemed unwilling to settle down. The others around him were content to remain in the spots they'd chosen and tend to their own affairs.

One pretty woman in her twenties fussed with a young boy's shirt collar while he told her why there were so many birds in the trees.

A preacher in his fifties sat perched upon the bench and stared quietly out at the water.

A man wearing a dented beaver hat leaned back with his legs stretched out in front of him. Only now did Jeremiah realize that this man was watching him from beneath the dark shadow created by the brim of his hat.

"You a rancher?" the man in the beaver hat asked.

Jeremiah looked around to make sure there was nobody else around him. Smiling affably now that he knew he was the target of that question, Jeremiah replied, "That's right. Do I know you?"

The man in the beaver hat remained stretched out as if he were taking in the sunset from his front porch. His arms were crossed over his chest, holding a worn jacket closed around him. A few beads of sweat rolled down his face, but that was to be expected on a warm spring day. In response to Jeremiah's question, the man only shook his head.

"Then I guess I must have seen you around town," Jeremiah said while hooking his thumb back toward the trail that led into the little town of Martha's Ferry.

The man in the beaver hat shook his head once again. "Nope. You just look like you're about to jump out of your skin since you can't take charge of what's going on. You're not wearing a badge and you're not long enough in the tooth to be a land or cattle baron, so that leaves rancher."

"That leaves a lot of things, I'd suspect," Jeremiah said.

"Perhaps, but you dress like you used to be a cowboy. That narrows the field down a bit more."

Jeremiah looked down at the clothes he was wearing. There weren't any holes in his pants, his boots were well maintained and his shirt was clean. He even wore the pocket watch his wife had given him with a new chain crossing his belly.

The man in the beaver hat chuckled to himself and shifted his eyes back toward the river. "No offense meant, mister. I was only saying."

"Saying what?"

"That you looked like a rancher."

Shrugging, Jeremiah stepped forward and extended his hand. "The name's Jeremiah Correy. What's yours?"

The man in the beaver hat glanced up at

Jeremiah and then down at the hand that was being stretched out toward him. For a moment, it seemed as if he were about to take hold of that hand and pull it clean off. Instead, he shook it in a quick, firm grasp. "Emmett Blaylock," was all he said.

"Waiting for the boat, Emmett?"

"I'd say all of us are."

Looking at the others sitting on the bench, Jeremiah nodded. When he realized that none of them were so much as looking in his direction, he said, "I suppose so. Did you book passage or are you waiting for cargo?"

"Why would you want to know?" Emmett asked in a tone that wasn't exactly menacing, but held the possibility that it might head that way.

"Just making conversation. Since I'm not allowed to oversee those workers, I've got to find some way to pass the time."

When Emmett laughed, it cracked the seriousness that had settled into his features. It was an easy laugh that seemed all the more genuine since it didn't thunder outward for everyone to hear. "I'm hoping to get a ride downriver."

"Hoping?"

"Yeah. I was supposed to meet up with this raft a few days east of here, but got held up. I just hope they still have room for me."

"And I just hope this is bigger than a raft," Jeremiah said. "The supplies I ordered should take up a lot of room."

Folding his hands behind his head, Emmett looked back toward the water and said, "That means there should be room for me after they unload."

Jeremiah felt uncomfortable standing still and it showed. The more he fidgeted, the more Emmett seemed like a statue in comparison. In fact, Emmett had picked a point along the river and was staring at it now that he'd gotten comfortable on the bench. Jeremiah, on the other hand, was already tired of looking at the water and had gone back to watching the men pile crates upon the pier.

"I'm pulling together an expedition," Jeremiah said proudly.

Emmett didn't take his eyes from the river. "That so?"

"Yes, sir. I'm packing up and headed into Oregon."

"That's passing for an expedition, huh? I was thinking you might be bound for Canada or California at the least."

"Why's that?" Jeremiah asked.

Emmett shrugged. "Sounds more worthy of being called an expedition."

"Look, Ma!" shouted the little boy who'd been enduring his mother's fussing. "The boat's coming!"

Jeremiah took his eyes away from the workers and looked in the direction the boy was pointing. It was also the direction that Emmett had been staring the entire time.

Less than a hundred yards away, a boat rounded a bend along a particularly narrow stretch of the Sweetwater River. It was about twice as long as it was wide and resembled a large raft with a shack toward the back of it. An engine chugged loudly to turn a short, wide paddle wheel while sending gouts of smoke into the air. The boat moved at a slow, steady pace down the middle of the river as several men scurried on the deck.

The boy on the shore was jumping around excitedly. "Are we going on that, Ma?" he asked. "Are we?"

"Yes, sweetie," the young woman said. "We are." Only now did she look around to acknowledge any of the others sitting around her. "We're heading to see my parents, and he's so excited."

The preacher put on an unconvincing smile, which Emmett mimicked perfectly. Since she didn't look at the others for more than a second, the young woman looked

14

back to her precious child and smoothed out his hair.

"This is gonna be a hell of a long trip," Emmett muttered.

Jeremiah looked at the woman and caught her shooting Emmett a scolding glare. "Here, now," Jeremiah said to the closest worker as he put the bench behind him and walked to the pier. "Let me give you a hand so we can be done faster."

"Go on back and take a seat," the squat worker told him. "Looks like we're gonna have all the help we need."

Stopping with his heels in the mud and his toes on the pier, Jeremiah squinted at the approaching boat. Sure enough, there were three other men standing on the deck. All of the workers on the boat wore blue scarves tied around their necks.

As the boat drew closer to the pier, the three men standing on the deck locked eyes with Jeremiah. They weren't wearing scarves.

Glancing around to be certain he was the one in those men's sights, Jeremiah saw that nobody else around him seemed to be concerned. On the contrary, the folks at the bench were getting excited at the prospect of boarding the craft and the workers were anxiously preparing to receive the vessel.

Since he didn't have much experience with boats, Jeremiah had to assume that things were moving along normally. By the time the side of the boat bumped against the pier, the workers were already tossing ropes. Two of the boat's crew caught the ropes and pulled the boat even tighter against the pier so they could start tying it off. Now that the boat was docked, Jeremiah realized the craft wasn't nearly as big as he'd been picturing it in his head. In fact, it barely seemed big enough to carry the things he'd ordered. After fishing the list of items he'd been expecting from his pocket, he got ready to check them off as they were unloaded.

"Where the hell is he?" asked a voice from the boat.

Jeremiah looked up from the crumpled piece of paper and immediately spotted two of the three men who'd been staring at him from the deck.

The man who'd spoken was short and had a muscular frame. Behind him stood another fellow whose face was twisted into a nasty snarl. Upon a second glance, Jeremiah saw that gnarled expression came from the fact that the man's right eye socket was covered by a thick mass of leathery, scarred flesh.

The shorter man was talking to one of the fellows wearing a blue scarf. They conversed for a few seconds before the worker waved his hand toward the shore where Jeremiah was standing.

Once the shorter man and the one-eyed fellow jumped off the boat, the workers got busy loading and unloading cargo.

Suddenly, all of the mystery of watching the boat's arrival faded away. Jeremiah was left standing in the sights of those two men with his back to an open stretch of land.

But the boat was quickly pushed from Jeremiah's mind as the third man who had stared at him from the deck stepped onto the pier. His bald scalp caught the sunlight and a dark beard covered most of his face. Narrowed eyes bored straight through to the back of Jeremiah's head.

Until now, Jeremiah had forgotten about the old Navy model Colt at his side. The pistol was used mostly for target practice. Other than that, there was the occasional wild animal or wounded horse that needed to be put out of its misery. At the moment, Jeremiah wondered if he even had the strength to pull the gun from its stiff leather holster.

"What the hell you think you're doing?" the shorter of the three men asked.

Jeremiah stepped back, but didn't take his eyes from the trio. His mind raced for a response to the man's question, but his mouth had already refused to do much more than suck in a few shallow breaths.

All three of the other men let their hands drift to the holsters strapped at their waists.

When he saw that, Jeremiah felt his heart slam against the inside of his ribs and his arm twitch toward the grip of his Colt in what he quickly realized was the worst possible move for him to make.

CHAPTER 2

All three of the gunmen walking off the pier cleared leather before Jeremiah could even pray to lift his gun from its holster. But no matter how much he wished he hadn't even reached for the weapon, it was too late for Jeremiah to do anything but follow through. The workers scattered as soon as they got a look at the guns in the three men's hands.

When he heard the first shot, Jeremiah felt every muscle in his body clench in expectation of being hit. His arm still moved of its own accord and lifted the old Colt up so he could tighten his finger around its trigger.

Another shot cut through the air, sending a loud ringing through Jeremiah's ears.

The scent of burned gunpowder drifted through his nose as he caught sight of those three gunmen moving forward.

So far, Jeremiah was still on his feet. That much, alone, was enough to make him wonder what kind of miracle was protecting him.

"Get down!" another man shouted into Jeremiah's ear.

When he turned toward that voice, Jeremiah wasn't quick enough to see who'd spoken before a rough hand took hold of his shoulder and shoved him to one side. Jeremiah staggered and started to fall over, but managed to catch himself with one outstretched hand.

Jeremiah looked up to see Emmett standing beside him with a gun filling one hand. Emmett's coat flapped open to reveal the holster that had been previously hidden from view.

The three men fired their guns as they fanned out at the base of the pier. The bald man dropped to one knee and sighted along his pistol barrel while the other two pulled their triggers at will. The shorter one took one step forward and fired while gritting his teeth and letting out a curse that was swallowed up amid the thunder of his weapon.

A bullet tore through the flap of Emmett's coat, causing him to step back with one foot so his body was lined up sideways to the other three men. From that position, Emmett fired a round that caught the shorter man in the chest.

Letting out a pained howl, the short man stumbled backward toward the river. Another round from Emmett's pistol sent him into the water as an inky cloud spread out from his wounds.

Emmett was sighting his target when a gunshot to his immediate right brought him spinning around on the balls of his feet.

The pistol in Jeremiah's hand was still smoking. Blinking quickly, Jeremiah watched as both of the gunmen along the riverbank ran away from the pier. "Did I hit one of them?" he asked.

"No, but you sent them running," Emmett replied as he reached down to offer a hand to Jeremiah.

Accepting the hand as well as some help to his feet, Jeremiah got his legs under him and let out a wheezing breath. "That's good."

"Not hardly."

As soon as he saw where those other two gunmen were headed, Jeremiah realized why Emmett hadn't been so optimistic.

The folks seated at the bench had been rattled at the sudden burst of gunshots, but had nowhere to run. Now that the bald gunman and his one-eyed partner were headed their way, the young woman and her son ran toward the river while the preacher froze in his spot.

As the bald man ran around the bench, the one-eyed gunman reached out for the preacher with his free hand.

Emmett aimed and tightened his finger around his trigger. Just as the hammer of his pistol was about to fall, Emmett shifted his aim. The one-eyed man in his sights had not only gotten a hold of the preacher, but was reeling him in like a bass at the end of a fishing line.

The gun in Emmett's palm barked once.

The one-eyed man snapped his head back and hopped away from the preacher as hot lead burned through the top of his shoulder. Blood sprayed from the messy wound, quickly causing him to forget about his prisoner.

Like a deer that had finally come to its senses after being surprised by a hunter, the preacher bolted away from the gunman as quickly as his legs would carry him.

Jeremiah swallowed hard and turned toward a movement he'd caught from the corner of his eye. Seeing the bald gunman trying to get a clear shot from that side, Jeremiah raised his Colt and pulled the trigger. He shut his eyes as the hammer dropped so he couldn't see much of anything. The rest of his senses weren't worth much either since his ears were filled with thunder and his nose was filled with the biting scent of acrid smoke.

When he forced his eyes open once again, Jeremiah saw the bald man running away.

Emmett fired at the bald gunman, but was rushed and his shot hissed through the air well over the man's head. By the time he shifted to put the one-eyed man back in his sights, Emmett was just about to squeeze off a quick shot when a gruff voice roared from the direction of the pier.

"That's enough of this!" the man announced before following up with a deafening shotgun blast.

Jeremiah hunkered down and tried not to panic. Only after he felt both of his hands pressed tightly against his ears did Jeremiah realize that he'd dropped the Colt.

The man who'd fired off the shotgun was a barrel-chested fellow wearing a blue scarf around his neck. He stormed onto the pier without taking his eyes from the men onshore. "Damned thieves!" he bellowed. "You ain't about to touch none of this cargo nor any of these passengers!"

The bald gunman, now returning from his retreat, locked eyes with Jeremiah before motioning toward his one-eyed partner. "Next move is yours," he said.

Jeremiah held up his empty hands as his tongue fumbled to come up with a reply. Thankfully, the man with the shotgun was more than happy to break the momentary silence.

"I told you to move on! Do it or I'll blast your head off your shoulders."

The gunmen holstered their pistols and raised their hands high.

"Now get the hell out of my sight," the man with the shotgun said. "I see either of you again and I'll send you to hell."

Looking down for his Colt, Jeremiah only found dusty ground at his feet.

"Here you go," Emmett said as he handed over the old pistol. "Best not to drop this again."

After taking his pistol back, Jeremiah looked for the gunmen. Between the workers that were now swarming from the pier and the others who'd been in the area, he couldn't see much of anything through all the chaos. Jeremiah spotted the preacher and finally let out a relieved breath when he also found the young mother and her little boy. By the looks of it, they were all alive and well.

The only gunman to be seen was the one lying half in and half out of the river.

The worker who'd shooed Jeremiah away

a little while ago now walked up to him and asked, "Do you know those men? Why were they shooting at you?"

"I . . . I don't know who they were," Jeremiah replied. "But didn't someone mention thieves?"

"Hell yes, I mentioned thieves," the man with the shotgun said as he stomped forward while cradling his weapon like a baby. "They boarded two stops before this one and I had my eye on 'em the whole time. I knew they weren't no good. You'd be the man here to pick up all this equipment?"

"I'm here for these things," Jeremiah said as he handed over the folded paper he'd already read over several dozen times.

The captain took the list in his free hand and nodded while glancing it over. "That's you, all right. You came here to pick up almost all the cargo I'm carrying and you only bring one man to watch your back?"

"Actually, I didn't bring anyone. I didn't think there would be a problem. It's just traveling supplies," Jeremiah said. "Nothing too valuable."

Laughing under his breath, the captain looked behind him at the workers gathered on the pier. "You must be the preacher we're set to pick up, mister. No other man I know would have so much faith in the kindness of others. I've seen thieves gut a man for the boots on his feet. Did you bring enough cash to pay for all these here supplies?"

Jeremiah might have been ready to shake the captain's hand before, but he sure didn't like the way the barrel-chested man was sizing him up now. "Yes, I did," he said.

"Then hand it over. Since you're on your own, my men can help load up whatever wagons you got. There'll be an extra fee, though."

"No need to charge extra," Emmett added while stepping up to Jeremiah's side. "This man isn't on his own."

Squinting at Emmett while handing the list back to Jeremiah, the captain said, "He just said he didn't bring anyone."

"He didn't bring me. I met him here. Besides, that's not any business of yours, now, is it?"

"I suppose not." Shaking his head as if to rid himself of the entire matter, the captain turned his back on both Jeremiah and Emmett so he could address the folks huddled near the bench. "Any of you waiting to come aboard needs to show me your papers. And I won't allow any weapons on board, neither. After this fracas, you can leave whatever firearms you may be carrying with me and I'll see you get 'em back when we drop you off."

The young woman waited for the preacher to start moving before she rushed ahead of him. Before she even reached the captain, she was explaining the special needs she and her son would require. Jeremiah walked over to the supplies stacked near the pier, and Emmett was more than happy to follow him.

"Are you all right?" Emmett asked. "You look rattled."

"Wouldn't you be? Those men were shooting at me. They shot at both of us!"

"It wasn't anything personal. They probably just wanted to come after whoever showed up to pick up those supplies."

"But why, for Christ's sake? It's nothing but food and gear for my expedition. Is there a sudden demand for tarps, bedrolls and wagon parts that men are willing to kill for them?"

Emmett watched Jeremiah without much of an expression on his face. He did grin a bit, however, when he asked, "Did you manage to get these things shipped for free?"

With his heart only now starting to slow to a normal rhythm in his chest, Jeremiah wiped the sweat from his brow and said, "No."

"And did you pay for all of these supplies

in advance?"

"No," Jeremiah said. "I brought the rest . . ." Faltering a bit as he patted the folded bunch of money in his pocket, he suddenly felt like the biggest, most oblivious fool west of the Mississippi. "I brought the rest with me," he finally muttered.

"You just need to think like a thief," Emmett said while tapping his forehead. "That's all. And you should try doing that before walking around with so much money in your pockets. I would've thought a rancher would know better than that."

"I do know better. That's why I feel like such an idiot right around now."

"I don't suppose you were also planning on carrying this stuff back to your house?" Emmett asked.

"No, but shouldn't you be getting onto that boat?"

Emmett glanced over his shoulder at the captain. The barrel-chested man stood at the base of the pier, overseeing the workers stomping on and off his boat while also talking to the passengers one at a time. When he turned back around to face Jeremiah, Emmett was shaking his head. "I'll catch another boat or maybe even a stagecoach. I don't trust those men and I don't want to hear what they tell the law when they show up to look into this shooting."

"That's one less worry you should have," Jeremiah said. "The closest lawman's got an office two towns away."

Jeremiah looked back at the pier and saw the workers moving back and forth between the boat and the growing pile of supplies he'd ordered on the shore. None of the men were particularly threatening, but none of them seemed to be put off by the shots that had been fired not too long ago.

"I hope those passengers aren't in any trouble," Jeremiah said.

"That captain's robbing them enough by charging them to ride on that heap," Emmett replied. "He doesn't strike me as the sort who'd go much further than that. I don't suppose you'd need a little help? I'd be willing to put in a day's work in return for enough to pay for a hot meal and a bunk for the night."

"Come on," Jeremiah said as he walked to the spot where he'd left his wagon. "Seeing as how you stood up for me back there, I might be able to accommodate you."

CHAPTER 3

Once the pier and boat were behind him, Jeremiah felt like he was stepping back into the world he knew. The supplies were loaded onto his wagon and had to be tied down since some of the crates were a bit larger than he'd expected. After cinching the last knot that tied down the tarp covering the back of the wagon, Emmett rode alongside it so he could keep an eye on the unwieldy load.

Jeremiah snapped his reins and made the clucking sounds with his tongue that seemed to catch his lead horse's attention more than anything else. Once the spotted gelding got moving, the other two horses pulling the wagon put their backs into their task as well. The wagon lurched and groaned a bit, but got rolling without too much fuss.

Glancing back toward the pier, Jeremiah shook his head and laughed quietly to himself.

"It's a damn shame," Emmett said.

"Pardon me?"

"The law. It's a damn shame there's no law coming around to see what all the shooting was about. That one fella is still in the water."

"There's usually not much trouble around here," Jeremiah said. "Most of the workers and sailors can handle themselves."

"I guess you're right about that," Emmett said. "That captain looked like he was about to clean those other two out as well."

Jeremiah nodded. "Which is probably why they ran out of there with their tails tucked between their legs."

As the wagon rolled along the trail leading away from the river, Jeremiah closed his eyes and pulled in a deep breath. It was good to fill his lungs with the scents of wet grass, river water and bur oak trees instead of the smoke that had filled his lungs during the day's excitement. Even the smell of the horses in front of him and the mud below were welcome additions.

"By the way," Jeremiah said as he leaned forward to rest his elbows upon his knees. "I never did thank you for helping me back there."

"You're thanking me with room and board, remember?"

"Of course, but . . . thanks all the same."

Emmett looked over at him without saying anything for a few seconds. It almost seemed as if he was waiting for Jeremiah to take back what he'd just said. When the words were allowed to stand, Emmett nodded and shifted his eyes back toward the mound of supplies stacked in the wagon behind Jeremiah. "Don't mention it."

"You're pretty good with that pistol."

Now Emmett laughed. "I am when compared to you. Why do you even bother lugging that old piece of scrap around with you?"

"Not every man who owns a gun can draw like lightning. You handled yourself better than most anyone I've ever seen in a situation like that," Jeremiah said.

"And how many times have you been in a situation like that?"

Rather than bend Emmett even further out of shape, Jeremiah conceded the point willingly. "Fine, fine. You've got my thanks and I'll leave it at that."

The road under the wagon's wheels wasn't much more than a set of ruts in some smoothed-out dirt. They led into Martha's Ferry, but Jeremiah didn't even stop to take a gander at the little town that earned most of its money from the nearby pier. Instead, he pointed his lead horse's nose to the south and kept on going.

Outside of town, the road became rougher. Every now and then, Emmett reached out to tighten one of the ropes holding the supplies on the wagon or to push a crate back into its place. "Are you headed out west to see the ocean?" he asked.

Upon hearing that, Jeremiah immediately perked up. "Not as such. I'm really not even one to get his feet wet unless I'm washing them. That's why I was sent to meet that boat instead of one of my men. My wife says I should stay home if I'm not inclined to cross a river when we come to it."

"Surely you've been on trail drives and such," Emmett pointed out.

"Ever since I was old enough to ride a horse. On one drive when I was eleven, I nearly drowned while helping rope in a stray who'd wandered into some deep water. The year after that, my brother died in a flood."

"I guess nobody could fault you for not liking water."

Jeremiah shrugged and let his eyes fix upon a point in front of him. He didn't focus on the ruts in the dirt ahead, or even on the backs of the horses pulling his wagon. Instead, he simply took in the world around him. Blinking a few times, Jeremiah straightened up and asked, "So where did you say you were headed?"

"I hope to end up in California. San Francisco maybe."

"I hear that's one hell of a town."

"I've heard the same. For now, I'd just like to work my way there however I can."

"There's plenty of room on my expedition," Jeremiah said. "Or westerly ride or whatever you'd like to call it."

Emmett grinned and pulled back on his reins so the wagon could roll ahead of him. He looked over all the knots holding the tarp in place and made certain nothing was about to fall from the back of the wagon. While steering his horse around the back of the wagon, he gave his reins a snap so he could approach Jeremiah from the other side. "I might just have to think about that," he said.

"I wish you would. My wife's been on me about hiring some protection to accompany us, but I didn't really know where to begin looking. The only thing I could think of was to post a notice or two in the spots where I usually look for ranch hands."

"You must have plenty of them working for you," Emmett said. "Aren't any of them good with a firearm?"

"There's a few hunters among them, but

that's about it."

"That's all you'd need."

Jeremiah nodded slowly, but frowned as he said, "Sure, but it doesn't matter much since they won't be coming along anyways. I offered to bring them to Oregon where they'd have jobs waiting for them, but they took on work at another ranch instead."

Emmett shook his head. "That's a shame."

"Can't say as I blame them. Beats the hell out of making a long ride and breaking their backs to build up a place before any money can come in. Hiring men in Oregon to be there when we arrive is all I got left, but most of them might not even show up."

"Sounds like a headache all around. Why even pack up and start fresh when you've got a place up and running already?"

A peculiar smile drifted onto Jeremiah's face just then. It made him look as if he was daydreaming while his eyes were still open. Even as he looked at the trees around him and the open sky above, it was plain to see that he wasn't really seeing those things. "You ever been to Oregon?"

Emmett shook his head. "Not yet."

"If you have, you wouldn't need to ask that question. The air just smells cleaner out there. Not as stale as it does here."

Pulling in a deep breath, Emmett held it

in his lungs and let it out through his nose. "Air smells just fine to me."

"Then perhaps it's just me. I've lived here all my life and that's good for some folks, but it's time to move along. I've taken on a partner who runs an outfit in Oregon and I've visited him twice as many times as I had reason to. Every time, I swear to the Lord above, I would have stayed if my wife wasn't waiting for me here."

"That good, huh?"

"Better."

As Jeremiah tried to come up with a way to describe what he was seeing in his mind, he closed his eyes and pictured it. The smile on his face grew wider and he opened his eyes to steer along the turn he knew to be coming up on the trail. Just the fact that he knew that turn was coming was enough to put a dent in the smile he wore.

"Sounds like you just got an itch to move," Emmett said.

"You'd understand if you saw for yourself."

"I know what it's like to want to get to any place that ain't where you are."

Wincing at the sound of that, Jeremiah felt something vaguely like what he'd felt when one of those gunmen's bullets had come a little too close to drawing his blood.

"We could have waited to hire on more men. We could have waited to save up more money. Fact is, there's always a reason to stay put. There's folks who traveled all the way to California from Nebraska and they didn't hire guards to protect them. They protected themselves, stuck together and moved along. The trail between here and Oregon is a lot shorter than that, so we can manage.

"I was worried that my wife wouldn't go, but she doesn't seem to mind," he said.

"If she did, she wouldn't go," Emmett replied simply. "No matter what they say or what reasons they give, folks do what they want to do. Duty and commitments of any sort boil down to that. Folks follow because they want to follow, lead because they want to lead, do what they want to do."

"Sounds like you've put a lot of thought into this sort of thing," Jeremiah said.

Emmett shrugged and stared at the trail ahead. "I've had plenty of time on my hands."

As the quiet settled in around him, Jeremiah heard the echoes of those gunshots rolling around in the back of his mind. It wasn't the first time he'd seen men trade shots with each other, but it was one of the only times he'd been on the receiving end of those shots. All things considered, he knew it could have turned out a lot worse.

They rode throughout the rest of that day and into the dusk. Once the sunlight had all but faded away, Emmett looked over to Jeremiah and asked, "You think we should get to your ranch before it gets too dark?"

"Sure," Jeremiah replied. "If I wasn't loaded down and if we'd both been running at a gallop since leaving Martha's Ferry, we might have gotten home before midnight."

"So we're camping, then?"

"If you'd rather have a bed under you, there's a town not too much farther along this trail. I'll warn you, though. It makes Martha's Ferry look like Cheyenne in comparison."

"You said there's a hotel there?" Emmett asked.

"A run-down one, but yes."

"Good enough for me."

Jeremiah let out a haggard breath as he tried to figure how much farther along the town was. After getting his bearings, he realized they should catch sight of the place after cresting the rise that was less than half a mile in front of them. "It's still a ways off," he said. "You sure you wouldn't rather —"

"If it's too far, we can just stop at that

settlement up ahead," Emmett cut in. "I'd guess it's only a mile or so away."

"You knew where it was the whole time?"

Emmett grinned and shook his head. "And here I thought you were an honest sort. I agree to do some work for you and you're already trying to work my fingers to the bone without hope of getting a good night's sleep."

"And you acted like you didn't already have this route planned."

"I didn't," Emmett replied. "I can just see smoke rising up ahead that looks like it came from chimneys rather than Injun signals."

Jeremiah squinted into the distance where Emmett was nodding. The sky was smeared with a dark purple, which made it just light enough to see a few clouds. Sure enough, there was also the faint hint of smoke trails leading toward the horizon. When he looked back to Emmett, he found the other man sitting smugly in his saddle.

"A man that don't have a wife tends to find plenty of other ways to sniff out a hot meal," Emmett said.

As much as he wanted to keep moving, Jeremiah resigned himself to getting to the town up ahead and stopping for the night. Even the prospect of a warm bed and a hot meal wasn't enough to ease his mind as the faces of those gunmen were pulled right back up from where he'd tried to tuck them away.

CHAPTER 4

When Jeremiah first rode into the town, he thought it might be abandoned. Emmett didn't bat an eye and rode right up to the largest of the town's five buildings.

"Looks like the hotel to me," Emmett said while pointing toward a broken sign that read HO EL. "Think you can find a place to put the horses up for the night?"

Suddenly, Jeremiah felt inspired. "Wait a second," he said. "We shouldn't stop here."

"Why not?"

"Because someone's already tried to rob me of my supplies. I need to get these back to my ranch or at least to somewhere I can keep an eye on them."

"Nobody tried to steal those supplies," Emmett said. "They wanted your money and that's already spent. If you'd prefer to sleep with the horses, that's fine. I'm staying in here. Whichever you chose, I'll meet you down here in the morning." And, without waiting for a reply from Jeremiah, Emmett climbed down from his saddle, hitched his horse to a post and walked into the hotel.

Despite the heat that had been in the air during the day, the night was turning positively chilly. As more and more of the sunlight had faded, the cold seeped into the air like pond water leaking through a drowning man's clothes. But Jeremiah wasn't concerned with the heat or the cold. He was anxious to get a few hours of sleep and knew he'd get plenty of hot meals once he was home.

Snapping his reins, Jeremiah drove the wagon through the little town and pulled it to a stop just outside its limits. It took more time for him to put a small fire together and when he was done, his eager smile had returned.

By the time the horses were unhitched from the wagon and tied to a nearby tree, Jeremiah wasn't even thinking about sleeping. In fact, he wondered if he might have been able to make the rest of the ride without stopping at all. Staring toward the southwest and into the inky blackness that swallowed up the hills he knew were ahead, Jeremiah grudgingly admitted that stopping was the proper thing to do. He couldn't even make out the ruts in the ground, and that could make the difference between riding toward home and riding toward the edge of a ravine.

Jeremiah rubbed his hands over the crackling flames of his campfire. No matter how good some hot coffee would have tasted, that would entail digging under the tarp that was tied down tightly over the wagon. Rather than try to dig through all those supplies, Jeremiah crossed his arms and leaned back against an old, dusty rock.

In the space of a few seconds, his eyes were wandering among the stars overhead. There were too many of them for Jeremiah to think of them as separate things. Smarter men than he had taken time to name the stars or tried to count them. His father had spent hours telling him and his brother about which ones were in the shapes of dogs or dippers or any number of things.

All of that was fine and dandy, but when Jeremiah looked up, he saw a brilliant, sparkling miracle overhead and didn't bother trying to figure out what it all was. Like a mess of silver dust scattered on a black velvet blanket, it was better to see it as a whole. Otherwise, Jeremiah would just see it as a confusing jumble.

As it stood, there was nothing confusing

about the night sky.

It was something put up there for all to see and make of it what they would. Jeremiah rested his head against that old rock and enjoyed the show.

When his eyes drooped shut, the bits of light were still floating behind his eyelids. He felt himself floating as well, settling into a better sleep than he could have gotten if his future was out of his reach.

When Jeremiah's eyes snapped open again, he felt as if he'd only just allowed them to close. The cramp in his neck and the cold that had soaked all the way down to the marrow in his bones, however, told a different story. Blinking a few times and listening to the pounding of his racing heart, he suddenly realized that his hand was clasped against the grip of his old Colt.

Jeremiah sat up and scrambled to his feet. Even after he'd stood up, he still didn't know why he'd awakened with such a start. He got the answer to that question when he heard the crunch of hooves against loose soil less than five paces from his wagon.

The campfire was out, but his eyes were accustomed to the dark well enough for him to see the smoke curling up from what remained of the wood he'd gathered. Jeremiah was about to pull his gun from its holster when he heard a voice from directly behind him.

"I wouldn't do that, boy," the voice said.

Jeremiah froze.

"If you're looking for that friend of yours, he ain't nowhere to be found."

"Who are you?" Jeremiah finally asked.

"We're the ones looking for a killer and I think we just found ourselves one."

Although Jeremiah had never had much reason to take his Colt from its holster in a rush, he had a reason now. Actually, he had two reasons since he could now see another figure on a horse positioned next to the wagon.

Jeremiah's hand closed around the grip of the Colt and he brought it up before he could think otherwise. His hands were trembling, but he managed to get the barrel of the gun pointed in the right direction. "I won't let you take this wagon," he said, barely able to believe someone hadn't shot him yet.

"We're not after the wagon. We're after the man who shot and killed a man up near the Sweetwater."

"Who the hell are you?"

The figure closest to Jeremiah was on foot and he stepped forward with both hands held up at chest level. There wasn't anything more than moonlight to go by, but that was enough for Jeremiah to get a look at the man's face. At least, he could see enough to know that it wasn't either of the two gunmen who'd taken a shot at him at the pier.

"I'll shoot you," Jeremiah snapped. "I swear I will."

"Now that wouldn't be a good idea, boy."

Jeremiah felt dizziness closing in on him as he flicked his eyes back and forth between the other two men. To go along with that, he'd positioned himself so neither one of those men could get a clear shot at his back. The Colt was a welcome weight in his hands, but began to slip within his sweating palms.

"You the man who shot that fella at the Sweetwater?" the closest figure asked.

"Who's asking?"

The closest man planted his feet and squared his shoulders to Jeremiah. His arms remained up and slightly out, but one of them started to slowly reach for the lapel of his jacket. "Don't get too jumpy," the man said.

Thinking that he might have to pull his trigger, Jeremiah felt his heart leap into the back of his throat. It slid back down into his chest where it belonged when he spotted the tin star pinned to the figure's shirt glinting in a few stray beams of moonlight.

"You're the law?" Jeremiah asked.

The closest figure nodded. "The name's Benjamin Tanner. I'm a marshal of this here county."

"And him?" Jeremiah asked as he nervously pointed his barrel at the other figure that was still on horseback.

"That's my deputy," Tanner replied. "Go on and show him, Art."

Art was a younger man who sat confidently in his saddle. His burly frame leaned slightly forward while he reached for his jacket as if he were one breath away from jumping off the horse's back and lunging for Jeremiah's throat.

In Jeremiah's rattled state of mind, he might have sworn he'd seen Art's eyes flash like a hungry coyote's.

Taking hold of his jacket in a loose grip, Art pulled it open to reveal a badge that was slightly smaller than Tanner's. Jeremiah didn't recognize them on sight, but he knew a lawman's symbol when he saw one.

"What do you want from me?" Jeremiah asked.

Grinning uneasily, Tanner replied, "First off, I'd appreciate it if you lowered that weapon." When he didn't see the old Colt move, he added, "I can take it from you if you'd rather, but nobody wants that."

Jeremiah let out a few choppy breaths that felt more like something was squeezing his innards to force the air straight out of him. He only lowered his gun because he didn't think he had it in him to shoot both, or even one, of those men if they turned on him.

"You made a good decision, boy," Tanner said. "Now why don't you hand over that pistol before someone gets hurt?"

"I'll keep it."

Much to Jeremiah's surprise, Tanner nodded once and said, "All right, but my deputy will have to keep an eye on you."

"Fine."

"Are you the man that shot that fellow at the river?" Tanner asked.

"There were three of them," Jeremiah said. "And they shot at me first."

"That's not what you were asked," Art said.

The sudden sound of the deputy's voice made Jeremiah twitch. And when Jeremiah twitched, he reached for his pistol out of reflex. Although he kept it holstered, Jeremiah had done enough to force the deputy's hand. Art straightened out his gun arm to take aim at Jeremiah, which brought Tanner rushing between them.

"Enough," Tanner said. "Both of you!"

Even through the sleepy haze that still lingered in his head, Jeremiah had seen plenty of differences between these men and the ones at the pier. Namely, these fellows had yet to pull their triggers. "All right, all right," he said while easing his fingers off the old Colt. "My gun's down." From there, Jeremiah held his empty hands up for both of the other men to see.

Art kept his weapon aimed at Jeremiah. His eyes still flashed in the shadows like those of a predator that wasn't about to look away from its next meal.

"You too," Tanner snarled.

"This man could be a killer, Marshal," Art said. "I ain't about to just —"

"You'll do whatever the hell I say and you'll like it."

Art did what he was told, but he most certainly didn't like it. His pistol lowered until it was out of sight, but the muscles in his arm stayed tensed as if he were waiting for any reason at all to go against Tanner's command.

Since that was about as good as he was likely to get, Tanner took his eyes away from his deputy so he could stare down Jeremiah. "We don't have time for this nonsense. Was there anyone else traveling with you?"

Jeremiah didn't know what to say. He

knew he didn't have much time to come up with an answer, but he also knew he'd taken too long to think about it when he saw the marshal nod.

"I'll take that as a yes," Tanner said. "Where is he?"

"I don't —"

"You tell me now and things will run a hell of a lot smoother. We're not the only ones out and about this evening, you know."

"What do you mean by that?" Jeremiah asked.

"Just what it sounded like. There was one dead man found on the banks of the Sweetwater. Word has it that blood won't go unanswered. Now, if you let us know where this partner of yours is, we may be able to get to him before he gets bushwhacked."

"In town," Jeremiah muttered. "The hotel."

"There's a hotel?" the deputy asked.

But Tanner was already nodding again and stepping toward his horse. "It ain't much of a hotel, but I know where it is. Art, you circle around the way we came and make certain there ain't an ambush in the works. You, come along with me."

Jeremiah felt his stomach clench even tighter than it already had been. "You mean me?"

"There ain't nobody else," Tanner said. "Come along and point your friend out to me."

While Jeremiah's brain wrestled with whether he'd done a favor for Emmett or not, his body was going through the motions of saddling up his spotted gelding.

"Here," Tanner said while offering a hand from atop his own horse. "Climb up behind me and I'll take you into town. It's less than a quarter mile away."

Accepting the marshal's hand, Jeremiah was pulled onto the back of the lawman's horse. For once, he had the instincts necessary for the situation. Having ridden a horse every way known to man, Jeremiah kept his balance while hanging on to the rear lip of the saddle. If he wasn't so rattled, Jeremiah would have been able to keep his balance even without the use of his hands.

In no time at all, they rode among the few buildings scattered along either side of the path. Jeremiah tapped the marshal's shoulder while sliding down from the horse. "This is it," he said. "This is where I left him."

Tanner hopped down from his saddle and slapped his hand against the grip of his holstered pistol. With his other hand, he flipped his reins around a hitching post and started walking toward the hotel's front door. "Let me walk in first, just in case —"

The marshal's warning was cut short as the hotel's door exploded open and a wild-eyed man staggered outside. Instead of the bald man or the one-eyed fellow from the pier, the man was one of the workers who'd helped unload the supplies from the boat.

"Jesus!" Jeremiah said as he locked eyes with the worker.

The next thing Jeremiah saw was the shotgun gripped in both of the worker's thick hands. A fraction of a second after the shotgun was brought up, Jeremiah heard the roar of a gunshot as Marshal Tanner pulled his trigger. The man with the shotgun winced and was knocked back by the blazing lead.

"You'd best stay out here," Tanner said.

As much as he wanted to obey that order, Jeremiah found himself numbly shaking his head and saying, "I'm going in there too."

"Suit yourself," Tanner grunted. "Just try to keep your head down and watch where you point that thing."

Jeremiah looked down to find his old Colt in his right hand. He didn't even remember taking the weapon from its holster.

CHAPTER 5

The gunshot woke Emmett from his sleep quicker than if he'd been splashed in the face with cold water. As soon as his eyes snapped open, he reached for the holster he'd hung off the back of a nearby chair. By the time Emmett's feet touched the floor, his gun was in his hand.

The room was sparsely furnished and smelled like it hadn't been properly cleaned in years. The bed creaked under Emmett's weight, so he stood up and watched the only door leading out to the hallway. The door was in as good a shape as the rest of the hotel, which meant Emmett could see something moving on the other side of it through several cracks.

Rather than wait for another shot, Emmett reached out and pulled the door open while hopping to one side. The hinges had barely started to creak when another shot filled Emmett's ears. This time, however, the shot didn't come from another room. It came from the hallway and was quickly followed by the sound of wood being cracked apart by lead.

Emmett sucked in a breath and pressed his back against the wall next to the door. He let that breath out slowly, doing his best not to make a sound as the shooter in the hallway began stepping into the room.

The first thing Emmett saw was the barrel of a shotgun. Smoke curled from the weapon, but he wasn't about to give it a chance to speak again. Gritting his teeth, Emmett reached out with his free hand to grab hold of the shotgun as far away from the end of the barrel as possible. Despite his efforts, Emmett still felt the hot iron burn the palm of his hand and his fingers. He used that pain to pull the other man into the room with even more force.

A tall man wearing a dark brown duster staggered a couple of steps forward before planting his boots and wrenching the shotgun away from Emmett. After pulling the gun back and over one shoulder, he sent the stock toward Emmett's chin while letting out a snarling grunt.

Emmett leaned back, which barely allowed him to steer clear of the incoming shotgun stock. His next movement was to lift his gun arm and end the fight right then and there.

Squinting over the top of his raised collar, the man in the duster twisted at the waist to swing the shotgun once again before Emmett could pull his trigger.

Emmett jumped back again, but wound up slamming his shoulders against the wall next to a dirty window. He fired a shot, but was in such a hurry that he sent his round into the wall.

Moving back into the hallway, the man in the duster leaned into the room so he could fire a shot of his own from cover.

Blinking away some of the smoke that was drifting through the air, Emmett cleared his eyes just in time to get a look at the business end of the shotgun's barrel. At that moment, Emmett realized he had less than a second to save his own skin.

The window beside him was dirty and cracked, but he would have tried his luck against a solid wall at that moment. Turning on the balls of his feet, he aimed his shoulder at the window and threw all of his weight behind it. The glass cracked on impact and shattered around him as his body spilled out into the cold night air.

Glass ripped Emmett's shirt as well as his bare legs, since he hadn't had enough time to pull on his jeans. As he flew through the air, he tried to recall how high up off the street he was. Since it didn't matter at this point, he simply closed his eyes and hoped for the best.

Another shotgun blast ripped through the room he'd left behind, filling Emmett's ears with a jarring ring. Another heartbeat later, he felt his shoulder slam against something solid.

Wood creaked beneath him as his body kept sliding along a rough wooden surface. Emmett opened his eyes just in time to see the end of an awning fast approaching him. He pitched his gun to free up his hand and then grabbed on to the awning as soon as the rest of his body slid over the edge.

With a painful strain in his shoulders, Emmett came to an agonizing stop and found himself dangling less than a foot above the ground. He let go and landed on his feet. From there, he looked for his pistol.

Against all better judgment, Jeremiah followed Tanner into the hotel even after he'd heard a shotgun blast coming from the building's second floor. Tanner didn't wait another second before rushing up the stairs.

The stairs were narrow and crooked, causing Tanner to slip after taking the first five or six in stride. When the marshal dropped to one knee and let out a curse, Jeremiah saw a man in a duster walk to the top of the stairs. The duster was buttoned shut and the collar was flipped up to conceal a good portion of the man's face, but the shotgun in his hands was plenty easy to spot.

"Watch out!" Jeremiah shouted.

Tanner stayed low and lifted his pistol to fire a shot. At that same time, the shotgun let out a smoky roar and tore a hole into the wall above Jeremiah's head. Splinters rained down upon both men at the bottom half of the stairs. Jeremiah squinted and fired his pistol again and again while choking back a panicked yelp.

As soon as Jeremiah's pistol was empty, the marshal straightened up and moved up the stairs.

Jeremiah's finger tightened on his trigger a few more times, but nothing happened. It took him a few more moments, but he soon realized he'd expended all his ammunition. He didn't know the reason behind it, but he kept the empty gun in his hand. Somehow, the weight in his grasp made it a little easier to keep from cracking under the circumstances.

As he crouched at the bottom of those stairs and breathed in the smell of burned gunpowder, Jeremiah wondered what he should do.

He wondered if Tanner was in trouble and needed someone's help to stay alive.

He wondered if he might be able to point his empty pistol at someone and convince them to drop their own weapon.

As more gunshots were fired on the floor above, Jeremiah wondered plenty of other things. One of those was whether or not Emmett was even still alive.

"What the blazes is going on up there?" asked a trembling voice from behind Jeremiah.

He turned and reflexively brought the Colt along with him, only to find the woman behind the front desk staring at him with wide, petrified eyes. She wasn't an elderly lady, but her hair was starting to go gray along the edges. After this night, Jeremiah figured the number of gray hairs on both his and the lady's heads would increase dramatically.

"Did anyone else go up there?" Jeremiah asked.

She thought it over for a second and started to nod. Before she could say another word, however, a few more shots were fired upstairs. Jeremiah took that chance to get away from the stairs and escort her behind the desk.

"There were two of them," she said. "One is . . ."

Jeremiah looked over to what had caught the lady's eye and spotted the dead man who had been shot by Tanner and was now lying in the front doorway. Setting himself between that grisly sight and the lady, Jeremiah got her attention once again.

"There were two of them?" he asked.

Grateful to have that body out of her sight, she nodded. "One came in later to ask if any strangers rented a room for the night. I told him just one and before I could say another word, he headed up there. That other one stayed down here. I thought he was going to hurt me, but he caught sight of you men coming to the door and . . . well . . . you know the rest."

"Everything's going to be all right," Jeremiah said. He prayed she wouldn't ask for any details confirming that claim and was happy to find that the lady was content to let it lie.

Once the shooting had stopped, she started to jump to her feet. Jeremiah pulled her back down again a bit too anxiously and caused her to hit the floor hard. She didn't seem to mind the impact against her knees, however, and even tried to climb back to her feet.

"You should stay down, ma'am," Jeremiah said.

But the lady kept straining to get back up as she said, "There was another fellow who fell out a window! I saw it happen while you and that other man were going up the stairs."

"What?" Jeremiah asked. "Who fell out the window?"

"I don't know who. I just looked out and saw him dangling from the awning and then he dropped. He might be one of the other guests. The only other one is some old woman from Montana." Suddenly, she nodded vigorously. "It was him. He didn't have any britches on."

"What?"

She nodded and leaned to the side so she could get a quick look at the bottom of the stairs. "I saw it with my own eyes," she told Jeremiah. "He hung there for a moment and then dropped. After that, all hell was breaking loose so I couldn't see much more."

The shooting upstairs had stopped, so Jeremiah stepped to the window that the lady had pointed to and took a look outside for himself. He couldn't see a half-dressed man lying with a broken leg in the street, but that didn't exactly calm Jeremiah's nerves.

"Anyone still down there?" Tanner shouted from the second floor.

Jeremiah rushed toward the stairs, but slowed down before he got close enough to look up them. Tentatively peeking around the crooked wall, he glanced up the staircase to find Tanner looking down at him.

"You hurt?" Tanner asked.

"No, Marshal. What about you?"

"Caught a scratch, is all. Where the hell's that deputy of mine?"

Jeremiah shook his head a few times before it occurred to him that Tanner might not be able to see the gesture. "I don't know," Jeremiah finally said. "He's not here, though."

"Then he should be nearby," Tanner said. "Take a gander outside and tell him to get in here!"

"What if he's not outside?"

"Then he'd better be dead because if he ain't, he might as well keep riding." With that, Tanner turned away from Jeremiah and stomped out of sight.

Now that he'd gone close to a minute without hearing gunshots, Jeremiah steeled himself and headed for the front door. "Stay put, ma'am," he said to the woman behind the desk. He could have saved his breath, however, since that lady wasn't about to move from her spot.

Jeremiah walked outside and felt as if he were walking straight into a dark abyss. Thick clouds had rolled in across the moon, drenching everything in shadow. There was more of a bite to the cold in the air as well, slicing through Jeremiah's skin like rows of gnashing teeth.

Unsure as to what might be waiting for him out there, Jeremiah stayed in the doorway of the hotel until his eyes adjusted to the dark. Even after that, he wasn't anxious to go exploring.

"Emmett?" he said from the relative safety of his doorway.

Jeremiah didn't get a reply, so he took a step outside.

"Emmett?" he repeated. "Are you out here?"

Just then, something caught his eye. Jeremiah glanced toward the dim gleam of metal lying in the street. When he picked out the shape of a gun in the dirt, Jeremiah scuttled toward it while twisting to try and look all around him. He made it to the discarded weapon without hearing a peep or seeing so much as a twitch anywhere around him.

"Emmett?"

Still no response.

"Anyone?"

Reluctantly, Jeremiah reached down and picked up the gun he'd spotted. Although he thought it could have been Emmett's, Jeremiah wasn't positive. The more he looked at the gun in his own hand, the less familiar it seemed. Finally, he lowered the gun and took another look around.

When he saw the boot sticking out from behind a nearby shack, Jeremiah wasn't sure whether or not it was empty. He walked toward it, still rattled enough to hold up his own empty pistol instead of the other gun he'd found that could very well have been fully loaded.

Jeremiah broke into a run as soon as he saw the leg emerging from the boot. He scrambled around the shack and found a man lying on the ground who wasn't in any condition to do harm to anyone.

"Good Lord," Jeremiah said as he dropped both of the guns he'd been holding.

Art was completely still as he lay on his side with both arms clenched to his body. When the deputy flopped onto his back and brought up his pistol, Jeremiah was actually relieved.

"It's just me," Jeremiah said. "What happened?"

Blinking and wheezing as if he wasn't sure

what he was seeing, Art kept his gun aimed at Jeremiah. "He got away," Art muttered.

Jeremiah reached down to try and help the deputy up, but stopped when he saw a wound on the deputy's forearm. In the faint glint of what little moonlight could push through the clouds, the blood looked almost black.

"Were you shot?" Jeremiah asked.

The deputy started to sit up, but winced and lay back down again. "No," he said while patting an empty scabbard that hung from his belt. "Stabbed. The bastard stuck me."

"Who did? Where did he go?"

"He's gone. Damn!"

Jeremiah wasn't a doctor, but he knew a cut on the forearm was more painful than serious. "You'll be all right," he said. "Let me just tell the marshal where you're at and see about getting a doctor."

"No doctor here," Art groaned. "If there is one, he'll probably stitch my shirt to my hand."

"Better that than bleeding out."

The deputy kept complaining, but Jeremiah didn't stay there to listen. Instead, he ran back to the hotel and pushed open the door. Marshal Tanner was standing at the front desk, listening to the lady who was speaking quickly and gesturing wildly with both hands.

"You find that deputy of mine?" Tanner asked.

"Yeah. He was stabbed. He's outside."

No sooner were those words out of his mouth than Jeremiah was being shoved out the front door again.

"Show me where he's at," Tanner insisted.

The next half hour or so was a rush in Jeremiah's swimming head. The town indeed had a doctor, who was roused from his sleep and dragged all the way from a small house at the end of the street. The doctor tended to Art's wound and had it dressed in a matter of minutes.

Much to Jeremiah's surprise, Marshal Tanner started giving his deputy no end of grief for losing his knife as soon as it was clear that Art wasn't about to die. The lawmen joked back and forth as the color slowly returned to Jeremiah's face.

"See, now?" Tanner said as he slapped Jeremiah's shoulder. "I told you things would turn out all right. Come along with me."

"Did you find my friend?" Jeremiah asked.

"That's . . . partly what I wanted to ask about."

Stepping back into the hotel was a mix of

good and bad. It was good to see a familiar place and to see the lady behind the desk was doing all right. On the other hand, it was bad to be so close to what felt to Jeremiah like the front lines of a battlefield.

Tanner led him up the stairs to a dirty hallway. Some of the mess looked fresh and the rest looked as if it had been there since the second floor had been raised over the first. The air still smelled of burned powder and the grit stuck to the back of Jeremiah's throat. Once the marshal stepped aside, the only thing Jeremiah could focus on was the body slumped in one of the doorways.

"That's the fellow who tried to shoot me. He your friend?" Tanner asked as he tapped the body with the toe of his boot.

Jeremiah leaned down to get a look at the dead man's face. Before seeing it, however, he spotted the bald head. Sure enough, there was a beard covering the man's chin and Jeremiah let out a relieved breath. "It's not him."

"You're sure?"

"Yes."

"Who is he?" Tanner asked.

"I wish I knew, Marshal."

CHAPTER 6

Sara Correy had nearly paced a rut into the floor of her kitchen. When her husband had left, she was glad to have some time in which she could pack up her things without him getting in the way. Now that he was overdue, all she could do was pace from one spot to another.

Her house seemed like miles of open space captured within a few sturdy walls. It seemed bigger now that it was nearly empty, but the place was becoming more and more unbearable with every day she had to spend there alone. The only thing that would make her feel any better was the sound of wagon wheels rolling up the road that led to her barn. Sara's ears were even sharp enough to know which creaks and rattles to listen for, so she didn't get excited when just anyone stopped by.

When she finally heard the exact sounds she'd been waiting for, Sara nearly jumped out of her skin. Part of her didn't even want to believe what she'd heard until her eyes could verify it. Sara ran to the kitchen window, pulled back the linen curtains she'd sewn especially for that spot and waited for a few seconds.

Sure enough, Jeremiah's wagon rolled into sight. Less than a second after seeing that, Sara was rushing through the kitchen door and shouting her husband's name.

Jeremiah set the wagon's brake and let out a slow breath. Seeing his ranch after the last couple of days was something close to getting a glimpse of the Promised Land. Just when he thought it couldn't get any better, he heard his wife's voice and saw her running toward him with her arms wide open.

"Jeremiah!" she shouted. "Thank God, it's you!"

He jumped from the driver's seat and landed just in time to catch his wife as she threw herself at him. Jeremiah swept her up like she was a feather wrapped in a soft cotton dress and squeezed her as if he hadn't done so for ten years. "Am I glad to see you!" he whispered into her ear.

After hugging him until some of the strength left her arms, Sara began peppering his face with fast, urgent kisses. "Where . . . have you . . . been?" she asked between pecks.

Waiting until he could set her down, Jeremiah held her face in his hands and planted a kiss on Sara's lips that curled both of their toes. "I went to get the supplies, Sara."

"But you should have been back days ago!"

"I'm only a day late, sweetheart."

"But I was worried something happened to you." Narrowing her eyes so she could study his face even more carefully, Sara asked, "What happened? I can tell something's wrong. Now tell me."

Jeremiah knew better than to keep anything from his wife. Hiding a birthday surprise or Christmas present was risky at best. Trying to keep from telling her what had happened in Martha's Ferry was positively futile. "There was a bit of trouble along the way," he told her as gently as he could manage.

"Oh my Lord," Sara gasped while placing one hand over her heart and the other in front of her mouth. "What happened? Were you hurt? I just knew something would go wrong, I knew it!"

Taking her hands in his, Jeremiah looked directly into her eyes and came closer than he'd ever come to lying to his wife. Not wanting to add that to all the other troubles he'd seen in the last couple of days, Jeremiah settled on telling her, "Some men tried to rob me at the boat."

"Oh no!"

"I would have been home earlier, but I forgot to take into account that I'd be traveling slower with all these supplies in the wagon. It was just a dumb oversight."

"Forget the oversight," Sara said angrily. "Tell me about those robbers!"

Jeremiah pulled in a breath and looked around. Everything from the curves of the landscape to the few shingles missing from his roof was known to him. The ground felt familiar under his boots and even the breeze brushed along his face in a familiar way. The ranch wasn't large, but it was home by every meaning of the word. Simply standing there was enough to put everything else out of his mind.

"Did those men try to hurt you?" Sara asked, unintentionally pulling Jeremiah out of the pleasant frame of mind that he had been settling into.

Jeremiah stepped back and held up his arms. "Do I look hurt to you?"

"Well, then tell me what happened. You can't just say someone tried to rob you and then leave it at that."

"Did the Bailey boys come over to pack up the house already?" Jeremiah asked as he glanced past his wife and to the house.

Sara stepped so she was once again all he could see. "Yes, they did. Now what did those men steal?"

"Nothing. How about I tell you what happened over dinner? Would that be a good compromise?"

Placing her hands upon her hips, Sara shook her head and stared her husband directly in the eye. After looking him over from head to toe once more, she nodded and turned toward the house amid a swirl of skirts. "All right. But you'll talk while I cook or you'll have to cook for yourself."

"Fair enough."

Sara tried to maintain a stern demeanor as she stomped back to the house, but fell into a laughing fit when she felt Jeremiah give her backside a pinch. Swatting at his hand, she was quickly wrapped up in his arms and kissing him all over again. After that, she took hold of Jeremiah's hand and led him the rest of the way to the kitchen.

As familiar as the ranch felt, Jeremiah couldn't help but notice how much emptier it was compared to how he'd left it. There were no workers wandering between the barn, the bunkhouse and the main house.

There were no chairs scattered along the front porch. There weren't even any other horses tied up in front of any of the buildings. In a way, the place reminded him of one of the sleepy, abandoned towns he'd passed on his way to Martha's Ferry.

Jeremiah's mind was brought back to the familiar when he heard the kitchen door creak open. He stepped inside to find the place where he'd eaten his last decade's worth of meals nearly as empty as the rest of the spread. But Sara didn't seem to mind. She bustled about, sifting through the crates set up here and there to fish out the things she needed to put together his supper.

"So, start talking," she said.

Being careful to skip the more gruesome details, Jeremiah told her about what had happened to him while he was away. Sara gasped every now and then, but made a point not to interrupt. Jeremiah could feel her eyes on him throughout most of his story, as if she wished she could skip to the last page of a book to be sure that her favorite character survived the tale.

When he was finished with the meat of the story, Jeremiah was about to dig into the meat that Sara had prepared for him. He picked up his knife and fork, cut off a slice of ham steak and then put it in his mouth. Just the fact that it was prepared with his wife's special glaze made it the best thing he'd tasted in a long time. At that moment, it seemed to make all the shooting and running worth the effort.

"So, where's this gunman you met?" Sara asked as she sat down across from Jeremiah at a small table against one wall of the kitchen.

"Gunman?"

"Yes. Wasn't his name Emmett?"

"Yeah. His name was Emmett."

"Was?"

Jeremiah finished the bite he'd been chewing and washed it down with some cool coffee. "It still is, I guess. I don't know exactly what happened. I suppose he was chased out of town by those fellows who ambushed him at that hotel."

"You don't know for certain?"

"There was no way for me to know, Sara. I stayed there for a while and there was no trace of him. I rode slower than I should have, even though I knew you'd be crazy with worry. I even circled the town a few times and still didn't see him."

"Maybe you missed him along the way," Sara offered. "There's more than one trail between here and there, right?"

"Sure, but it's a lot of open land. I would

have spotted him." Jeremiah hung his head and poked at his supper. "I should have stayed longer. You're right."

Soon, he felt a soft finger beneath his chin. Jeremiah allowed his face to be tilted upward until he was looking into his wife's eyes.

"I didn't mean to pass any blame," she said earnestly. "I just asked where he was."

"He got away from there, is all I know. None of Marshal Tanner's other deputies found a . . . found Emmett. I just hope he's alive and well."

"I'm sure he is." Sara turned around and quickly rinsed off the dishes she'd dirtied using a bucket of water and a single cloth. After drying the dishes off, she asked, "What about the deputy that was stabbed?"

"He got stitched up and was on his feet the same night," Jeremiah told her. "I offered to stay on for a bit, but the marshal wouldn't hear of it. To be honest, I don't know if there was any good in me staying around anyway. Those men who tried to ambush me and Emmett both wound up dead."

Sara nodded and continued fidgeting with the couple of boxes needed to hold what still remained in the mostly empty kitchen. After she'd fussed with the same box for

74

more than twice the amount of time she should have needed, it became clear that she was occupied with something other than the task at hand.

Jeremiah got to his feet and faced her. He had to wait less than three seconds before Sara was rushing at him again. She wrapped her arms around him so tightly that Jeremiah's ribs felt the strain. But he didn't try to push her away or even get her to ease up. Instead, he placed his arms around her and started rocking her slowly.

"You could have been killed," she sobbed against his chest. "You could have been shot any of those times and I never would have seen you again."

"But I wasn't, sweetheart. I'm here and I'm just fine."

"For now. But what about the next time?"

Forcing himself to laugh a bit, Jeremiah told her, "The next time I plan on getting into a gunfight, I'll let you know."

She balled up a fist and smacked it against his chest. Although there was some strength behind it, she obviously wasn't trying to hurt him. She hit him a few more times while letting out another couple of frustrated sobs. "We should just stay here," she said. "We've never had anything like this happen here."

"There's been trouble," Jeremiah replied. "Remember when those men tried to steal half the herd?"

"Those were just a few rustlers and you scared them away with a shotgun."

"Not just me. A few of the hands had to ride out with me too. We all carried guns. It could have been dangerous."

Sara looked at him as if she was close to smacking some sense in to him. "Are you trying to make me feel better or worse?"

"Sorry."

Shaking her head, she said, "We should stay here. That's all there is to it."

Jeremiah took her by the shoulders and held her at arm's length. Looking directly into Sara's eyes, he said, "We're doing what we've been planning on doing for the last year. There's no reason why we should let an opportunity like this slip away."

"It's not worth getting killed over."

"There's a danger in everything we do," Jeremiah insisted. "I could snap my neck falling off a horse. You want me to plant my rump into a rocker and not take it out again?"

"No," Sara muttered.

"And what about those others who've signed on to ride along with us? Should we just tell them to hang whatever their plans were because we're too frightened to step foot off of this ranch?"

"They can do whatever they please."

"And so should we," Jeremiah said. "This place has been great for us, but the land's picked clean and there's no more opportunity here. Our future is in Oregon. Whether there's more money to be made or not, we both want to go there, so that's what we'll do. I'll be damned if I'm going to let some animals with guns tell me where I can or can't live."

"I just don't want to see any harm come to you," Sara whispered. "We still need to have babies someday."

Smiling at the sound of that, Jeremiah said, "And I wouldn't want a child of mine growing up thinking that his pa was afraid of a few ignorant robbers. This isn't a safe world, Sara. You know that just as well as I do."

"But it's a long way to Oregon."

"Plenty of others have traveled a whole lot farther. Old Man Jenkins drove his wagon all the way from Missouri and he did it when he was older than us. We're taking a good trail and we won't be alone. That's going to make a big difference, you know."

Although there was still plenty of redness around Sara's eyes, the fear had dwindled down considerably. "Are you sure about that?"

Jeremiah nodded. "Once I had just one other fellow along with me, I made it through all the lead those robbers shot at me. For this ride, it'll be us and three other wagons. We'll be armed and looking for whatever trouble there is."

"And what about the trouble that takes you by surprise?" she asked. "You can't look for all of it, you know."

"I know, darling. Between the two of us, we should be able to spot anything." Seeing the scolding wince on his wife's face, Jeremiah sighed and said, "Just about everything. And what we don't spot, someone else will. One of the Inglebrechts used to be a scout for the army. Did you know that?"

Nodding, Sara replied, "Yes. I told you about him, remember?"

"That's right," Jeremiah said with a smile. "You did."

Looking at her husband's face, Sara couldn't help but smile herself. She nuzzled her cheek against him and gave him another hug before taking a deep breath and stepping away. "I guess it would be foolish to stay since everything we own is already packed up and ready to go."

"Yep."

"I only wish that friend of yours could come along as well. Someone like that would be awfully useful."

Jeremiah tried not to show it, but he felt a stab of guilt when he heard that name. Since there wasn't much of anything else for him to do in that regard, Jeremiah forced it from his mind and thought about what else needed to be done before the house was handed over to the newly married couple intent on buying it.

There was plenty more to do, so Jeremiah stopped kicking himself for things beyond his control. "I'm going to unhitch the horses from that wagon," he announced. "They're gonna think I forgot about them."

"You did forget about them," Sara replied.

Stepping behind her and giving her a kiss on the back of the neck, he whispered, "Who could blame me?"

She giggled and shooed him away. Even though Jeremiah knew there were still plenty of fears and doubts lingering in her mind, he had enough faith that Sara could fight through them just as well as he could fight through his own. Besides, there would be plenty of time for consoling one another during the ride to Oregon.

Jeremiah busied himself with leading the horses to the barn, opening the door and

79

leading them inside. Once there, he un-hitched them from the wagon and put away each hitch, harness and bit in its proper place. He'd completed the task so many times that he didn't even need to think about what he was doing. That way, when he heard something out of the ordinary, it was enough to startle him out of his peaceful trance.

Something shifting against the straw-covered floor, making Jeremiah's heart skip a beat and his hand drop down to the gun at his side. He froze and squinted into the shadows of a nearby stall. "Someone there?" he asked.

He took one step forward before he heard the shifting sound again. This time, however, it was followed by another series of scrapes as a figure straightened up from where he'd been sitting in the back of that stall.

"No need for all that," Emmett said. "I didn't come all this way just to be shot at again."

CHAPTER 7

Jeremiah rushed forward so quickly that he forgot he was holding the old Colt. "Where have you been?" he asked. "I thought you might have been killed!"

"I was chased out of my hotel room and I just kept running," Emmett replied while dusting a few bits of straw from his arms. "You told me where your ranch was, so I rode ahead a ways and waited for you here. I didn't want to spook your wife, so I thought it'd be best to wait until I could be introduced by you."

"I looked for you, but I never found a trace of where you were."

Emmett shrugged. "I would have waited around longer, but I dropped my gun somewhere along the way. After what happened with those gunmen, I wasn't about to just kick my feet up and wait out in the open."

"I'll be damned. You must have been

ahead of me the whole way."

"Why? Did the law insist you stay in that one-horse town?"

"That marshal practically booted me out," Jeremiah said. "I think he was afraid I'd attract another round of trouble."

"Who could blame him?" Emmett said. "I was starting to think you were nothing but bad luck."

"So, what happened to you at that hotel?"

"Someone knocked on my door with a shotgun is what happened. I barely got out of there before I got to know that shotgun even better."

"The fellow with the shotgun was there when I went back," Jeremiah said. "The marshal was there too."

"I wasn't feeling too welcome after falling out the damn window. Once I hit the street without breaking my legs, I kept right on going."

"Did you run into the other gunman that was out there?"

Emmett blinked a few times and asked, "What other gunman?"

"There had to be another one out there, because someone stabbed one of the marshal's deputies."

Lowering his head, Emmett let out a tired breath. "I didn't see anyone else. I was running too damned fast. All I could think about was getting away from there alive. Is that deputy all right?"

"Sure. All he needed was some stitches."

"Then that's what matters. If I would have had my gun . . ."

"Today is your lucky day, my friend," Jeremiah said as he brightened up a bit. Walking over to the wagon, he reached into one of the bags just behind the driver's seat and took out the pistol he'd found in the street that night. He held it out and asked, "Does this look familiar?"

When he spotted that pistol in Jeremiah's hand, Emmett looked like a kid on Christmas morning. He grinned from ear to ear and took the gun away as if he was being reunited with a long-lost child.

"Where the hell did you find this?" Emmett asked. "I looked everywhere for it."

"Not everywhere, apparently. It was in the street right outside the hotel."

"Really? I must have been dizzier than I thought." Taking the gun in one hand, Emmett gave it a quick spin around his finger, dropped it into its holster and patted it for safe measure. "I hope you've still got some space on that expedition you've been going on about."

"You have any experience as a scout?"

"A bit."

"Good," Jeremiah said. "Because I'd rather not leave the task solely in the hands of some rich man's son."

"Now what about that hot meal? Is it presumptuous to ask for that as well?"

Jeremiah slapped Emmett on the shoulder good-naturedly and motioned toward the barn's door. "My wife can cook you up something, but it won't be anything fancy. I can give you that introduction you've been waiting for."

"Don't tell her I was hiding in here. I just thought that, knowing my luck, she would have shot me out of pure nervousness."

"You're probably right."

Between the two of them, they got the horses unhitched and put into their own stalls in a short amount of time. The supplies were left in the wagon and the barn door was locked up behind them. As Emmett had predicted, Sara looked a bit frightened when she saw the unfamiliar face. Fortunately, Jeremiah was there to ease her mind.

"Sweetheart, this is Emmett Blaylock. Emmett, this is my wife, Sara." After saying that, Jeremiah stepped back and beamed from a distance.

Emmett stepped forward and offered his

84

hand. When Sara reached out to shake that hand, he enclosed hers in a grasp that was strong without being too strong. "Nice to meet you, ma'am," he said.

Looking at his eyes and then down to the weathered holster at Emmett's side, she nodded. "Likewise."

Jeremiah was happy to see that she didn't let his hand go straightaway. Instead, Sara seemed to tighten her grip for a moment before finally taking her arm back. When she turned around, her cheeks were slightly flushed.

"Can I get you something to eat?" she asked.

Emmett nodded. "I'd like that. It's been a while since I've had my fill."

Over the course of the next few days, Emmett was put to work. He wasn't alone in that, since both Jeremiah and Sara were also moving so much that they hardly seemed to stand still. There were more things to pack away, more rooms to clear and more chances for them to try and discover new ways to get those things packed onto two covered wagons.

More and more of their things wound up being hauled away by neighbors or local store owners. As much as Jeremiah or his wife hated to see something of theirs go, neither one of them could think of a way to take it with them.

"We'll get a better one in Oregon," was what Jeremiah usually said upon seeing another of his possessions find a new owner.

More often than not, Sara showed a more practical side by stating, "We don't need it," to whatever had to go and then moving on to the next thing on her list.

It was during one of those busy days that Jeremiah spotted a pair of covered wagons approaching his fence line. He rode back to the house and made the excited announcement to his wife. "They're here," he shouted.

Stepping onto the porch, Sara asked, "Who's here?"

"There's a couple wagons heading up the road and there's a few cows trailing behind. It's got to be someone for the expedition."

"Yes, but who is it?" she asked slowly and patiently.

Jeremiah blinked and then grinned. "I don't know, exactly. Maybe I should ride out to meet them."

"That'd be a good idea."

Watching her husband pull his reins to one side and point his horse's nose back in the direction from which he'd come, Sara chuckled and turned to walk back into the house that felt more and more empty the longer she was in it. Nervousness sank into her features as she slowly dragged one of the kitchen chairs outside to the front porch and dropped herself onto it.

"Good Lord," she exclaimed when she saw Emmett standing near the corner of the house.

"Sorry," he said. "I didn't mean to startle you."

"Well, that's sure what you did. I think I lost a few years of my life."

He grinned and walked up to the porch. "Sorry about that. I thought I heard Jeremiah."

"You did. He thinks he saw someone from the expedition."

"Good. Hopefully they'll all be here soon."

"Are you anxious to leave?" she asked suspiciously.

Without batting an eye, Emmett replied, "Yes. Aren't you?"

Sara let out another breath and rubbed her eyes. "Everything's been moving so fast, I hardly know what to think of it anymore. It seems like Jeremiah just got back and we've all been so busy and everything I own has been either sold off or packed onto a wagon. . . ."

Emmett had been making some last-minute repairs to the bunkhouse's roof and still wore a belt with pouches of nails around his waist. Dropping a hammer through a loop in that same belt, he walked over to Sara and leaned against a rail to face her. He then leaned in for a look inside the house. Since there were no shades or curtains on any of the windows, seeing inside wasn't too difficult.

"Looks like everything's pretty well cleaned out," he said. "I don't believe I've ever seen a house that empty."

Sara lowered her hands and thought about that for a moment. "You know something? I don't think I have, either. Maybe that's why my head feels like it's spinning all the time."

"Something tells me that's only going to get worse once we get those wagons rolling," he said. "There's still some work to be done. If those are folks from the expedition starting to arrive, then I need to get finished."

"Nobody will notice whether the work's done or not," she told him. "As long as the house is standing and the fences are up, the couple buying this place won't complain. Considering the price that Jeremiah gave them, they've got no right to complain even if there are holes in the roof."

"Yeah, well . . . I should go all the same."

Emmett started to walk away, but stopped when he felt Sara's hand close around his. She gazed at him and leaned forward while staring directly into his eyes.

"I didn't mean to chase you off," she said. "I know I haven't talked to you very much, but that's just because I wasn't expecting someone like you to be here."

"Someone like me?"

She started to reply, but couldn't find the words. Instead, she simply shook her head and pulled her hand back. "I don't know. Like I said before, my head's still spinning with all that's been happening lately."

Emmett stepped away from the chair, stopped to look back at Sara and then kept walking toward the edge of the porch. The sprawling ranch house and the bunkhouse and barn all looked and felt like just another set of formations on the open acres of Jeremiah's property. Without any of the trappings from the people who'd lived there, the buildings simply blended in with the rest of the acreage.

Seeing Sara in front of that empty house situated in the middle of all that empty land made her appear even more alive and vital than when she smiled or locked eyes with him. Emmett had to force himself to turn away and start walking in the other direction. It was an effort, but he managed to walk to the bunkhouse without once looking back.

On the porch in front of the main house, Sara closed her eyes and lowered her head. She kept her eyes closed as she thought quietly to herself. Since there wasn't much left for her to do, she walked back into the house and wandered from room to room.

Each room was as empty as the one before it.

Each room was cleaned out so well that there wasn't a stray bit of dust or forgotten piece of clothing to remind her that she'd spent years of her life rattling around in that space.

"Maybe it is good to move along," she said to herself. "It's not like I've got a choice any longer."

Jeremiah rode all the way to the southernmost expanse of his property as if he were in a race. Leaning forward over the neck of his horse, he snapped his reins and grinned so wide that he was in danger of catching flies in his teeth. He steered around the couple of rough spots that had tripped him up over the years without even realizing what he was doing. Once his fence was in sight, he eased back on the reins and fixed his eyes upon the sight that had caught his attention in the first place.

The wagons were almost at the gate. Jeremiah rode ahead so he could push it open and let them pass. He stopped short, however, as some of the caution he'd acquired over the last week or so made its presence known in the pit of his stomach.

Bringing his small team to a stop, a man with a thick head of gray hair and a well-trimmed beard sat in the front wagon's driver's seat. He spoke quickly to a plump woman in her fifties who sat beside him. A man who was obviously a younger version of the wagon's driver rode around to the front of the line atop a dusty brown mustang that seemed anxious enough to clear the fence in one jump.

"This'd be the Correy Ranch?" the young man asked.

"It sure would," Jeremiah replied with a grin. "And who might you be?"

"My name's Paul Inglebrecht." Pointing toward the couple sitting in the lead wagon, he added, "This is my father, Harold, and my mother, Noelle."

Jeremiah tipped his hat. "Pleased to meet you folks. You're the first ones to arrive."

"You gonna introduce yourself?" the older

man driving the wagon snapped.

Although Noelle didn't say anything, she shot the old man a glare that could have melted copper.

Reaching out to pull the latch holding the gate shut, Jeremiah said, "Pardon my manners, but things are a bit hectic as of late. I'm Jeremiah Correy."

"Pleased to meet you," Harold said. Glancing toward his wife, he muttered, "That wasn't so hard." He then snapped the reins and got the wagon moving through the gate that Jeremiah held open.

"We're all going to get along just fine," Jeremiah said. "Just fine, indeed."

CHAPTER 8

The Inglebrechts were followed by another wagon that arrived an hour later. Jeremiah raced out to greet this arrival with as much zeal as he'd greeted the first. This time, however, some of his excitement was returned in kind by another smiling face that seemed even more eager to get the expedition under way.

"And what might your name be?" Jeremiah asked as he escorted the wagon back to the ranch house.

"I'm Claire Mays," a little girl with an upturned nose and apple cheeks replied. She sat bolt upright next to the blond woman driving the wagon.

"Hello, Claire. My name's Jeremiah." After shaking the little girl's hand, he offered the same hand to the blond woman. "Jeremiah Correy. I hope you had a safe ride here."

"So far so good," the blonde replied.

"Her name's Anne," Claire announced. "Just like my grandmother."

The blond woman seemed apprehensive when looking at Jeremiah, but she couldn't keep herself from smiling for very long once she glanced at her daughter. Looking back to Jeremiah, she told him, "She's right. My name is Anne. Are the others here?"

"Yes, but we're still waiting for another family."

"Thank goodness. I thought I might miss everyone since I wasn't able to leave home until later than I'd planned."

"Seems like we've all had some troubles here and there. Come along and we'll get you settled until the others arrive."

"So, how did the others hear about this expedition?"

"The Inglebrechts are related to some friends of mine who knew we all were itching to head out a bit farther west. I work with plenty of cowboys and a few other ranchers and I just had them spread the word to folks they knew. You got word from Jordy Pickerell, didn't you?"

Anne nodded. "He says hello, by the way."

"I hope he didn't tell you too many stories about me. There should be another family headed this way and they're second cousins of one of my former ranch hands. There's not many of us, but that should make things go a little easier."

"Hopefully," Anne said.

Jeremiah rode beside the wagon on Anne's side. Even though he barely knew the woman and wasn't even close enough to reach out and touch her, he could feel a weight in the air around her. It almost seemed as if something heavy were settling in on his shoulders the closer he got to the blonde.

"I hope there wasn't any trouble in getting here," Jeremiah said.

Shaking her head reflexively, Anne glanced over to him and then shrugged. "A little, but it wasn't much, really."

"Pop-Pop didn't want us to go," Claire said.

Jeremiah put on a concerned face and addressed the little girl directly. "Really? Why's that?"

Before the girl could answer, her mother said, "My father . . . he told me I was being foolish to pick up and leave. But, since I lost my husband, I haven't been so quick to settle just because a place is familiar."

"That's very admirable," Jeremiah said.

Sitting up and cocking her head like a scholar, Claire said, "I think it's honorable too."

Jeremiah caught Claire glancing at him using the corner of her eye, so he sat up to reflect the posture she'd taken for herself. "You're quite the proper young lady, Claire," he said.

Trying to keep her chin held higher than Jeremiah's, Claire replied, "I'll be ten years old this fall."

"Ten years, huh? Maybe you can help us scout one day."

"We'll see about that," Anne said quickly before the girl could get too excited.

Both Jeremiah and Claire rode to the ranch house like Washington crossing the Delaware. Anne smiled at Jeremiah, but eventually had to look away.

"I say we give the other family until morning," Harold Inglebrecht declared. "After that, we should leave without them."

Noelle swatted the old man's shoulder and whispered, "That's terrible. We can't leave anyone behind."

"We can't leave anyone behind until we're on our way. We're not even a proper expedition yet."

Emmett sat with the rest of the group on the front porch of the main house. Various chairs and stools had been scavenged from all the wagons and arranged in a crooked row along with two chairs that had once been in Jeremiah's own dining room. Being on the end of the row, Emmett had to lean over so he could nudge Jeremiah with his elbow.

"Did you get that word from him?" Emmett asked.

Jeremiah chuckled and Harold fixed a stern glare upon him.

"What was that, sir?" Harold asked.

Emmett wiped the grin from his face and shook his head like a boy who'd been caught sticking his tongue out when the schoolteacher's back was turned. "Nothing," he said.

Grunting as he shifted on the stool he sat upon, Harold grimaced and said, "We can't wait around forever. I could have ridden to Oregon on my own, but I signed on here to travel in a group. I didn't sign on to sit around some empty house on a milking stool."

"My father's right," Paul added in a much more polite tone. "We shouldn't use up supplies just to stay here waiting. Any food we eat, wood we burn and time we waste is taking away from the resources we'll have on the trail to Oregon."

"What about the other family?" Sara asked. "Do we just leave them behind?"

As folks started talking back and forth to one another, Jeremiah could feel the community spirit that had been there a few minutes ago beginning to dissolve. Unsure as to how he would be received, he stood up and cleared his throat noisily. To his surprise, all the smaller conversations stopped and everyone looked to him expectantly.

"We were all supposed to meet here and leave by the end of the week," Jeremiah announced. "That was yesterday. As we discussed already, Mr. Inglebrecht, we were all a bit behind schedule."

Harold groused a bit, but couldn't dispute the truth.

Looking around to the others, Jeremiah saw that Paul and Noelle Inglebrecht were nodding contentedly. Anne waited patiently for Jeremiah's next words and Claire just seemed happy to be sitting on her mother's lap among all the other adults. Sara watched him with quiet confidence written across her features.

"Mr. Inglebrecht is right about one thing, though," Jeremiah continued. "We can't sit around here and wait for very long. The weather's been holding up nicely, but I wouldn't want to waste another fine day that could be better spent traveling. Paul's also got a point in that we're eating food now that could be saved to eat along the way."

"Won't we be able to resupply?" Anne asked.

Jeremiah nodded. "Sure. There's towns along the way, but resupplying means spending money or wasting ammunition on hunting. The point is that we've all got things to do and a schedule to keep. If the rest of our group can't keep up their end, they shouldn't be allowed to drag the rest of us down. For all we know, they might have decided against coming along with us in the first place."

"Hear, hear!" Harold said while stamping his foot approvingly.

Although his first reaction was to accept the old man's praises, Jeremiah quickly found himself waving them off. "We'll wait until morning," he said. "After that, we'll head out and be on our way just as we would if we weren't even waiting for another group."

"We could leave right now if we weren't waiting for those vagrants," Harold muttered.

Paul responded quickly and spoke in an exasperated voice. "No, we wouldn't, Father. It's almost dark and we've still got to

99

organize before we just venture out half-cocked."

Harold stood up quickly enough to knock his stool over. "Don't you forget who's in charge of this expedition, boy."

"Looks to me like he is," Paul replied while pointing toward Jeremiah.

For a moment, Jeremiah waited and watched along with everyone else. Once he realized they were all looking at him, he choked on a breath and then tried his best to make it look like he was only clearing his throat.

"I don't . . . we really don't need to have anyone as a leader," Jeremiah blustered clumsily. "I mean . . . do we need a leader?"

"Of course we do," Harold grunted.

"Whose idea was it to organize this group?" Anne asked.

Jeremiah straightened his collar and rolled his eyes. He could feel Sara's gaze boring a hole straight through him. "It was my idea," he said before his wife beat him to the punch.

Anne smiled and nodded once. "Then if we need a leader, it should be you. Is that all right with everyone else?"

Shaking his head and patting the air, Jeremiah said, "We don't need to do this. We all know where we're —"

"I'll second it."

Hearing that voice nearly knocked Harold over. He spun around with his mouth hanging open and his fists clenched. If not for the fire in his eyes, the sight of the enraged old man might have been comical. "What did you say, Noelle?"

The old woman shrugged and kept her hand raised. "I said I'd second the motion. Aren't we voting?"

"We are, but I'm your husband!"

"And that young man is the leader of this expedition," she replied simply. "Are we heading out tomorrow?"

Jeremiah nodded and kept his open hands in front of him as if he were holding a tray. "Yes. We really should leave tomorrow."

"Sounds like the right decision," Noelle said. "Keep making right decisions and you'll be a fine leader."

Harold started to speak several different times. Each time he stopped short with a sound that was half squeak and half growl. He barely even noticed that Claire needed to put her hand over her mouth to keep everyone from hearing her laugh at him.

"If that's all it takes to be a good leader," Sara said, "he's got my vote also."

If Harold's expression had been comical before, it was even more so when he spun on the balls of his feet to glare at Sara. "What? You think that's all it takes? A man's got to be . . . he should . . . it's not just . . ."

"Me too," Emmett said.

"Who the hell is that?" Harold asked. "Is he even a part of the expedition?"

"I sure am," Emmett replied. "I was hired on as a scout."

"My son's the scout and he's all we need."

All the eyes in the group settled upon Paul. The youngest Inglebrecht shrugged and said, "You can never have too many scouts."

"And I suppose you'd vote for him as the leader, eh?" Harold asked.

"Does it matter?"

"Of course it does."

"Fine," Paul said. "He's got my vote."

Sara clapped her hands together as if she was literally ridding herself of the whole thing. "Fine. Now that that's over, how about we get some sleep? Or would you rather start voting on who's second in command?"

Everyone glanced around with more fatigue showing in their eyes than interest in the conversation going any further. Although he was the only one who seemed ready to keep a debate alive, Harold could tell that he wouldn't have any takers. Finally, he threw up his hands and shut his mouth.

"Good," Sara said. "Now who wants something sweet before going to bed?"

CHAPTER 9

Jeremiah awoke before dawn, saddled up his horse and rode out to tour his property. Even though it would be the last time he'd see it while it still belonged to him, he wasn't looking at the land to say good-bye. He wasn't even looking for stray heads of cattle, which was an activity that normally took up a good portion of a rancher's time. Every last steer had been sold off weeks ago and the broker who'd made the deal to sell the ranch was in charge of handing it over to its new owners.

Jeremiah's last tour of his ranch had nothing to do with sightseeing or business. He wanted to give some more time to that last family before he and the rest of the group moved along. He didn't know the family personally, but had corresponded with them several times to arrange their spot in the expedition.

Shaking his head, Jeremiah swore off even

thinking that word anymore since he only heard Harold's voice when the term came to mind.

After he'd ridden along every last inch of his fence line, Jeremiah still hadn't seen a trace of the last family anywhere in the area. Since he'd stopped at a spot with a good view of the main trail leading to his ranch, Jeremiah stayed there and folded his hands over his saddle horn.

He didn't know how long he should wait or if there was even any good reason to wait at all. What he did know was that he needed to wait a bit longer just to be certain he'd done all he could.

Only a few minutes passed before Jeremiah felt an anxiousness in the pit of his stomach as though everyone else in the group were staring at him impatiently. Letting out a breath, Jeremiah pointed his horse's nose back toward his house and snapped the reins.

On the way down that well-worn trail, Jeremiah didn't look over his shoulder or even to the sides. His eyes were firmly set upon the trail. It wasn't long before he spotted the wagons that were lined up along the front of the bunkhouse. The others must have been busy because those wagons had been scattered all around the main house when he'd left for his early morning tour.

As he rode even closer, Jeremiah could see people moving back and forth between the wagons and the houses. Some carried crates, others carried sacks of supplies on their shoulders and others bustled about the houses themselves. Jeremiah didn't need to see details or faces to know his wife was in the latter category.

Riding through the gate in front of his house, Jeremiah felt a change in the air. As the others spotted him, they nodded or waved in his direction as someone might expect. But there was more to it than that and Jeremiah couldn't quite put his finger on what it was. Thankfully, Sara walked up to him and gave him a smile that made him feel immediately better.

"There you are," she said. "We were all starting to worry about you."

"Worry?" Jeremiah asked as he jumped down from his saddle. "Did you think I'd go to Oregon without you?"

"I don't know. We were just concerned. Is that so awful?"

"I suppose not."

She stepped up close to him and straightened the collar of his shirt. Even though he only wore a simple rumpled shirt under his battered jacket, Sara fussed as if she were gussying him up for a ball. "It doesn't set too well with you, does it?" she asked quietly.

"What do you mean?"

"What they said last night. About you being the leader. That makes you nervous. I can tell."

"I just hope they don't expect me to make all the decisions. I've been on plenty of cattle drives, but I've never led an *expedition*." When he said that last word, Jeremiah put an exaggerated amount of haughtiness in his tone.

His sarcasm wasn't lost on Sara and she chuckled while reflexively glancing over to where Harold was standing. The old man was lugging crates from one of his own wagons and loading it onto Anne's. When she looked back to Jeremiah, she found him still studying Harold.

"What's he doing?" Jeremiah asked.

Sara didn't need to look at the old man again. In fact, the look on her face made it fairly clear that she'd already seen more than enough of him. "He's loading some of his things onto Anne's wagon."

"Why?"

"Because he overloaded his own and won't admit it. Even after the thing nearly tipped over, he wouldn't accept any blame."

"He probably had his wife do all the heavy lifting," Jeremiah muttered.

Sara laughed. "I wouldn't doubt it. Actually, we've all been doing some rearranging here and there to make the most out of our space. I figured it would keep us busy until you came back. Next time you go off on your own, just let me know, all right?"

"I will." Jeremiah took a moment to watch the rest of the folks go through their motions. Now that he'd had a little while to take it in, the overall picture didn't seem so chaotic. "I trust you thought about being able to tell whose things are in what wagons?" he asked hopefully.

"I had everyone pack their things away and then section off the leftover space so that . . ." Sara paused when she recognized the confusion creeping into the edges of Jeremiah's face. "We'll be able to tell," she said. "And what's more is that we're able to get all of our things into even less space than we'd originally thought. There's a few things I'm leaving behind for the new couple that's going to be living here. I'm sure they can put it to better use than we could."

Patting Jeremiah's chest and then turning away from him, Sara added, "And don't worry. Most of the things I'm leaving were yours, anyway."

"Not my personal things?"

"Oh no. I burned those a long time ago."

If he hadn't known the woman for so long already, Jeremiah might have been troubled by the nonchalant way she threw those words at him. But he saw the sly grin on her face even though she did her best to hide it. In fact, it was that grin that made the uneasiness in the bottom of his stomach finally fade away.

As Jeremiah led his horse to the barn, he saw Paul rush up to him.

"We should be ready to go," Paul said. "Just doing some rearranging."

"Great." Jeremiah started to walk away, but stopped and turned back around to face the younger man. "For some reason, I feel like I should return a salute."

Paul grinned and shuffled his feet. "I served for eight years in a cavalry division. I guess it's a bit hard to shake the army off my skin."

"How long have you been out of uniform?"

"Just over a year and a half."

"Well . . . cluster the troops," Jeremiah said.

Paul stood motionless before asking, "Do you mean muster?"

"Sure. Let's just get moving before I make

109

myself look like an even bigger fool."

Paul laughed and gave him a quick salute before heading back to the spot where his parents were huddled together discussing something between themselves.

Jeremiah led his horse back to the barn, but suddenly realized he'd done so out of sheer force of habit. Not only was the barn cleaned out, but there was no reason for him to be there. He couldn't take the saddle off his horse or even pause long enough to give the spotted gelding a rest.

When he saw a mostly empty grain sack in one corner, Jeremiah led his horse to it. He climbed down, dipped his hands into the sack and removed a small portion of oats from inside. Holding his hand under his horse's nose was all it took to get the animal to start eating. At least now he felt like he hadn't just wandered into the barn out of sheer addle-mindedness.

"Guess this isn't your home anymore," Jeremiah said to the horse.

The animal just kept eating. Its ears twitched every now and then, but there wasn't much more of a reaction than that.

"You want some more?" he asked once the oats were gone.

The horse glanced around and then stared at the floor. Although he didn't have anyone complaining in his ear, Jeremiah felt awkward remaining inside that barn. It was almost as if he'd suddenly become a stranger in his own home.

He let out a breath and climbed back into his saddle. Once he rode out of the barn, Jeremiah didn't look back. In fact, he didn't even bother looking at the house since everyone was present and accounted for near the wagons.

"Is everyone finished with what they were doing?" Jeremiah asked.

He got responses from the others ranging from Harold's reluctant grunt to the excited yelp from Claire.

"All right, then," Jeremiah said. "I suppose we should get moving."

Even when there had been hired hands working for him, Jeremiah had never gotten such a quick response from his words. Everyone climbed onto their wagons and got themselves situated while anxiously chattering to the people closest to them. Once they were ready to go, they looked over to Jeremiah expectantly.

Jeremiah looked around for the one face he hadn't seen in the last few seconds. "Where's Emmett?" he asked.

"Right here," the familiar voice replied. Emmett rode around from the back of the house and tossed Jeremiah a wave. "Just had to, uh . . . see to a personal matter."

Since Emmett had come from the direction of the outhouse, it didn't take much for Jeremiah to figure out what personal business Emmett needed to handle. "We're all here, then? All right." He pulled in a deep breath and steeled himself for the moment he knew would be coming, but was still partially dreading.

Jeremiah took one last look at the bunkhouse. It was empty, but there had been plenty of times throughout the good and bad seasons when the bunkhouse had been empty.

The barn looked fairly close to how it always looked when boarded up for a storm.

Jeremiah was stricken by the difference, however, when he took a final look at the main house. His home had never looked so barren. Even when he'd first arrived and the house had been empty, it still seemed to be filled with promise and expectations.

Now the house was just empty.

Not cleaned out.

Not deserted.

Just . . . empty.

The longer he looked at that old house, the less it seemed like Jeremiah had ever even lived there. He wouldn't feel right again until he'd turned his back on the place for good.

"Come on," he said while flicking his reins. "Let's get a move on."

Jeremiah led the way through the gate with Sara driving the lead wagon. A team of three horses pulled that wagon as well as a smaller cart that was hitched to it. For the moment, Jeremiah didn't care too much about the rest of the group or what order they fell into. All he wanted was to get off that property.

It was just under an hour later before he could take an easy breath again.

CHAPTER 10

The clouds had rolled in early that morning, but slowly burned away as the sun climbed higher into the sky. Once his property was behind him, Jeremiah felt his spirits climb as well. Now, a few days later, a slow breeze rolled in from the north, caressing his face as he rode ahead and to the left of the wagon Sara was driving.

Jeremiah twisted around to get a look behind him. The wagons had remained in a fairly straight line since they'd left. Only once when one of Harold's wheels snagged on a rock while crossing a shallow creek did any of them falter. There was some loud swearing and rattling from that wagon, but they'd continued along just fine. Considering that was the only incident so far, Jeremiah had to admit he was getting off to a good start.

Behind the smaller cart being pulled by Sara's wagon, Anne rode with Claire excitedly bouncing beside her. The little girl never stopped talking, singing or making some other sort of noise. Between the wind, the horses and the rumbling of the wheels, her voice sounded like a bird's chirping.

The Inglebrechts had two wagons to worry about. Harold drove one while Noelle drove the one bringing up the back of the entire train. The suggestion had been made for Harold to be the one at the end of the train, simply because he was better suited to start shooting in case of an ambush from the rear. But he wouldn't have any of it. After grousing at length about how it was more important to keep his eye on Anne's wagon than for anything else, it became easier to just let the old man have his way.

Jeremiah wasn't too happy about the decision, but he didn't want to cross Harold so early in the journey. Besides, Emmett didn't seem to mind hanging back to ride alongside Noelle to make certain nothing happened to her. The elderly woman took kindly to the company and cheered up immediately when she realized she'd have someone other than Harold with whom to pass the time.

Now that he'd had some time to think, Jeremiah had to wonder if something was bothering Emmett. Whenever they stopped,

Jeremiah couldn't see anything outwardly wrong with the man. He always rode at the end of the line, content to be there and nodding along with whatever Noelle was saying to him.

"What's the matter?" Sara asked. "You look like something's bothering you."

"Have you talked to Emmett very much?"

An odd look slipped onto Sara's face as she shook her head and shifted her eyes away from her husband. "No, but we've all been busy. This is a big day, after all."

"It is, but . . ."

"But what?"

"I've just got a feeling, is all. Kind of like when a stampede was about to break when I used to drive cattle through Kansas."

Sara furrowed her brow and looked over at him. "You mean you think there's going to be a stampede?"

"No," Jeremiah snapped. Realizing he'd raised his voice, he steered his horse a little closer to the wagon and leaned over so she could hear him when he whispered, "It just feels like something bad's gonna happen."

Nodding slowly, Sara asked, "Something bad with Emmett?"

"I don't know. He seems awfully quiet."

Sara chuckled at that. "He probably just can't get a word in edgewise. Mrs. Inglebrecht has been chewing his ear since we left."

Reluctantly, Jeremiah allowed himself to grin. "That's true. She does seem to have taken a shine to him."

"Sure beats the alternative."

From the distance behind them, a voice rattled among the clatter of the wheels to reach Jeremiah like a wayward mosquito.

"Mr. Correy! Where'd he go? Did he wander off again?"

The voice was easy enough to pick out. Harold Inglebrecht wasn't exactly the sort to blend into his surroundings. Even though nobody could have missed his barking, Jeremiah closed his eyes a bit and sighed as if that would make him disappear.

"He's up here!" Sara shouted. Seeing the mix of anger and surprise on her husband's face, she lowered her voice and told Jeremiah, "You need something to distract you. Since riding halfway across the country isn't getting the job done, maybe this will."

"Remind me to appreciate what I've got next time," Jeremiah mumbled.

"I should think this would serve as a good enough reminder for a while," Sara said.

Shaking his head at the pure cruelty that reared up from within his wife's mind, Jeremiah pulled back on his reins to bring his horse to a stop. The rest of the wagons rolled past him, giving him a quick view of everyone else. After getting an enthusiastic wave from Claire, he saw Harold's gruff face glaring at him. Jeremiah leaned back to check on Mrs. Inglebrecht, only to see she was still chattering away with Emmett.

"Mr. Correy, there's a situation," Harold announced.

"Really? What situation is that?"

Staring at Jeremiah through narrowed eyes, Harold asked, "Are you taking this seriously or should we elect another leader?"

Jeremiah fought to keep from giving the first reply that came to mind and settled upon the second. "I'm taking this seriously, Mr. Inglebrecht. What's the situation?"

Harold kept staring him down before finally letting out an exasperated breath and stomping his foot against the boards in front of him. "I think we're being followed."

"What?"

"Look for yourself if you don't believe me," he snapped while stabbing a finger to point toward the north. "They're right there plain as day."

Jeremiah looked in that direction and then shook his head. "I don't see anyone."

"Well, they're not there right now! That don't mean they weren't there before.

Besides, you didn't even give a proper look."

Normally, Jeremiah was tolerant of folks. He was certainly tolerant of older folks, since he'd been the only one in his family to look after his mother once she became too weak to look after herself. Even so, Jeremiah had never come so close to slapping one of his elders. It wasn't just the contempt in Harold's voice or the disgust in his eyes, but the combination of those two things could test the patience of a saint.

Jeremiah dug into his saddlebag and fished out a telescope. It was a battered piece of equipment that he'd bought on a whim from a little shop in Wichita, but it had gotten more use over the years than the gun on Jeremiah's hip. He lifted the telescope to his eye and gazed through the lense.

Although he got a closer look at the landscape, the motion of the horse beneath him didn't do Jeremiah any favors. He adjusted for the bounce and was able to take a fairly good look at the horizon from the west all the way around to the northeast. After that, the wagons blocked his view.

Lowering the telescope, Jeremiah looked back to Harold and said, "I don't see anyone."

"You calling me a liar?"

"No, I'm not calling you anything. I'll keep an eye out for anyone tracking us, but it could have been anything, you know. We're not the only souls riding to or from Oregon. Besides that, there's plenty of stops along the way that don't have anything to do with where we're headed."

"I saw what I saw."

Jeremiah nodded and almost patted the old man's elbow the same way he'd comforted his mother when she used to have one of her spells. "I'm sure that you did. It could have just been Indians out riding to —"

"Indians?" Harold snapped. "There are Indians about? Good Lord!"

"What was that?" Noelle asked from the wagon behind Harold's. "Did you say there are Indians coming?"

From ahead of Harold's wagon, Claire's little voice rose into an excited pitch. "Indians! I want to see Indians, Mommy!"

"There's no Indians!" Jeremiah said to everyone who could hear him. "I was just talking, that's all."

"Can you guarantee there's no Indians?" Harold asked.

"I can guarantee we'll leave you behind if you insist on stirring up so much discord. If you see someone following us, point them out to me. Otherwise, keep your damn mouth shut."

Harold looked positively appalled by what Jeremiah had just said to him. For the time being, he kept his mouth shut, gripped his reins tightly and hunched forward like a child sulking in a corner.

Jeremiah felt his heart slamming in his chest as he steered his horse away from Harold's wagon and snapped his reins. When he got alongside Anne, he saw the blonde looking at him anxiously. After taking on bits and pieces of everyone else's things as well as a portion of the group's supplies, her single wagon was full to bursting. Even so, Claire found plenty of ways to wriggle her skinny little body in among the crates, trunks and furniture.

"Where's the Indians?" the girl asked.

"They're not around here, sweetie," Jeremiah replied. "That was just talk." Shifting his eyes toward Anne, he added, "Sorry about that. There's really nothing to worry about."

Anne nodded.

Suddenly, Jeremiah heard hooves coming up behind him. He turned in his saddle and found Paul riding up next to him before slowing so he could keep pace.

"You didn't see any Indians, did you?"

Jeremiah asked.

Paul chuckled and shook his head. "Not yet, but I wouldn't rule them out. The trail ahead don't look much more interesting than that map of yours."

"Then perhaps you should tell that to your father. He sure put a scare into everyone."

Lowering his voice to a whisper, Paul said, "He's been afraid of being attacked by Indians since we all agreed to make this trip. I think I frightened him with some of the stories I told him from my cavalry days."

"There's some hills to the south of us. In your opinion . . . should one of us go have a look at them?"

"You did used to lead trail drives and such, right?"

"Sure, but this is a little different."

"Is it really?" Paul asked.

Jeremiah stopped before answering that. He'd had plenty of experience in trail drives when a few cowboys and a lot of cattle were concerned. For the most part, he'd figured that was enough to lead a few wagons along a well-established trail into Oregon. They weren't exactly blazing any new frontiers. For the most part, they were following a path that had been followed many times before by plenty of other folks.

Thinking along those lines, Jeremiah was less inclined to think he'd bitten off more than he could chew. "You feel like taking a ride up those hills in a bit, Paul?"

Paul nodded. "My horse hasn't even broken a sweat yet."

"Then why don't you scout those hills and then circle around to check our northern side? If you see anything peculiar, be sure to head straight back and let us know."

"And if I can't make it back in time, I'll fire two shots in the air close together so you won't miss them."

Jeremiah nodded and extended his hand, which was immediately shaken by the younger man. "Glad to have you along, Paul."

As Paul snapped his reins and tore away from the wagons in a rush, Jeremiah sat up a little straighter in his saddle.

"You send my boy to find them Indians?" Harold shouted.

"He's out scouting, is all," Jeremiah replied. "The next time you mention Indians, you'd best be able to point them out."

Although Harold did plenty of blustering and sputtering from where he was sitting, he didn't give any lip back to Jeremiah.

"Emmett!" Jeremiah shouted. "Come on over here!"

After about a minute, Jeremiah heard the sounds of Emmett's horse galloping to catch up to him. Once beside him, Emmett pulled back on his reins to match the plodding speed of the wagons.

"I owe you one for getting me away from that old woman," Emmett whispered.

"I thought you were going to say you owed me something worse for leaving you with her so long."

After pondering that, Emmett shrugged. "Nah. I don't mind her so much."

"I sent Paul to scout ahead," Jeremiah told him. "Now I'd like you to scout behind us."

"Scout behind? Did you let that old fool get under your skin?"

"No, but it wouldn't be wise to wave him off so quickly. Just ride back and see if you can spot anyone that might be following us. It's better to be overly cautious than to get caught with your pants down."

Emmett shrugged. "I suppose. You know what I might be looking for?"

"No. Just look."

"And will you be taking some of this scouting duty yourself, or will me and Paul get the honors?"

"I wouldn't let you two have all the fun," Jeremiah assured him. "Besides, I still need to get a feel for this group."

Emmett chuckled. "Driving these wagons like you were driving steer, huh?"

"The two seem to have plenty in common. Both groups can be worked a whole lot easier if you think of them as one big thing. Right now, I need to get an idea of what sort of mood this big thing is in."

Emmett grinned and said, "Next town we see, you're buying me a bottle of whiskey."

"Why would I do something like that?"

"It's the price I'm asking to keep it to myself that you consider these good people just another herd of cattle."

Jeremiah winced and shot a quick glance toward the wagons to see if anyone else caught that. Deciding to nod in the face of Emmett's extortion, Jeremiah faced forward and waved for the other man to get moving.

After Emmett had turned and bolted away from the wagons, a single voice sliced through the air to catch Jeremiah's ear.

"Did I hear that someone spotted a herd of cattle?" Harold shouted.

Chapter 11

Once Jeremiah had put himself into the proper frame of mind, he felt the hours slip through his fingers like fine dust. His self-appointed duties included making the rounds from wagon to wagon, keeping an eye on the horses and making certain the other folks in his charge were healthy and accounted for.

Jeremiah knew his appointment as leader wasn't exactly legal, but he took it to heart. At least that gave him enough to think about to keep from falling into the lull that most everyone else had.

By nightfall, conversation among the travelers had dwindled away to practically nothing. Tired eyes remained fixed upon the back of the wagon in front of them. Sara was the only one with a different view, but even she seemed to have grown weary of looking at the same stretch of flat ground for hours at a time. Backs were aching.

Reins were gripped within callused hands. Claire was the only one in the line not driving a team of horses and even she'd taken to curling up in the wagon just behind her mother's seat.

All those eyes perked up again once Jeremiah signaled for the wagons to slow down. He started at the back of the line and began shouting for everyone to ease up and make for a patch of open grassland next to a small stand of trees. The wagons remained in their formation as they rolled to a stop, and soon preparations were being made for supper.

"We'll need to plan this a little better next time," Sara said to Jeremiah. "It's almost dark and I don't even have a fire to work with."

"I know," Jeremiah said. "I should have stopped us sooner."

"No wonder all those boys used to complain when you'd lead the drives. You must have run them until the moon came up."

Jeremiah simply shook his head and kept searching the horizon. "Where the hell are Paul and Emmett?"

"They haven't come back yet?"

"No," he snapped. "Have you seen them?"

She flinched and looked at Jeremiah as if he'd bared a set of fangs and snarled at her.

"No need to be so cross."

When Jeremiah looked at his wife, the tenderness he normally showed her returned. "Sorry about that. I'm just worried, is all."

"Well, you shouldn't be too worried," Sara told him as she nodded toward the north. "Here come one of your scouts right now."

Jeremiah spun in that direction and squinted at a shape in the distance. For a moment, it was hard to see whether that shape was even moving. After another couple of seconds, even the darkness wasn't able to hide the outline of a man on horseback racing toward the camp.

In the blink on an eye, Jeremiah was planted in his saddle and racing to meet the approaching rider. He ignored the flurry of questions Harold Inglebrecht shouted at him and kept snapping the reins until he was close enough to catch a better glimpse of the other rider's face. It was Emmett.

"Where have you been?" Jeremiah asked breathlessly.

Emmett pulled back on his reins and steered his horse to one side before charging straight into Jeremiah. Once the horses were both slowed down and calmed after the near collision, Emmett shouted to be heard over the rush of blood going through his ears.

"You damn near killed me," Emmett said. "What the hell's wrong with you?"

"Where have you been?" Jeremiah repeated.

"Out scouting. Where should I have been?"

"Did you see Paul?"

"Was he supposed to find me?"

"No," Jeremiah replied. "We just haven't seen him since he left to scout those hills."

"Then he's probably still out there. You've done your share of riding. You know just as well as anyone how easy it is to lose track of time once you get out in the open. He probably just got too far out before he realized he wasn't even going to reach those hills."

Jeremiah slowly nodded. "I suppose that could be."

Glancing past Jeremiah, Emmett asked, "Is that a cooking fire? I'm about to starve to death."

"Sara's putting something together, but it'll probably just be some more ham and grits. Help yourself."

"Don't mind if I do." With that, Emmett snapped his reins and rode to the camp. "You coming?"

"In a bit," Jeremiah replied.

Emmett shrugged and kept riding.

Sitting in his saddle, Jeremiah looked out at the rest of the world spread out in front of him like a massive, patchwork quilt. His eyes had become somewhat accustomed to the dark, but he still couldn't see well enough to pick out every last detail. Even in the afternoon sun, he knew he wouldn't be able to spot a rider that was miles away unless he just happened to know the exact spot in which to point his telescope.

Jeremiah remained where he was until hunger gnawed at his innards. Once he felt that first stab, he knew it would only get worse until he got something to fill his belly. The wind grew colder as he sat there, bringing with it the smells of fertile ground and burning wood. When the first whiff of cooking ham drifted into his nose, Jeremiah muttered a curse and turned his horse back toward camp.

He rode back and ate what was on the tin plate Sara handed to him without tasting any of the food. It chewed up fine and filled the void inside him, which was all Jeremiah needed. After his plate was clean, he handed it back to Sara and walked to the wagon she'd been driving.

"I've already unloaded the bedrolls," she said to him.

"That's not what I'm after," he replied.

She kept her eyes on him as he stepped up to the wagon and searched through the things that were packed behind the seat. When she saw him take the rifle that was stashed there, Sara ran over to him.

"What do you need with that?" she asked.

"I'm taking it with me."

"Taking it where?" When she didn't get an answer right away, she grabbed his arm and pulled him toward her so Jeremiah was forced to look at her directly. "Taking it where?" she repeated urgently.

Jeremiah looked around at what the others were doing. Although a few glances were pointed in his direction, the rest of the group seemed to be more concerned with getting themselves squared away so they could get some sleep. Only Anne kept her eyes on Jeremiah consistently because Claire was already curled up under a blanket right beside her.

When he looked back to his wife, Jeremiah lowered his voice to a whisper and told her, "Paul hasn't come back yet. I'm going out to look for him."

"Do you think something's wrong?" Sara asked.

"I don't know, but I should go and check."

"But it's getting so dark. You won't be able to see much of anything out there."

Jeremiah didn't respond to that because he couldn't think of anything to say. In fact, the more he thought about what he'd intended to do, the less it seemed like a good idea. Finally, he said, "I can't just stand by while he may be out there hurt. If he's wounded somewhere and hears me nearby, maybe he can catch my attention. Look, I don't really know what I can do, but I've got to try. We can't lose anyone this soon."

Sara nodded and let go of his arm. Soon, she was straightening the sleeve she'd rumpled only a few moments ago. "Just be careful out there. You can barely see where you're riding."

"Don't worry about that. I've spent plenty of nights chasing down strays or running off rustlers." Jeremiah gave her a quick wink and turned his back to his wife so he could walk over to where the Inglebrechts were sitting.

Before Jeremiah or Harold could say a word, Noelle jumped to her feet and rushed forward.

"Where's my son?" she asked. "You sent him away and he hasn't come back. Where is he?"

"I'm going to find him now," Jeremiah said. "I know which way he went, so I have an idea of where to start looking."

"You have an idea?" Harold snarled. "An idea? I knew it was a mistake to elect you as leader!"

"That vote was just short of a joke and everyone knows it," Jeremiah said. "I'm taking charge because nobody else wants to or they're just too lazy to step up when they'd rather flap their gums. I'm going to look for Paul, so either come along with me or shut your mouth."

Harold looked stunned, but stood and picked up his coat from where it had been hanging from the harness of the wagon behind him. "I'm coming along," he said.

"Are you sure about that?" Jeremiah asked, suddenly feeling guilty for what he'd said before.

Harold nodded and then looked down to the rifle in Jeremiah's hand. "I brought along my Sharps. Should I get it?"

"It might not be a bad idea."

As Harold turned back toward the wagon, Emmett walked up to them. He carried a tin plate heaped full of ham and grits and was shoveling them both into his mouth using a bent fork.

"You two going hunting?" Emmett asked while spraying out bits of chewed ham.

"We're looking for Paul," Jeremiah replied.

"You want me to come along?"

"Sure. Harold, why don't you stay here with that Sharps?"

The old man looked stunned again, but that was soon replaced by the anger that had become a permanent fixture upon his face. "He's my son, damn it!"

"And this is your wife," Jeremiah told him. "She's staying here with the rest of the women as well as one child and I won't have them staying here alone. Stay put and keep an eye open for anyone that might be following us."

When he heard that, Harold practically snapped to attention. "You're right."

Jeremiah patted the old man's shoulder and walked to his horse with Emmett at his side.

"Should we light some torches?" Emmett asked.

Jeremiah shook his head. "They won't do much good once we're moving. Besides, there's enough of a moon out to ride by."

"Whatever you say," Emmett replied.

The rifle in his hand might have come from the wagon, but Jeremiah usually carried it on his saddle. He dropped it into its more familiar spot so it was held close to his horse's side. After that, Jeremiah flicked his reins and rode away from the camp at a quick trot.

Emmett followed right alongside him and soon both of their eyes were adjusted to the darkness. Snapping his reins again, Jeremiah brought his horse up to an even quicker gait, but not quite up to a full gallop. Fortunately for him and Emmett, the ground was mostly level and only had a few trees or rocky patches to cause them any concern.

As he rode, Jeremiah kept his reins gripped tightly in both hands so he could steer the horse with a twitch from either side of its neck. His back was hunched over the animal's neck so his eyes were that much closer to the ground. After a while, he pulled back on the reins and brought the horse to a stop. Jeremiah waited for a few seconds, but didn't hear Emmett riding beside him. The sounds of hooves against the ground reached his ears and soon Jeremiah saw another horse approach him.

"We're gonna break our necks out here," Emmett hissed.

"We're a bit farther out than I thought," Jeremiah said as he squinted back at the campfire that flickered in the distance behind him.

Emmett didn't need to glance behind him. "You want to go back?" he asked. "I don't know what you expect to see out here."

"I wasn't expecting to see much. I was hoping to hear something, though. Paul said he would fire some shots into the air if he was in trouble."

"If he's in any condition to pull a trigger."

Jeremiah fixed his eyes upon Emmett and felt the muscles in his jaw clench. Reluctantly, he nodded. "Yeah, I know." From there, he let his eyes wander among the shadows, hoping for one that would give him any measure of hope. When he actually did see a shadow that was moving, Jeremiah pulled in a surprised breath. "What's that over there?" he asked.

Emmett was quiet as he looked in the direction Jeremiah was pointing. Suddenly, he leaned forward in his saddle. "I see it. Looks like it may be someone riding out there."

"Could be Paul."

"No," Emmett replied. "Not unless Paul decided to trade that mustang he was riding for something lighter and bigger."

Jeremiah saw that Emmett was right. "So who is that?" he asked.

"There's one good way to find out," Emmett replied before snapping his reins and setting his horse into motion.

Jeremiah caught up with ease. While he was straining to get a better look at the other rider, he saw that pale horse turn and race away.

"You try to catch up to him from here," Emmett said, "but be careful. I'll do my best to flank him on the right."

"But we should probably —"

It was too late for Jeremiah to say anything about it. Emmett had already veered off to the right and galloped away. Jeremiah had the choice of chasing down Emmett or that other rider he'd spotted. He picked the latter. There were some questions Jeremiah wanted to ask this stranger.

CHAPTER 12

Jeremiah wasn't much of a churchgoing fellow, but he knew better than to fool with the man who rode a pale horse. Even so, with Paul still out there and unaccounted for, Jeremiah simply couldn't afford to let this man get away.

Snapping his reins, he kept his eyes on the terrain directly in front of him while also doing his best to keep the stranger in his sight. The man on the pale horse had gotten a head start, but was a bit more reluctant to gallop for very long once the shadows grew thicker. Either that, or he hadn't counted on Jeremiah being quite so tenacious in his pursuit.

Something in Jeremiah's gut told him to take a shot at the stranger now that he had his chance. Since his only clear target was the man's back, however, Jeremiah passed on that opportunity and used both hands to work the reins.

Jeremiah focused upon the stranger as if that man and his horse were the only other living things on the face of the earth. When the stranger sped up, so did Jeremiah. When the stranger slowed down, Jeremiah grinned to himself and was certain he was about to catch up and get a better look at the man's face.

When the stranger's horse suddenly veered to the left and jumped over a fallen log, Jeremiah nearly ran his own horse directly into that log, which would have sent them both face-first to the ground.

Jeremiah reflexively pulled his reins, but knew he was too late. Every muscle in his body prepared to be thrown from the horse and feel the unwelcome impact of the cold, hard ground.

Fortunately, Jeremiah's horse wasn't as surprised. It jumped over the log and barely managed to clear it. Its hooves knocked against the front of the log, scraped against the top of it and kicked the back of it, but the horse managed to get over without being tripped up.

It took a few moments for Jeremiah to realize he wasn't lying on the ground with a collection of broken bones. A grateful laugh sprang from the back of his throat, but was quickly choked back again when he saw a second stranger and his horse standing in wait no more than ten paces away from that log.

That second horseman seemed to have appeared from out of nowhere. He rode a darker horse and wore a dark coat. If not for the subtle glare of moonlight coming from the rider's face, Jeremiah might not have seen him at all.

It was too late for Jeremiah to do anything more than pull his reins and steer his horse away from that second rider. Although that kept him on the first one's tail, he wasn't too happy about putting his back to the second. While leaning down close to his horse's neck, Jeremiah reached for the rifle hanging from his saddle. The weapon felt comforting in his grasp, even if he couldn't take proper aim using only one hand.

Jeremiah glanced over his shoulder, which was enough to see that the second rider was coming after him. Cursing under his breath, Jeremiah did his best to keep looking back and forth between the two riders. When he looked behind him again, he saw a third rider explode from between a pair of trees like a murder of crows flying from cover.

Once Jeremiah saw the familiar markings of Emmett's mustang, he breathed a little easier. Jeremiah shifted around to look ahead once more, which was when he heard the horses behind him veer off and ride in another direction.

As the thunder of hooves behind him faded away, Jeremiah concentrated on the pale horse in front of him. That rider had gained a bit of ground, but that lead dissipated quickly once Jeremiah snapped his own horse's reins. As he closed in on that other horse, Jeremiah took a deep breath and hollered as loudly as he could.

"I don't want to hurt you," he shouted. "I just want to —"

But Jeremiah was cut short when he saw the rider ahead of him turn in his saddle. He couldn't get a good look at the rider's face, since the man was sighting along the top of a pistol.

Jeremiah gritted his teeth and pulled hard on his reins. His horse responded well enough that its hooves skidded along the ground and it had to struggle to keep itself upright while turning sharply to the left. Jeremiah gripped the reins in one hand and dug his boots into the stirrups to keep from slipping from the saddle.

Just as Jeremiah was regaining control, he heard a shot fired from somewhere ahead of him. Even as he heard lead slap into flesh, Jeremiah braced himself for the rush of pain that was surely to come. He'd seen men shot and was always amazed at how long it took for the pain to set in. Sometimes it was a matter of seconds and sometimes it was minutes. Sometimes, he'd been told, a man didn't feel much pain at all. He simply fell over and landed in his Maker's arms.

All of this flashed through his mind in a rush, but Jeremiah still didn't feel any pain. He did, however, notice that the horse was becoming harder to control.

"Jesus Christ," he muttered as he felt the large animal begin to topple over.

The horse wasn't responding to the reins or even the spurs as Jeremiah fought to keep it from dropping. Jeremiah could feel the horse's ribs shudder as it wheezed one last time. After that, its hooves scraped against the ground and its massive body keeled over to one side.

Rather than jump clear straightaway, he kicked his legs back so they were free of the stirrups. After that, he waited until he could feel which way the horse was falling and then jumped clear so he landed on his back.

The fall seemed to take forever and Jeremiah was gritting his teeth through every second of it. He knew the landing was going to hurt, but at least it was a kind of hurt he was familiar with.

When he hit the ground, he felt pain explode from his ribs and another burst from his right knee. As he skidded along the loose gravel, Jeremiah kicked his legs straight and reached out to stop himself. His left fingers dug into the dirt and his shoulder ached from the sudden stop. Jeremiah could still move and he seemed able to get up, so that's what he set out to do.

Every muscle in his body ached.

Jeremiah's head felt like it had been cracked like an egg, but he couldn't feel any blood after a few quick pats. The first thing he saw when he took a look around was the horse lying on its side nearby. Jeremiah walked up to the animal and placed his hand upon its side.

The animal rattled and let out a groaning breath.

As near as Jeremiah could tell, the other rider's bullet had dug in from the front and raked along like a talon before digging farther into the animal's gut.

Suddenly, Jeremiah was shaken back to his senses by the sound of approaching hooves. He didn't even know he'd been standing there in a daze until he was snapped out of it.

When he looked for the rider, Jeremiah

felt as if he were standing under the pale glow of silver lanterns. He'd been in the dark for long enough that his eyes soaked up every bit of moonlight to be had. Jeremiah stared toward the approaching sounds and quickly picked out the shape of the other rider.

That sight was more than enough to put Jeremiah's mind on nothing but survival. His rifle had been tossed, so he reached to the holster at his side and grabbed the handle of the old Colt. As he tried to draw the pistol, he was instantly reminded of why the gun hadn't fallen from the holster earlier. The leather strap looped over the hammer had kept it in its place then just like it kept it there now.

Swearing under his breath, Jeremiah fumbled with the strap as the rider drew closer.

When the old Colt cleared leather, Jeremiah was in such a hurry to defend himself that he sent his first shot straight into the dirt somewhere between himself and his intended target.

The rider came to a stop and stayed put.

"Come on!" Jeremiah shouted breathlessly. "You can shoot a horse, but you can't hit me? When'd you lose your nerve?"

Jeremiah watched the rider, but couldn't

make out more than a shape in the darkness. He was glad to make out the rider at all, but only an owl would have seen more than the figure in the saddle and the faint glint of light off the iron in the man's hand.

The instant Jeremiah saw that gun in the rider's grasp, he straightened out his own gun hand and pulled his trigger.

In the distance, the horse shuffled from one leg to another as the rider snapped the reins and hunkered down low in his saddle.

Jeremiah steeled himself for whatever the next couple of seconds would bring. It was too late for him to think about getting away from the rider, so all that remained was to survive the next few seconds.

This time, he raised his gun and took a moment to aim before firing off another shot. The Colt bucked against Jeremiah's palm, but was quickly answered by a shot from the approaching rider. Lead whipped through the air and hissed to Jeremiah's right. He reflexively hopped in the other direction and landed upon the ankle that had been aching since he'd fallen from his horse.

Unlike the first spill he'd taken, Jeremiah caught himself before hitting the ground. He fired another shot, but quickly realized there was no more target in front of him.

The only trace of that pale horse was the dust it had kicked up when it galloped out of sight.

Jeremiah stood his ground, twitching at every noise he heard. He was almost certain he'd heard gunshots in the distance not too long ago. Then again, he knew that could very well have been echoes within his own battered skull.

Hearing another labored groan from his horse, Jeremiah walked over to the fallen animal. Squatting down next to the horse's head, he rubbed its ears one last time.

"Sorry about that," he whispered. "But you won't be hurting much longer."

With that, Jeremiah straightened up and put the horse down with one merciful shot.

While he was checking to see how many rounds were left in his cylinder, Jeremiah heard another horse approaching. He snapped the gun shut, aimed in the direction of those sounds and waited for a threat to present itself.

Another horse sped over to Jeremiah and was quickly brought to a stop.

"Easy, now," Emmett said. "Don't shoot. I came to see if you need any help."

Jeremiah let out the breath he'd been holding and lowered the Colt. "Thank God, it's you."

"I heard shooting. Were you hit?"

"No, but damn near every piece of me is screaming for mercy. What about you? I thought I heard some shooting myself."

Emmett rode up close enough for Jeremiah to see the haunted look in his eyes. "You heard right, but I wasn't hit."

"Who were those men? Why were they after us? And where the hell is Paul?"

"I found Paul," Emmett said in a tone that didn't inspire much confidence.

"Where is he?" Jeremiah asked, even though he wasn't looking forward to the answer. "Is he all right?"

After shaking his head, Emmett said, "No. He was killed."

"Oh, Jesus."

Emmett offered him a hand. "Come along with me. I'll take you back to camp."

"No! Not yet."

"It sure don't look like that horse is gonna be of much use."

"We can't go back with those men out there," Jeremiah said. "They might circle back toward our wagons!"

"Which is why we should get back there and protect them," Emmett replied in a voice that was as steady and cold as the underside of a rock.

After taking a few more breaths to steady

147

himself, Jeremiah asked, "What happened to the one you found? Where did you find Paul? Did you . . . did you kill that other man?"

"I chased him off," Emmett replied quickly. "And while I was headed back this way, I saw the one you were after running from here like his tail was on fire. Neither one of them was headed for camp."

Jeremiah filled his lungs with cool night air. Although it went a ways to help calm his nerves, the simple action strained his ribs something terrible. "Where did you find Paul?"

"He was at a smaller camp not far from here. It must have been where those other two came from. Paul probably stumbled on them and was shot for it."

Jeremiah felt his head spinning, and it wasn't solely because of the beating he'd taken in the fall. "What am I going to tell the Inglebrechts?"

"You'll tell them the truth. If you'd rather, I can tell them."

Pulling in a breath that wasn't deep enough to hurt, Jeremiah shook his head. "No. I'll tell them."

Emmett stared down at Jeremiah for a bit before saying, "We'll need to tend to the body. Should we do that now or later?"

"Let's go to that other camp you found and then check on our wagons. Hopefully we'll find those bastards somewhere along the way."

CHAPTER 13

Nobody was there when Jeremiah and Emmett arrived at the little campsite. In fact, the spot was so barren that Jeremiah wondered why Emmett was stopping. Since he was forced to sit up straight in the saddle behind Emmett, Jeremiah was having a hard time seeing much. What little night vision he'd gained was washed away by the constant pain that flooded his entire body.

"You all right?" Emmett asked.

"Yeah. I'm fine. Where's Paul?"

Emmett pointed ahead and to the right. "Over there."

Despite the pain it caused, Jeremiah slid down from the saddle before Emmett even had a chance to dismount. Emmett walked around the horse toward a shape that looked more like a fallen log in the shadows than a man. Jeremiah followed and looked around at the rest of the camp.

There wasn't much to see apart from a

few rocks and a pile of twigs. The smell of burned wood still hung in the air and when he got closer, Jeremiah could see wisps of smoke drifting up from the twigs. Even though there had been a fire there, Jeremiah still felt like he was looking at the wrong spot. "Are you sure this was a camp?" he asked.

"Yep," Emmett replied. "It's a camp set up by men who don't want to be seen. It was set up and broke down in a hurry, and my guess is that Paul probably caught sight of the fire before it was put out."

Reluctantly, Jeremiah looked at the shape that was stretched out on the ground near Emmett's feet. Somehow, that shape seemed to be standing still while everything else moved along. Dirt rustled in the breeze and burned twigs from the campfire stirred every now and then.

But that shape didn't move one bit.

It was dead.

It was also Paul.

"Good Lord," Jeremiah whispered. "Why would this happen?"

While Jeremiah glanced down at the body and then turned his eyes away, Emmett kept his eyes on that unmoving figure while slowly shaking his head.

"Like I said," Emmett replied, "the men

who made this camp didn't want to be found. Paul found them."

Suddenly, Jeremiah tensed and slapped his hand against his holstered Colt. His eyes locked upon something nearby that had moved.

Emmett looked at what had caught Jeremiah's attention and held out a hand. "Don't bother with the gun. It's just the kid's horse."

Jeremiah squinted through the haze that was collecting behind his eyes and saw no rider in that animal's saddle.

"Go ahead and take him," Emmett said. "You need it more than Paul does."

As much as Jeremiah wanted to argue, there was no sense in it. He didn't have any other horses to choose from. "You go back to make sure the others are safe," he said to Emmett.

"What are you gonna do here?"

"Put this body under a bit of ground. I don't want his parents to see him like this."

Emmett rode away to head back to the wagons, leaving Jeremiah with the dead man's horse.

When Jeremiah rode back to his own camp, the campfire made his eyes hurt. Looking at those crackling flames felt like staring up at the blazing sun until his eyes readjusted. But looking at the expectant faces of Harold and Noelle Inglebrecht was a whole lot harder.

"Where's my son?" Harold asked. "Where's Paul?"

Sara gave Jeremiah a temporary reprieve when she rushed forward and nearly pulled him from his saddle. "Oh my God," she said. "What happened to you? Are you hurt?"

"I'm all right," Jeremiah told her as he eased himself down from the horse's back. "I just took a fall from my horse."

"What?"

"I'm fine. It wasn't the first time I've fallen from a saddle."

"You could have broken your neck."

"But I didn't," Jeremiah said with a bit too much venom in his voice. After taking a breath, he looked his wife in the eyes and held on to both of her hands. "I'll be all right," he said earnestly. The look in his eyes told Sara that there were much bigger problems to be addressed.

"That's Paul's horse," Harold said as he stomped over to Jeremiah and spun him around with a rough hand upon his shoulder. "What happened to my boy? Tell me, damn you!"

Jeremiah winced with the pain of being shoved like that. When he spoke, his voice came out through gritted teeth and sounded much harsher than he'd intended. "Didn't Emmett tell you anything?"

"I want to hear it from you!"

"Your son was shot, Mr. Inglebrecht."

Harold froze. Behind him, Noelle went pale as a sheet.

"Shot?" the old woman asked. "Emmett said there was trouble, but . . ."

While Jeremiah tried to choke back the lump that had formed in his throat, Emmett stepped forward. "Yes, ma'am," he said. "I was the one who found him. I'll tell you whatever I can."

Both of the Inglebrechts fixed their eyes upon Emmett, and Jeremiah couldn't have been more grateful for it. Everyone in camp listened as Emmett relayed the news of what he'd found. Jeremiah couldn't help but notice how few words it took to describe the end of a good man's life.

When he was done, Emmett stood with his arms folded across his chest and his eyes on Noelle Inglebrecht's face. She seemed too stunned to do much of anything but stare back at him, until Emmett bowed his head to look at the ground near his feet.

"So you say these men killed my boy?"

Harold asked.

"Yes, sir," Emmett replied.

"And why would they do that?"

"I'd only be guessing, sir. The fact is that I don't rightly know."

"Do you know who they are?"

Emmett let out a slow breath and chewed on the inside of his cheek.

Although he'd been watching quietly for a while, Jeremiah wasn't about to stand by any longer. He stepped forward and put a hand on Emmett's shoulder. "We were both shot at by those men."

"Or you were shooting at my son."

"Why in the hell would we want to do that?" Jeremiah asked.

"Because he helped fund this whole expedition of ours," Harold snapped. "Don't stand there and tell me you didn't know that!"

"Why would I know that?" Jeremiah stopped himself from saying another word and took a breath. "Look. This has been a hard night for all of us. If you want to turn back, I'd understand. Just say the word and we'll —"

"We're not turning back," Noelle said in a quiet, yet stern voice. "We knew this ride wouldn't be easy. There's no reason for us to turn back."

"Our boy's dead!" Harold snarled.

"And nothing will change that," Noelle replied with enough strength to put her husband's gruff demeanor to shame. "The last thing I want to do now is go back to the house where we raised him, walk the streets where I walked with him as a child and stand in the same spots where we all stood when we were a whole family."

Slowly, the rage in Harold's eyes subsided. When it left him, it took away some of the fire that had always been present in the old man's face, leaving him noticeably lesser for it. By the time he nodded to her, Harold didn't have enough strength to get out one more word.

The camp became quiet after that. Apart from the occasional crackle from the fire, it was as though the whole world had held its breath until the solemn moment passed.

"We need to get some rest," Jeremiah said. "I'll stand watch." With that in mind, his next thought was to take his rifle along with him. It was then that he realized the rifle was probably wedged under the carcass of his horse. Rather than consider going back to that spot, Jeremiah walked over to his wagon and dug out the box of spare rounds for the Colt.

Sara tried to comfort him, but he wouldn't

have any of it. Jeremiah was through with talking. All he wanted was to keep anyone else from getting hurt. Despite his silence, Sara rubbed his back for a few seconds and then left him in peace.

The Inglebrechts kept to themselves for the rest of the night.

Emmett double-checked the rounds in his pistol and dropped it back into its holster. As he walked over to the bedroll he'd laid out in a dark corner of the camp, he never let his hand swing more than an inch or so from his gun. Even after stretching out on his bedroll and sliding his hat partway over his face, he crossed his arms so the pistol remained in his reach. It was impossible to say whether he was asleep or not, but Emmett didn't move once he'd settled in.

Jeremiah walked a few paces from the perimeter, picked a spot where he could see anyone approaching the wagons and got as comfortable as he could. His gun was holstered as well, but Jeremiah kept flinching toward it as if he didn't know whether to keep it in hand or leave it be. He chose the latter since he didn't want to mistakenly shoot himself in the foot.

A few minutes later, he heard light footsteps approaching and turned to get a look. Expecting his wife, Jeremiah instead found

Anne making her way to his post. She smiled when she saw she'd been spotted and showed him something Jeremiah had not been expecting from her.

"Here," she said while handing over a Winchester rifle. "You could probably use this."

Jeremiah took the rifle from her, but looked at it as if he wasn't sure what to make of it.

Anne shrugged and sat down beside him. "I'm sure you're a fine shot with that pistol, but this one's got much better range."

"Thanks for letting me know," Jeremiah said with a weary smile.

"Not that you wouldn't know the difference," Anne quickly added. "I just thought . . . oh, forget it. Just take the damn rifle."

Jeremiah took it and propped it against the tree beside him. "I appreciate it. I'm just a little tired. It's been a hell of a long day."

"It sure has." Anne stayed next to him and stared out at the dark land stretched in front of her. The longer she watched the shadow-covered hills and swaying trees, the tighter she wrapped her arms around herself, as if bracing against the cold. "Do you think those killers are out there?"

Although Jeremiah started to shake his head, he couldn't get himself to commit to it. As his head swayed slowly like the trees in the distance, he replied, "I don't think so. Come to think of it, they might have been run off for good."

"Really?"

"I shot at one and Emmett chased down another. Both of us managed to convince them to turn tail and run." Blinking away memories that were all too fresh in his mind, Jeremiah looked over to Anne and then to the spot where Claire was curled up asleep in a little ball. "I'll see to it that no harm comes to you or your daughter."

"I know," she said confidently. "And I know you already put yourself in harm's way to keep us all safe. Looks like you were hurt as well."

Jeremiah looked down at his rumpled clothes, which were still stained with blood as well as mud that had soaked through during his fall. "Looks worse than it is," he muttered.

Reaching out for him, Anne ran her fingers along a spot on his side that was particularly bloody. "That looks pretty bad," she said. "Are you sure you don't want someone to take a look at it? I used to be a nurse, you know."

Despite the pain that had been filling him up since the fall, Jeremiah could only think about his wife at that particular moment. More specifically, he was concerned with where Sara was and whether or not she was watching him. He spotted her right away, sleeping in her bedroll next to their wagon. Even though Jeremiah was only fifteen or so paces from her, he felt as if he was close enough that he needed to whisper to keep from waking her up.

Before Jeremiah could say anything, he felt Anne pulling his shirt from where it was tucked into his waistband. Even when she began running her fingers along his ribs, Jeremiah kept quiet.

"This looks pretty bad," Anne said. "It's bruised up and cut in a few places. Does this hurt?" she asked while pressing against a specific spot.

Jeremiah pulled in a sharp breath and nodded. "Yeah. A bit."

Despite the reaction she'd gotten, Anne smiled and nodded. "You're right," she said while pulling his shirt back down. "It looks worse than it is. If your ribs had been broken, you would have done a lot more than squirm."

"So, that's your test, huh?"

"Yep, and it works pretty well. You got

knocked around, but I'd say you'll be all right. I've been watching you."

Hearing the way her voice lowered a bit when she said that last part was enough to bring a grin to any man's face, married or not. "You . . . uh . . . you have?"

Anne nodded again. Her hair wasn't tied back, so it hung around her face naturally. Although she probably would have said otherwise, she looked beautiful just then. Jeremiah had always preferred to look at women before they gussied themselves up too much. It was a way to get a glimpse into who they truly were.

She didn't fuss with her hair or avert her eyes the way some women did when they weren't made up to what they thought was their best. She looked at him easily and didn't back down from a thing she said. She was tired, frightened and also brave enough to keep going. What was more important was that she let all of that show in her eyes without hiding or drawing attention to it. That said a lot about any person.

"I've been watching you ever since you got back looking like you were dragged behind a horse," she told him. "You're walking all right, breathing all right, moving as good as one could expect. That means you at least don't have any broken bones. Maybe a sprain or two, is my guess, but I was just a nurse. We could spot a few things, but I won't pretend to know all there is to know about how to make them better."

"You seem pretty smart to me," Jeremiah said.

Anne grinned and held his gaze for a few seconds. "Thank you. And you're very brave for what you've done."

"I got a boy killed," Jeremiah whispered.

"No. Those men were the ones who killed him. You chased those men away. That means you saved me, my daughter, your wife and the Inglebrechts from getting shot as well. I'm sure Paul wouldn't have wanted it any other way."

Jeremiah reluctantly nodded. "Thanks."

"Now that I see you're all right, I can get some rest. We've still got a long way to go." Leaning forward, Anne gently kissed Jeremiah's cheek. "Thank you so much. You truly did a brave thing."

The kiss was quick and sweet. Jeremiah might have expected something similar if Claire had been the one thanking him. Still, he couldn't help but feel guilty about receiving it. What cut him even deeper was the part of him that hadn't wanted it to end so quickly.

Jeremiah glanced over to his wife again.

She was sound asleep, just as she had been the last time he'd checked. He then watched Anne go over to where Emmett was lying.

She jumped a bit when she saw him stir, but stepped closer as Emmett rolled onto his side. Emmett sat up and exchanged a few words with Anne, smiling and keeping his voice low so as not to disturb any of the others. After a few more seconds, Anne unbuttoned Emmett's shirt and took a quick look at him.

Even from a distance, Jeremiah could see the dark patches of dried blood caked on Emmett's sides. The firelight illuminated the camp just enough for Jeremiah to see a pattern of rough and leathery scars covering Emmett's chest like a thick spider's web.

Anne's hands moved along Emmett's wounds quickly and then she pulled his shirt closed again. After a few words that were too quiet for Jeremiah to hear, Anne gave Emmett a quick kiss.

Turning his back to the camp, Jeremiah focused on the shadow-covered landscape until his eyes adjusted to the absence of firelight. He let out an aggravated breath and then looked at the rifle Anne had brought him. Unless he saw a group of gunmen riding straight toward him, Jeremiah intended to leave that rifle right where it was.

CHAPTER 14

The next morning, Jeremiah was awakened by the sound of crates slamming into the backs of wagons and pans clanking against one another. He was so tired that he barely recalled Emmett relieving him of watch duty. It must have happened, though, since Jeremiah was wrapped up in his bedroll without his boots and Emmett was sitting on a log, hunched over a cup of coffee.

When he saw Jeremiah stir, Emmett raised his cup and then pointed to the campfire. Fresh branches had been stacked beneath a kettle and a pan that fought for space above a crackling flame.

"Rise and shine," Sara said as she leaned down to rub the top of Jeremiah's head.

He twitched and looked up to find his wife standing behind him. "Why didn't you wake me up sooner?"

"You needed your rest. I saved some bacon and griddle cakes for you. I woke up early, so I thought I'd fix something other than beans for a change."

Jeremiah sat up and filled his lungs with crisp morning air. The scent of breakfast drifted into his nostrils as well, bringing a tired smile to his face. "Reminds me of home," he said.

"This is home, remember?" Sara asked good-naturedly. Seeing that her joke had the opposite of its intended effect on Jeremiah, she added, "At least for a while anyway."

"Yeah," he said as he took the plate and cup Sara handed to him. "For a while. How are the Inglebrechts?"

"They're doing better. They didn't eat much breakfast and haven't been talking, but nobody could blame them for that. I think they'll be better once they can pay their respects."

"Respects?"

Sara blinked and then took a quick look around. When she saw that everyone was distracted by making preparations to leave, she leaned down and whispered, "We are going back to where you buried Paul, aren't we?"

"I didn't have time to do much. It's not a proper grave."

"But he's buried?"

"Yes."

"We need to go there," Sara told him. "Aren't we supposed to ride in that direction anyhow?"

"More or less."

"Then we need to stop. They need to see their boy. Even if he's under a pile of dirt, they need to see him. Can't you understand that?"

Jeremiah didn't need to hear another word. All he needed to do was watch the Inglebrechts as they tied down their wagons and hitched their horses into their harnesses.

Noelle was keeping her head up, but she moved as if lifting her feet was an effort. Harold was quiet and reserved. Compared to how he'd been before, the old man seemed defeated and broken down.

Before he took his eyes from the elderly couple and started in on his breakfast, Jeremiah was planning the best route to get his wagons close to the campsite he and Emmett had found.

They arrived at Paul's grave well before noon. Jeremiah led the Inglebrechts to the spot while Emmett remained behind to keep an eye on the wagons as they continued west. Neither Harold nor Noelle said a word

167

as they followed on one horse. Even when they saw the mound of freshly turned soil, neither one of them seemed to have much of a reaction.

Harold took his hat off and held it in both hands as he looked down upon the grave. "This is where you found him?"

"No," Jeremiah replied. "It wasn't far from here, though. This just seemed like a better spot to . . . I mean . . . for him to be."

Harold nodded slowly and stared at the ground.

As she dropped to her knees, Noelle began to sob. Her husband didn't reach out to comfort her and she looked as if she wouldn't have accepted comfort anyway. Her tears traced lines along her cheeks and stopped before dripping onto her lap. Noelle wiped them away with the back of one hand and then reached around her neck to carefully remove a necklace she'd been wearing.

Jeremiah watched reverently as Noelle took the silver chain from around her neck, looked at the simple cross hanging from it and gathered it all up in her hand. She placed that hand upon the ground and pressed it into the soil.

"You did all you could," Harold said in a

voice that was as cracked as the floor of a desert.

Snapped from the weight of the moment, Jeremiah thought he must have misunderstood the old man's words. But there was no anger on Harold's face as he placed a hand on Jeremiah's shoulder and gave him a fatherly pat.

"I'm sure you wouldn't have just let him die without doing your best to stop it," Harold said as if he was thinking out loud rather than addressing another person. "If I said anything other than that . . . I apologize."

Jeremiah didn't have a notion of what he should say to that. He simply kept quiet until Harold wandered away and stood behind his wife.

After another few moments, Noelle patted the ground and scooped up some dirt to cover the cross she'd pressed into the earth. Harold helped her to her feet and they walked back to their horse.

"I need to make another stop," Jeremiah said. "Do you think you can find your way back to the wagons?"

"We'll go with you," Harold said sternly.

"No, I just need to get my rifle."

"Then we'll come along." Before Jeremiah could protest again, Harold added, "And I won't hear another word about it. If those gunmen are still about, you shouldn't go off on your own."

"They're probably nowhere around here," Jeremiah said. Of course, he neglected to mention that if those gunmen were still around, they wouldn't be frightened off by an old couple in mourning.

"If they're gone, then there's no reason for us to leave your side," Harold said.

"Fine. I'll be quick about it." Since he didn't want to let any more time go by, Jeremiah snapped his reins the moment he climbed into his saddle. He headed back to the spot where he'd taken his fall and almost missed it since it looked like a completely different place now that it was drenched in sunlight.

Unfortunately, the sight of the horse's carcass was a difficult thing to miss. Jeremiah rode up to it as his head filled with memories from the night before. Those memories were a nightmare compared to the tranquility he felt now. Even the dead horse lay there like just another one of nature's unfortunate victims. If he hadn't delivered the killing shot himself, Jeremiah might have thought the horse had simply run out of time and died right there.

He spotted the rifle protruding from

under the horse right away. Jeremiah dismounted and dropped to one knee beside the carcass so he could grab the weapon with both hands while pushing with the foot that was braced against the ground. After a few tugs, the rifle started to budge. It took several more tries, but it finally came free and Jeremiah got back to his feet.

"Got it?" Harold asked from where he and Noelle were waiting.

Suddenly, Jeremiah caught sight of something else that he hadn't been able to see the night before. His eyes wandered from the carcass as he relived the attack in his head. With his sights set on the spot where the gunman on the pale horse had been, Jeremiah spotted a stretch of hard-packed soil that covered most of the area.

"I got something," Jeremiah replied, without taking his eyes from the tracks embedded in that soil.

"That's your rifle, isn't it?"

Jeremiah looked down at the rifle in his hand as if he'd almost forgotten it was there. "Yeah. It's my rifle. Just stay put for a second."

Before taking another step, Jeremiah looked at his feet to study the ground upon which he stood. Sprigs of tall grass erupted from the earth here and there, occasionally broken up by large rocks, a few trees and a couple of fallen logs. The sun beat down upon Jeremiah as well as everything else, making it easier for him to pick out the impressions in the soil.

By the looks of it, the dirt had soaked up a good deal of water. Since there hadn't been much rain the last few days, Jeremiah had to assume that moisture had come from an earlier storm or dew that had collected overnight. Whatever caused it, that moisture made the ground soft enough to hold the impressions of what were unmistakably tracks left behind by horses that had recently trampled this spot.

Jeremiah did his best to see where the tracks led as he tried even harder to think back to what Abe Saunders would have done in this same spot. Abe had been one of the first men Jeremiah looked into hiring whenever setting out on a cattle drive. Abe was a tracker who could tell which way a stray had gone by picking out one set of tracks amid a jumble of others. More often than he could recall, Jeremiah had seen Abe study a patch of ground for a bit, think to himself and then point which way they all needed to go.

The first time he'd seen that trick, Jeremiah had thought Abe was full of beans.

But every single time, Abe had led them straight to whatever they'd been looking for, whether it was man or beast. Even though he'd learned a thing or two from Abe, Jeremiah would have given anything to have Abe Saunders by his side right now.

"What are you looking at?" Harold asked after several moments passed in heavy silence.

"I think I found those gunmen's tracks," Jeremiah replied.

"Is that a fact?"

"I think it is." Straightening up, Jeremiah kept his eyes focused upon the tracks and then started walking.

He'd asked Abe on several occasions to explain the miracles he'd performed. While the tracker never tried to hide his secrets, understanding them was something that had proven to be out of Jeremiah's reach. It was akin to listening to a watchmaker explain his steps as he put a clock together. After hearing and listening to every word, a man couldn't exactly put together a clock for himself.

As far as Jeremiah could remember, there were ways to tell which direction the horse had been facing when it had left its tracks. There were ways to figure how fast it had been running. There were even ways to figure out what it was carrying, but Jeremiah didn't know any of that. The one advantage he did have was that he'd been there when the horse had been there.

He knew which way it had been facing, how fast it had left and didn't much care to know what it had been carrying. What he didn't know was where the gunmen had ridden off to. By the time he'd walked more than thirty yards without losing sight of the tracks, Jeremiah was feeling confident that he could get a notion as to where those men had gone.

"Where are you going?" Harold asked from not too far behind Jeremiah.

Turning to see the old man following a few paces behind, Jeremiah said, "Bring my horse up here, will you?"

"Sure. I've got the reins right here."

Jeremiah saw his horse standing beside Harold's. He reached up to take the reins from the old man and felt deathly afraid that he wouldn't be able to find the tracks again. Much to his relief, Jeremiah saw the impressions in the ground as clearly as he saw the boots on his feet.

"How long have we been away from the others?" Jeremiah asked.

After fishing a dented watch from his pocket, Harold flipped it open and took a look at its face. "Just over an hour, I figure."

After a bit of calculating, Jeremiah said, "Good. I've got a pretty good idea of where they should be."

"If they stayed on course," Harold muttered.

"They're on course. There's not many other ways for them to go. I should be able to follow these for a while and then catch up with them without too much trouble. Since you've got two on one horse, maybe you shouldn't come along."

"And you think we'll be safer heading back to meet up with the wagons on our own?"

Even though he could tell that Harold was just trying to get him to second-guess his own actions, Jeremiah couldn't help but be swayed by the argument. Whether the old man truly believed it or not, there was a genuine possibility that they could run into some serious danger no matter which way they rode. It was just safer to stick together either way.

"Fine," Jeremiah said. "Come along, but don't distract me. I need to follow these tracks and I can't do that with you barking at me."

Harold held up his hands and said, "I'm not the one holding us up here."

"Don't be so difficult," Noelle said as she swatted his shoulder. "That's all the boy is trying to tell you."

Although it was clear to see the old man had plenty more to say, he kept it under his hat long enough for Jeremiah to reacquaint himself with the tracks and get moving.

Jeremiah wasn't able to ride very fast and he still lost sight of the tracks when he got overly anxious or accidentally snapped the reins. After having to double back a few times, Jeremiah got into the habit of marking certain rocks, trees, roots or other landmarks that were near the tracks so he could find them again if need be.

After less than half a mile, Jeremiah's task became a lot easier since the tracks he'd been following were joined by several other sets that converged upon the first. From that point on, the riders of those horses didn't seem too concerned with staying hidden. A blind man could tell they were riding in a column headed in a very specific direction.

"Good Lord," Jeremiah said as his head snapped up.

"What is it?" Harold asked. "You lose the tracks again?"

"No, I can see the tracks just fine."

"Then what's on your mind?"

"Those riders mean to intercept our wagons," Jeremiah said. "That is, unless an ambush has already started."

CHAPTER 15

Jeremiah raced back to the wagons so quickly that he thought he'd lost the Inglebrechts several times along the way. When he finally caught sight of the row of covered wagons slowly plodding to the west, Jeremiah was both happy and anxious. He was happy to find them all well, but was anxious because he was fairly certain that wellness wouldn't last for very long.

Before Jeremiah and the Inglebrechts joined up with the wagons, they were met by Emmett. He rode out to them with his rifle already drawn, but appeared relieved when he got a look at their faces.

"Glad to see you again," Emmett said. "What the hell took you so long?"

"I had to get my rifle." Waiting until the Inglebrechts passed him by and headed for their wagons, Jeremiah added, "I think I found some of the tracks left by those gunmen."

"Let me guess. They led back in this direction."

"How'd you know?"

"Because I spotted a few riders following us like a damn shadow," Emmett replied. "I nearly took a shot at you when I saw you rushing up on us like that."

"Jesus. Where are they?"

Emmett motioned for Jeremiah to follow him as he rode up to the head of the line of wagons. Along the way, everyone else took a long look at Jeremiah as if they were seeing a ghost.

The Inglebrechts' wagons were connected to the others by a tether, which was enough to keep the horses moving along behind the rest. As Harold rode up alongside the wagons, he glanced over to inspect what he could from his spot. The old man appeared to be almost anxious enough to try hopping into the driver's seat from his saddle.

"Now, don't make any quick moves," Emmett said. "But they're just up ahead on that ridge. You see 'em?"

Jeremiah didn't have to strain his eyes much to catch sight of the figures lined up on a hilltop less than half a mile or so away. It took all the restraint he had to keep from pointing or making a move toward his gun, but Jeremiah knew that Emmett was right to be cautious. For all they knew, those figures were sighting in on them at that very moment. "I see four of them. Maybe five. How long ago did you spot them?"

"Not long," Emmett said. "Less than half an hour, maybe."

"Do you think they're the ones from the other night?" Jeremiah asked.

"From what I can see, they could be those gunmen, Injuns or the law. I didn't want to study them too carefully. If they are those gunmen, then they might just decide to charge before we get a chance to prepare ourselves. I didn't want to take the chance seeing as how it was just me, the women and that little girl."

"Glad you waited." Jeremiah stared up at the figures in the distance and felt his stomach clench. "What do you think we should do now?"

"Didn't you have a plan for this sort of thing?" Glancing over at Jeremiah, Emmett added, "You are the leader and all."

"I made sure we all had rifles and that we had at least three men along who could use them. I didn't exactly bank on losing one of the most capable men of this group so quickly. Paul was supposed to be our best asset for situations like this."

Emmett nodded and looked around as if

he was merely taking in the scenery. "Well, they're positioned up there and haven't moved much. We could scout ahead for a way around those hills. Maybe we don't even need to get any closer to them."

"That's a good idea. Should I ride ahead?"

"Nah, I'll do it. You should stay here. I think your wife is pretty anxious to have a word with you."

"Mr. Correy?" Noelle shouted. "Could we stop for a moment? My husband and I need to get back onto our wagons."

"Sure," Jeremiah said. "Let's get situated. In fact, Emmett's gonna scout ahead to check on the condition of the trail."

"Is everything all right?" Sara asked from the front of the line.

Jeremiah gave her a quick nod, which was enough to keep her quiet for the moment. It was also enough to let her know that he would talk with her as soon as he could.

Pulling back on his reins, Jeremiah went to the first of the Inglebrechts' two wagons and then made sure the horses stopped smoothly once Sara brought the line to a stop. The crunch of the wheels grinding against the ground slowed down and before long, fell into silence. As everyone got themselves situated, Jeremiah could think

181

only about the figures that were watching them.

Were those figures even looking down at the wagons?

Were they friendly? Hostile? Or did they even give a hoot?

Finally, Jeremiah couldn't rid himself of a single thought that plagued him until he rode up to where Sara was waiting for him. Even seeing his wife's face wasn't enough to shake that thought free.

"What the hell was I thinking?" Jeremiah asked, giving voice to that nagging thought.

"What?" she asked.

"This whole thing," Jeremiah said. "This whole ride to Oregon. What in God's creation got me to think I was capable of leading anyone, even you and me, all the way into Oregon?"

"We've talked about this before," she said soothingly. "Folks do this sort of thing all the time. Some folks pack up their things and head west to dig for gold, and others just need a change of scenery."

"There's plenty who live their entire lives in one spot and love every day of it."

"You're not one of those folks, mister," she said. "Neither am I. Now tell me how the Inglebrechts took seeing their son."

Jeremiah sighed. "As good as can be

expected, I suppose."

"Did they need extra time with him? Is that why you were gone so long?"

For a moment, Jeremiah debated whether or not he should tell Sara about the tracks he'd found. His main concern was to avoid worrying her over nothing. Then again, since they were already being watched, he figured there was plenty worse she could be worried about.

"I found some tracks," Jeremiah told her. "They're from those gunmen."

"Good Lord. Is that who's watching us from that ridge up ahead?"

Glancing toward the ridge, Jeremiah laughed and looked back to his wife. "You knew about that, huh?"

She shrugged and told him, "Emmett didn't say much, but he was riding up ahead and staring at those hills long enough for me to get a hint."

As if on cue, Emmett bolted past them and headed toward the hills before veering off to the left.

"He's going to get a closer look at them now," Jeremiah said. "If we can, we'll try to steer around them altogether."

"That sounds smart." She reached out with one hand and leaned toward Jeremiah so she could rub his cheek. "You're plenty capable of doing this. Nobody said it was going to be easy." Sara's proud smile didn't fade in the slightest. "You've been doing just fine. And stop kicking yourself about Paul. That wasn't your fault."

Jeremiah nodded, knowing better than to argue. That didn't, however, make the bitter memories any easier to stomach. When he looked over to the ridge again, Jeremiah felt as if he'd been kicked in the chest. "Where'd they go?" he asked under his breath.

"What was that?" Sara asked.

But Jeremiah didn't look to her. His eyes were glued to those hills and he looked for a trace of the riders who had been there only moments ago. All he saw was the contours of the land the way God had created it. No longer concerned with maintaining appearances, he dug into his saddlebag for the telescope he kept there. His hands were trembling as he brought it to his eye.

He didn't see any more through the telescope's lense than what he'd seen without it. Swearing under his breath, Jeremiah lowered the telescope and looked around.

"What is it?" Sara asked insistently. "Tell me."

"Whoever was up on that ridge isn't there anymore," Jeremiah said.

"Do you think they're coming this way?"

"I don't know."

"What should we do?"

"I don't . . ." But Jeremiah stopped himself before completing that statement. Instead of throwing up his hands and surrendering, he took a moment to catch his breath and go through the possibilities.

When he'd been arranging this expedition, he'd consulted with plenty of men about what to do if various things should befall them. As it turned out, Jeremiah already knew a good deal about dealing with most emergencies that could crop up. All he needed to do was think of the expedition as another cattle drive instead of a small wagon train.

"Gather everyone up and keep your eyes open," Jeremiah said as if reciting the instructions from memory. Now that he'd gotten a grip on himself, everything else seemed to shrink down to a manageable size. "There's already a man riding ahead, so we'll wait here for him to come back."

"What if something happens to Emmett?" Sara asked.

"Then we'll hear the shots. Either they'll shoot at him or he'll fire to signal to us. Do you still have the shotgun?"

"You took the rifle from —"

"Not the rifle," Jeremiah corrected. "The

185

shotgun. It should be toward the front where you can get to it."

Sara turned and sifted through some things before finally taking hold of a shotgun that was over half as long as she was. "You haven't used this in a long time."

"What's important is if you can use it. Can you?"

She nodded. "It's not that difficult."

Jeremiah looked her in the eye and then leaned over so he could get closer to her. Sara met him halfway so he could give her a lingering kiss. Without taking his lips more than an inch from hers, he said, "You don't hesitate to use that shotgun if need be, understand?"

"I understand."

"This may be nothing, but just in case . . ."

"I understand," she insisted. "Now go see to the others. I can hear them getting restless back there."

Knowing that his wife was more than capable of handling herself, Jeremiah turned his horse around and rode alongside the other wagons. Before he could get a look at Anne, he saw Claire lean out from her mother's wagon and stare at him with wide, curious eyes.

"Hello, Mr. Correy," the little girl said cheerfully.

"Hello, Claire," Jeremiah replied with a tip of his hat. By now, he was in line with that wagon and able to see Anne just fine. "You might want to get in where it's safe."

"Into the wagon?" Anne asked.

"That's right. Just to be cautious."

"Is there a problem?"

"Not yet," Jeremiah said with a stern look that got his point across without needlessly worrying the little girl. "But you'll want to be extra safe."

"Will I need my rifle?" Anne asked.

Only then did Jeremiah remember that he was still carrying the rifle Anne had lent him as well as his own rifle, which had been retrieved earlier. Taking the borrowed rifle from the boot in his saddle, he handed it over and said, "You might want to keep this handy."

As he rode down the line, Jeremiah heard Claire anxiously questioning her mother.

"Are there Indians out there?" Claire was hushed and quickly helped into the wagon behind the driver's seat.

"Why aren't we moving?" Harold asked as soon as Jeremiah was close enough.

Lowering his voice a bit, Jeremiah replied, "There might be some trouble brewing."

Harold nodded and reached behind him for his rifle. Nodding toward the horse under Jeremiah, he said, "Try to keep that one alive, boy. That horse was my son's favorite."

Jeremiah blinked as he was pulled out of the thoughtful trance that had kept him on task this long. He had to quickly look down to verify that he was riding a horse other than the one he'd used to leave his ranch. For a man in his line of work, horses were a valuable commodity. While most men tended to befriend theirs to some degree or another, Jeremiah saw plenty of horses get injured, die or get sold off. It had just proven easier to treat whatever horse he rode the way others treated their wagons. He kept them in working order, treated them right, but didn't go much further than that.

"His name's Lockjaw," Harold said with a smirk. "You might want to be careful in taking the bit from his mouth."

"Understood."

From there, Harold shifted his focus onto the rifle in his hands. "There's any trouble, you just let me know."

"Don't worry about that. If there's trouble, you'll know."

Jeremiah rode to the end of the line, where Noelle was getting herself situated in her seat. "Don't get too comfortable, ma'am," he told her. "It's best you get in under cover until we move out. There might be a spot of trouble."

She grumbled, but kept it to herself as she climbed over the seat and into the cramped confines of the wagon behind her.

As he circled around the back of the last wagon, Jeremiah pulled in a breath and then let it out. With the wagons stopped, all he could hear was the whistle of the wind and the horses shifting from one leg to another.

Soon, another noise reached Jeremiah's ears. By the sound of it, Emmett was on his way back. Jeremiah snapped his reins and rode ahead to meet him. Whatever Emmett had to say, it seemed prudent to make sure it wasn't overheard by everyone else right away.

Jeremiah was about to call out Emmett's name when he got a clear look at the trail ahead. One horse was approaching and after a few seconds, another couple of horses fell into step behind it. Not one of those riders was Emmett.

"Get ready!" Jeremiah shouted. "They're coming!"

CHAPTER 16

Jeremiah raced ahead, thinking he should have told the others to hold their fire and wait for a signal. As far as that went, he should have arranged a signal.

But there was no more time to work out details. Nobody was firing yet and he guessed they would if he needed them to. For the moment, Jeremiah was more worried about the four riders approaching at full gallop.

No, he realized as the riders drew closer, make that five.

There were five of them and Jeremiah could see rifles in at least three of their hands.

Coming to a stop in the middle of the trail ahead of the wagons, Jeremiah dropped his rifle into the saddle's boot and then raised his hands over his head to show they were empty. He waited until they got a little closer before shouting to them, but he made sure to wear a friendly smile in case those riders were just passing by.

The first shot came from the lead rider. It cracked through the air and hissed a few feet over Jeremiah's head. His hands reflexively dropped, but his eyes remained fixed upon those riders. The one who had fired the shot was the one-eyed gunman from the pier at Martha's Ferry. As soon as he saw that ugly face, Jeremiah knew he'd made a bad move in stepping forward.

The move seemed even worse once the remaining four started firing shots of their own. A second or two later, Jeremiah heard the first pained groan come from one of the horses in Sara's team.

Sara braced her feet against the boards and pulled back on the reins with all her strength. The rest of the team didn't like it, but they slowed to a stop before the weight of the wounded animal dragged them all down. By the time bullets started cutting through the rest of the horses, the brake had been set and Sara was scrambling to pick up her shotgun.

"No!" Jeremiah shouted. "Just get down!"

Sara got the shotgun firmly in her grasp before climbing into the back of the wagon. More lead cut through the air around her, but those bullets were either shredding through the top of the wagon or digging into the horses.

"Bastards!" Jeremiah shouted. Although he could hear that word himself, it was mostly swallowed up by the roar of the rifle in his hands as he raised it to his shoulder and returned fire.

The riders scattered, but didn't move far from the trail. Instead, they raced toward the wagons from five different angles.

Jeremiah fired off a quick shot at the one-eyed rider since he was the closest one to him. He focused upon that man as if his ugly, wounded face were the only one in sight. Even as he fired the shot, Jeremiah knew it would miss. A split second before he could pull his trigger again, Jeremiah heard another shot. This one came from behind him, however, rather than from the riders up ahead.

"Get to some cover, you damned fool!" Harold shouted as he sighted along his rifle and levered in another round. The old man leaned to one side from his wagon and pulled his head back as a few rounds whipped past him.

Snapped from whatever it was that had rooted him to his spot, Jeremiah flicked his reins and rode back toward the wagons. The horses at the front of the team had been shot into a bloody mess and the ones behind them weren't in much better shape, but those animals weren't Jeremiah's concern.

"Sara!" he shouted. "Are you all right?"

First Jeremiah saw the barrel of the shotgun emerge from between two slats making up the backboard of the driver's seat. Since there wasn't anyone else riding with her, he took that as all the indication he needed.

"Keep your head down," Jeremiah said as he wheeled around to deal with the approaching riders.

Only a few more shots had been fired by the other men in the last few seconds. Now that they were closing to within thirty yards, however, their pistols were drawn and they were lining up their shots.

With no other options available to him, Jeremiah took aim with his rifle and pulled his trigger. The gun barked once and sent a piece of hot lead toward the one-eyed rider. That man ducked down low and squeezed off another round from his pistol.

"Go on and circle all the way around," one of the other riders commanded. "Dave and I will take care of this side."

The one-eyed man grinned and sent another two rounds at Jeremiah before holstering his pistol and drawing another one. That gun was spitting fire almost as soon as the one-eyed man could touch the trigger. After a few seconds blazed by, another rider appeared behind the one-eyed man and lent his own lead to the hailstorm flying at Jeremiah.

The rider who took up position next to the one-eyed man was a big fellow who wore buckskins and had thick hair that surrounded his face like a horse's mane. His skin was leathery and tough and he held a pistol in each hand while staying perfectly balanced in his saddle. He fired one shot at Jeremiah before his attention was diverted by something away from the trail.

Until now, Jeremiah had been doing his best to fire back as bullets tore through the air around him. He was vaguely aware of others firing their guns, but quickly realized that everyone except Claire had entered into the fray. Rifles were blazing from most of the wagons and a few shotguns roared every now and then. Jeremiah did his best to keep moving while pulling his own trigger when he could.

As he fired and the smoke began catching in the back of his throat, Jeremiah was barely able to keep his wits about him. Despite all the planning and preparations he'd thought he'd made for this moment, there was no way for him to go through it

194

the way he'd hoped.

Jeremiah pointed his gun at the one-eyed rider and pulled his trigger. He didn't have time to take proper aim. After that, he pointed his gun at Horse Mane and fired. He tried to think of how many shots he'd fired, but just kept pulling the trigger of his old Colt until his hammer slapped against an empty shell casing. After that, Jeremiah wondered if it would hurt when he was killed.

"Duck, you damned fool!" Harold shouted amid the chaos.

Before he had a chance to think twice about it, Jeremiah did as he was told and heard a shotgun blast explode from a nearby wagon.

Blood sprayed from One-Eye's arm and side as buckshot tore through him. He twisted around in his saddle as Horse Mane moved forward to fill the gap. Jeremiah managed to get his rifle back in hand, but wasn't quick enough to fire a shot before Horse Mane had him in his sights.

Suddenly, Jeremiah realized what had split the two gunmen's attention. Like an answer to several sets of prayers, Emmett raced in from the side of the trail with his gun blazing. Jeremiah took advantage of the temporary confusion among the gunmen by steering toward the wagons and jumping down from his horse.

Horse Mane swung his upper body around so he could point both his guns at Emmett. His fingers clenched around the triggers, sending forth a storm of lead from both barrels.

Emmett hunkered down low over his horse's back, using the animal as a makeshift barricade. Horse Mane's shots might have been quick and plentiful, but they were also wild. A bit of fancy riding was all it took for Emmett to get away from the incoming lead before catching any of it for himself.

Watching all of this as he ran to the closest wagon, Jeremiah was able to drop his Colt into its holster so he could take up his rifle with both hands. His fingers fumbled through the motions of plucking fresh bullets from his jacket pocket and he even managed to slide some of those rounds into the rifle where they belonged.

"Are those Indians?" came a frightened little voice from inside the wagon.

Jeremiah looked into the wagon and could see Claire peeking out from beneath a pile of toppled boxes. For the moment, he was glad to see her tucked away in a much safer spot than the ones he had to pick from. "No, little girl," Jeremiah replied as calmly as he could. "They're not Indians. Where's your mother?"

Although the girl was too scared to say anything else, she looked toward the opposite side of the wagon. That was all Jeremiah needed to see and he climbed onto the driver's seat to look in that direction for himself. What he saw on the other side was enough to knock all the wind from his lungs.

The other three riders were still in their saddles and lined up alongside the wagons. Compared to the scene on the other side, they were a picture of tranquility. Their guns were still drawn and aimed at Anne and the Inglebrechts, but these riders held everyone in check more with the coldness in their eyes than the iron in their fists.

Just as he'd caught the eye of one of the riders, Jeremiah was almost knocked to the ground by a heavy impact against his side of the wagons. He turned and saw the back of Horse Mane's head as his shoulders slammed against the wagon. Jeremiah didn't know how the man left his saddle, but he wasn't much the worse for wear.

Horse Mane let out a strained groan and raised both hands to unleash a torrent of thunder from his pistols. More shots were fired, causing Horse Mane to buck and twitch against the wagon. Jeremiah could only watch as Horse Mane's arms finally dropped and swung uselessly from his shoulders like ropes dangling from a tree branch.

When Horse Mane finally spun around and dropped against the side of the wagon, Jeremiah could see Emmett kneeling behind him. His gun was still in hand, smoking from the shots it had put into Horse Mane's chest. Jeremiah could also see the one-eyed gunman moving around to get behind Emmett.

"Look out!" Jeremiah shouted.

But it was too late.

Emmett started to turn, but only made it a quarter of the way around before he felt the touch of iron against his head. The one-eyed gunman glared down at Emmett and leaned forward as if anticipating the kickback from his pistol when he pulled his trigger.

"Ain't no way out of this," the one-eyed man said. "Maybe I'll just put you out of your damn misery right here and —"

"Enough of that!" one of the gunmen on the other side of the wagons shouted.

Jeremiah turned and saw that gunman standing up in his stirrups so he could get a clearer look between the wagons. When he started to move his gun arm, Jeremiah saw the other two gunmen on that side fix him with deadly stares and bring up their own weapons to cover him.

Confident in the men beside him, the gunman who'd shouted didn't take his eyes off Emmett and the one-eyed man. "Take his gun from him, Dave," the gunman commanded as he continued to stare between the wagons. "Don't hurt him any more than that."

Dave blinked his one eye furiously as sweat trickled down his forehead. His gun hand trembled, but more as a side effect from the tremendous amount of restraint it cost him to keep from following up on his previous threat. Finally, Dave raised his gun and gritted his teeth. "Drop the shooting iron, Natham," he said.

Emmett let out a sigh and reluctantly lowered his gun. Before he could set it down all the way, the butt of Dave's pistol cracked against his temple and dropped Emmett onto his side.

When he looked up at the man still watching him from the other side of the wagons, Dave shrugged and said, "Sorry about that, Sam. I thought he might be trying to make a move."

Sam lowered himself back into his saddle as his eyes narrowed into angry slits. "Get his hands and legs tied," he said. "I want the rest of these folks rounded up as well. If any of them get it in their heads to fight back, shoot them after you shoot one of the others."

Those words sent a chill down Jeremiah's spine and settled all the way down to the marrow in his bones. Since every last one of those men seemed capable of carrying that order through to the letter, Jeremiah set his gun down and held out his empty hands.

Jeremiah caught sight of Anne's pale, terrified face. He wanted to tell her he was sorry, but the words seemed pointless.

CHAPTER 17

Jeremiah had plenty of time to think things over once he was hog-tied and dropped against a wagon wheel. Although only a few minutes had passed, it felt like an eternity since that first shot had been fired. He could think of everything that had happened in that short stretch of time, but he couldn't think of anything he could have done differently that would have made a lick of difference. Finally, he had to close his eyes and force the thoughts from his head before the bile rose any higher in his throat.

"They all here?" the one called Sam asked.

Jeremiah opened his eyes and got a look at the man who appeared to be the leader. Sam was a bit shorter than the rest and had light sandy hair. He wore a holster around his waist, which remained mostly hidden by a fringed buckskin jacket. There were no scars on Sam's face. In fact, he was the sort of fellow who looked as if he had no problem convincing a woman to spend time with him. Of course, the women in the immediate vicinity weren't included in that assumption.

Horse Mane was dead. Jeremiah knew that for certain when he saw one of the others drag the body farther off the trail and dump it into some bushes.

Dave, the one-eyed gunman, hadn't stopped swearing under his breath since his scuffle with Emmett. Blood had soaked through the shoulder of his shirt and he favored that arm as if it was constantly giving him trouble. Jeremiah thought back to the fight at the pier, since that was when Dave got that shoulder wound. The wounds he got earlier today seemed to bother him less.

Another of the gunmen was a large Indian who wore clothes from several different sources. His pants looked like the jeans any cowboy wore. His shirt was a Mexican design and the coat he wore was standard army issue. Although the Indian didn't look like a Cheyenne or Crow, Jeremiah wouldn't have sworn on it. The only Indians he'd ever dealt with had been honest traders or quiet craftsmen. This one was neither.

The Indian lugged the Inglebrechts like sacks of grain and dumped them against their own wagon not far from Jeremiah. He then pulled Anne from her wagon without feeling any of the blows she rained down upon him using her tightly balled fists. On a somewhat more promising note, the Indian had also not been able to find Claire or hear anything that would make him look any deeper into Anne's wagon.

The final member of the group was tall and lanky. He wore a dented bowler hat and had a formal vest underneath his battered duster. A gold watch chain crossed his belly and caught Jeremiah's eye because that watch might have been stolen from Harold Inglebrecht. Before Jeremiah could be certain of that, he saw the lanky man stare at him as if he were watching a lizard try to crawl up and lick his boots.

"I believe this is all of them, yes," the lanky man said with a thick English accent.

"Did you check all them wagons?" Sam asked.

"Of course I did. They're all stuffed to bursting with what you might expect."

"Any valuables?"

This time, the Englishman turned the same annoyed glare toward Sam while letting out a sigh. "That would require us to dump out these wagons and go through every last parcel, wouldn't it?"

"You got somewhere else to be?"

The Englishman sputtered for a few seconds before Sam started to laugh.

"Don't get your britches in a knot, Charlie, I was only joshing you. Just see what you can find. We're not here to unload a bunch of wagons anyhow."

Although Charlie let out the breath he'd gathered up, he didn't seem too relieved. The Englishman shook his head and wandered back over to the Inglebrechts' second wagon.

The Indian had stepped out of Jeremiah's sight, but returned with Sara slung over his shoulder. She was kicking and trying to scream, but was only making a muffled squeal thanks to the bandanna that had been stuffed into her mouth.

"Looks like you got a real fiery one there, Pointer," Sam said.

The Indian looked over to him, but didn't say a word. He just put Sara down so she was sitting with her back to one of the wheels and moved along.

Seeing his wife treated that way was more than enough to stoke the fire in Jeremiah's innards. Without making it obvious, he tested the strength of the knots holding his arms together behind his back. Whoever had tied them knew their job pretty well. As he squirmed, Jeremiah snarled, "Who are you men? What do you want?"

Nobody took any notice of Jeremiah. They all had their jobs to do and they kept right on doing them.

"Answer me! Whatever you're looking for, you're not going to find it! We're just traveling to —"

"I don't give a rat's ass where you're traveling," Sam said as he wheeled around to fix his eyes upon Jeremiah. "So why don't you do us all a favor and shut yer mouth before one of my men shuts it for you?"

"You're leading these men?" Jeremiah asked.

"That's right. You want to lodge a complaint? Tell it to London Charlie. He's the formal one."

That brought a chorus of laughter from the rest of the men. Even Dave chuckled loudly, but he was in fairly high sprits since Emmett was still slumped over and unconscious not too far away.

"Why did you do this?" Jeremiah asked. The words spilled out of him and since he couldn't move, he felt he was doing his part by keeping at least one of the men preoccupied. If that man happened to be the leader, that was all the better.

"We're not carrying anything valuable,"

Jeremiah pleaded. "Just our personal things and such. If you're going to rob us, just do it and get it over with."

Suddenly, Sam whispered a few quick instructions to the Indian he'd called Pointer and turned back around to face Jeremiah. He took a few quick steps, but then lunged down to grab Jeremiah's shirt so forcefully that he lifted him an inch or so off the ground.

"When I tell you to shut your mouth, you'll do it. Understand?"

Sam's voice had been smooth and collected before. Now it reminded Jeremiah of the noise a dog made when its teeth were clamped around an enemy's leg and wasn't about to let it go. The smooth, unbroken lines of his face made it look like a perfectly carved demon mask.

"You want to make this easier for us?" Sam asked. "Then keep right on talking. Believe me, it's a hell of a lot easier to lug dead bodies around than put up with your damn mewling all the time. You talk when you're spoken to or we start having fun with these women here. How'd you like that?"

"Don't you touch her," Jeremiah growled in a savage tone that even surprised him. "Don't you touch any of them."

Sam grinned now that he saw he'd

touched a nerve. Shifting his eyes a bit, he shouted, "Hey, Dave! You see anything you like?"

The one-eyed man was breathing heavily as he walked back into Jeremiah's sight. His eye drifted back and forth between Sara and Anne while he licked his lips. "Sure do."

"I'll bet Pointer might even give the old woman a ride," Sam said. Although he didn't get a reply from that, he looked to be plenty happy with himself. He was still laughing under his breath as he walked away and met up with the Englishman toward the end of the row of wagons.

Jeremiah struggled a bit more against his ropes, but it didn't take long for him to realize it was futile. The ropes weren't budging and it felt as if nothing short of a sharp blade would change the situation. When he looked over to his wife, he found her going through the same motions. After coming to the same realization Jeremiah had, she let out a breath and hung her head.

Not wanting to catch any of the gunmen's attention, Jeremiah didn't say a word to Sara. Instead, he did all the talking he could using his eyes. He didn't even need to mouth his question for her to understand and nod her head. He could read her face just fine and knew that she was trying to tell him that she wasn't hurt.

Jeremiah took some comfort from that, even though he knew Sara would probably have kept it to herself if she were injured. The very thought of those men hurting her was enough to make Jeremiah's blood boil. Despite all that had happened recently, he'd never felt so capable of killing another human being than when he let the possibility of Sara being violated pass through his mind. He kept his eyes on her for a little while to watch and make certain she was all right.

Sara was tired. She was aching. There was some pain and plenty of fear written on her face, but Jeremiah didn't see enough to make him think the worst had actually happened.

With that thought still lingering like a disease in his skull, Jeremiah looked over to Anne. She was leaning forward and gritting her teeth without so much as glancing in Jeremiah's direction. Since he'd been propped up closer to her than to his own wife, he could see the muscles in her arms tensing as she continued to pull her wrists against the ropes that bound them. Even though she wasn't making any progress, she kept on trying.

Jeremiah saw blood trickling from her

wrists, which caused him to lean over and speak to her in a fierce whisper. "Stop that," he said. "You're just going to hurt yourself."

"I have to try," she insisted. "They haven't . . ." When Anne glanced up to her own wagon, she forced herself to look away. The next thing she did was look around to see if any of the gunmen had taken notice of what she'd done.

Just to make sure he was thinking along the same lines, Jeremiah leaned forward and looked around. Sure enough, the others were tied up and sitting just as he was. Anne was to his left, Sara was a bit farther down in that direction, the Inglebrechts were to his right and Claire was nowhere to be seen.

"She's going to be fine," Jeremiah said as he stared intently into Anne's eyes. "We all are. I'll die before I let anything happen."

What he meant to say was that he would die before letting anything happen to the little girl who was hopefully still hiding nearby.

Anne slowly nodded as she turned her head away from Jeremiah as well as her own wagon. "I know," she said softly and unconvincingly. "I know."

As much as Jeremiah wanted to catch her attention again, he stopped himself from doing so. He didn't think she doubted that he was earnest. What he wanted to tell her was that she should believe that he could back up his words.

At the moment, even he couldn't believe that.

CHAPTER 18

"Round 'em up," Sam told the Englishman in a low rasp. "Get 'em all in one spot. It'll be easier that way."

Those words struck a fear deeper within Jeremiah than he'd ever thought possible. For a second, he considered breaking his arms, cutting his wrists or anything else to make it possible to get out of those ropes. The fear inside him ran like a cold stream directly through his innards, making it difficult to think of anything else.

The Englishman nodded and turned to face Jeremiah and the rest. He gave the ladies a smile and the gentlemen a tip of his hat as he walked by. He did keep walking, however, which was enough to let Jeremiah breathe once more.

After the Englishman had walked around to the other side of the wagons, where most of the gunmen were convening, Jeremiah turned toward Harold. "Are you two all right?" he whispered.

Harold didn't seem to hear him at first. When he did look over in response to Jeremiah's voice, the old man looked calmer than at any other time during the expedition. "I'm not hurt. Neither is my wife."

"Are you sure?"

"I think I'd know if I was hurt," Harold grunted.

Noelle leaned forward and smiled consolingly. "I'm fine," she said. "Thanks for asking. I saw what you did, Jeremiah. That was very brave of you."

Jeremiah blinked and tried to think about what she could have been talking about. Considering their predicament, it was difficult to imagine himself doing anything that was of any help whatsoever.

"What about Emmett?" she asked. "And . . ."

Jeremiah saw the way Noelle glanced quickly toward Anne's wagon and he nodded. "She's fine. I'd say she's probably doing better than most of us right now."

"Are you certain about that?"

"Yeah."

Noelle let out a breath and leaned back against the wagon wheel.

"We need to do something," Jeremiah told Harold quietly. "Before they do."

"What are they going to do?"

"I don't —" Suddenly, Jeremiah heard footsteps coming toward him. The Indian walked around the end of the wagons, past Noelle, Harold, Jeremiah, Anne and Sara and then squatted down to study something. Jeremiah couldn't see much, but he could see enough to know that the Indian was taking a closer look at Emmett, who wasn't even moving.

Jeremiah waited for the Indian to stand up and walk away before trying to catch Sara's attention. When he finally caught her eye, Jeremiah asked, "Can you see if he's hurt?"

She turned around to face the other way and then shifted back toward Jeremiah. "He's bloodied up, but breathing. I don't know when he'll wake up, though."

"Just so long as he does."

"Did you hear what they called him?"

Jeremiah fought through the pain that filled his head and body so he could answer that question. "Natham."

"I thought his last name was Blaylock."

"So did I. Maybe it's another name he goes by."

"If they called him by name," Sara stressed, "they know him."

Taking a moment to think it over again,

Jeremiah tried to walk through what had happened without being sidetracked by everything else. For the most part, those memories were a tangle of gunshots, galloping horses and terror. Even so, Jeremiah could still recall Emmett giving his last name as Blaylock.

"How could they know him?" Sara asked. "And is Emmett Blaylock or Natham?"

"I don't know what any of this means, but we can try to figure it out once we're out of here."

"When will that be?" Anne asked.

She'd been quiet for so long that Jeremiah and Sara had taken to speaking over her as if she weren't even there. But Anne made her presence known again by speaking in a fierce whisper. Her hands were slick with her own blood and she was even starting to strain against the ropes around her ankles.

Jeremiah looked into her eyes and forced himself to think about anything but what so desperately wanted to rise up and swallow him whole. He put a calm expression onto his face and wore it like a Sunday suit. He might not have been comfortable in it, but he needed to make it look good.

"I don't know exactly when it'll be," he told her. "But I know it's going to be sooner rather than later."

"Honestly?"

"Yes," Jeremiah lied. "I'm going to do the best I know how." At least that second part had been the truth. Still, as long as he got her to stop tearing her wrists and ankles apart, Jeremiah felt he was doing Anne a favor.

Once she stopped pulling at the ropes, Anne seemed to feel the pain coming from her bloody wounds. She clenched her eyes shut and gritted her teeth as tears started to flow. "Don't let them take her," she said in a trembling whisper. "Please, Jeremiah. She's all I have."

"You stop that talk right now, you hear?" he replied as his eyes began darting to and fro in search of any trace of movement. Even though he didn't see any of the gunmen in the vicinity, he couldn't shake the memory of Sam glaring between the wagons and seeing everything happening on the other side as if he could look straight through walls.

"If she's gonna stay safe, we all need to work to keep her that way," Jeremiah continued. "Do you understand?" He lowered his head a bit so he could put himself more within Anne's sight. "Do you understand?"

The tone in Jeremiah's voice cut through the fear in Anne's heart more than his words did. She blinked once and looked at him with a calmness in her eyes that surely hadn't been there before. Nodding, she whispered, "I understand."

"Good. Now tell me what happened to you after the shooting started."

"I saw you ride off and I got my rifle ready. I told . . ." She paused before mentioning her daughter and then forced herself to rethink what she was about to say. When she started speaking again, her voice was even steadier than it had been a few seconds ago. "I made sure everything was squared away and then I tried to help. I fired a few times, but they came so fast. I couldn't get a clear shot."

Seeing the tears well up in the corners of her eyes, Jeremiah quickly told her, "You did all you could. Just tell me, when they took you . . . did they hurt you?"

"No," she replied. "Not more than putting some marks on my arms and such when they dragged me from the wagon and tied me up. One of them wanted to hit me, but that English one stopped him."

Jeremiah nodded. "All right. Which one tried to hit you?"

"The leader, but he didn't exactly try. He . . . wanted to hit me. I could see it in his eyes."

Jeremiah soaked up every word and took another quick look around. The Inglebrechts were talking to each other, but it sounded like they were simply calming each other down. Jeremiah let them have their time, since they would be more of a comfort to one another than he would. Shifting his focus back to Anne, he asked, "Did any of them say anything to you?"

"Like what?"

"Like who they are or what it is they want?"

She thought about it for a few moments while keeping her head cocked to one side. Although the way she positioned herself might have looked odd, Jeremiah knew she was keeping an eye on the spot where she'd last seen her daughter. After a few seconds, Anne let out a frustrated breath. "I can't think of anything," she said. "It was all so horrible. It happened so quickly."

"I know. Believe me, I know," Jeremiah said. "Just try to gather your strength."

"Are you going to try to get out of here? Do you want me to help?"

"You just stay put and keep your ears open. Maybe you can overhear something that might be useful."

"Or maybe I could get one of them to talk," Anne offered. "The leader of those men . . . I think his name's Sam . . . I think he likes me." Those last couple of words seemed to turn her stomach, but she forced them out anyway. "I might be able to get him to say some things if I let him —"

"No!" Jeremiah said fiercely. He was quick to collect himself and looked around to see if he'd drawn any unwanted attention. As far as he could tell, the gunmen were still preoccupied with their own tasks. The Indian was watching them from afar, but he was standing a ways off with a rifle in the crook of his arm. It was a good spot for keeping watch over the prisoners, but hopefully not so good for listening in on them. Judging by the stoic expression on the Indian's face, he wasn't too interested in what was being said anyway.

"You won't need to do anything like that," Jeremiah said.

"Then what else is there? I need to do something. I can't just sit here and wait."

"That's exactly what we're going to do," Jeremiah said. "All of us. Even if we could get out of these ropes right now, we'd have to leave Emmett behind and that wouldn't be right after all he's done to help us."

Anne looked over to where Emmett was lying and nodded. When she turned away from the unconscious man, she lowered her

218

voice even more, as if she were afraid he might hear her. "What you were saying to Sara . . . about these men knowing Emmett. What if it's true? What if he's not who he says he is?"

"What if it is true?"

"Maybe they just want him. Maybe they'll just leave once they get whatever they're after."

Those words stuck in Jeremiah's craw like a thorn. "Then we should ask him about it," he finally said. "But we can't do that until he wakes up. Besides, they're going to be watching us like hawks for a while."

"Do you think they'll let up?"

"I don't know, but there's not much else for us to do until they do. In the meantime, we need to think about any other choices we have."

Anne pulled her legs up close to her and lowered her head as if she wanted to rest it upon her knees. It was awkward for her to do so, but she curled up as best she could without letting her wagon out of her sight.

It was an eternity before the rest of the gunmen reappeared. Jeremiah had spent what felt like hours testing his ropes, watching the others, keeping track of the Indian and listening for a hint that Emmett might be waking up. The only way to keep track of the time was watching the position of the sun overhead. No matter how accurate that method had been for untold thousands of years, Jeremiah still thought it could be wrong.

Could he have been sitting there for only an hour or possibly just a little longer?

His entire body ached as if he'd been leaning against the spokes of that wagon wheel for an entire night. His throat was parched and his joints were sending sharp jabs of pain throughout all of his limbs. Once he saw the other gunmen walk into sight, however, Jeremiah set all of that aside.

"Charlie," Sam said as he walked along the line of prisoners, "keep an eye on these good folks for a spell so Pointer can do something else for a bit."

The Englishman went over to the same spot and took the rifle from Pointer. He took Harold's watch from his pocket, checked the time, snapped it shut and then dropped the timepiece back into his vest.

Jeremiah could hear someone rummaging through one of the wagons before moving on to the next. He tried not to be too obvious, but he made certain nobody was making a move toward Anne's wagon. So far, they seemed more interested in what was packed inside the Inglebrechts' wagon.

Soon, another sound caught Jeremiah's ear. Something scraped against the dirt, followed by pained, labored groaning.

"You may want to come over here, Sam," Charlie announced. "It appears our friend is rejoining the world of the living."

"Huh?" one of the gunmen asked.

Dave poked his head out of Jeremiah's second wagon and took a look for himself. "The asshole's wakin' up," he announced. "Why didn't you just say that, Charlie?"

Sam took his time walking into Jeremiah's sight, but did so before Emmett had had a chance to straighten up. He stepped over to get a closer look at Emmett, but didn't get close enough to put himself within arm's reach of the other man.

Jeremiah watched all of this with interest. Even though none of the prisoners had made a wrong move or even managed to slip out of any of their ropes, none of the gunmen were allowing themselves to be careless. It made Jeremiah glad he'd convinced Anne not to try anything, but that still didn't bode well for any future opportunities.

"Good," Sam said with a nod. "By the time we're done searching these here wagons, he should be ready to have a little chat."

Upon hearing that, the first thing that sprang to Jeremiah's mind was one of those gunmen stumbling upon Claire's hiding spot. Before he could think of anything else, Jeremiah leaned forward and shouted, "You want to chat? You can start with me!"

"Well, you're still feelin' your oats, huh?" Sam asked.

"I just want to know what the hell is going on here."

For a moment, all of the gunmen stopped what they were doing. Then they gathered around to get a look at the prisoner who'd decided to stand up to Sam.

Sam looked at Jeremiah and grinned. "Maybe I should be the one askin' you about that."

"We're just trying to get to Oregon," Jeremiah replied.

"And I suppose you're bringing along a known killer for companionship?"

"What?"

The grin on Sam's face grew even wider. Studying Jeremiah, he added, "Or maybe you just didn't bother to ask many questions of the folks you ride with."

CHAPTER 19

If Jeremiah thought he was hurting before, he was shown another level of pain when Pointer hauled him to his feet and dragged him away from the wagons. The Indian's rough hands took hold of Jeremiah's arms as if he were hanging on to a length of rope. After dropping Jeremiah onto his feet, the Indian clasped one hand under Jeremiah's chin to keep him propped upright. Once Jeremiah got his balance, he saw the Indian extend one arm to point toward Sam.

The Indian didn't say anything else. He simply pointed. Jeremiah guessed that was how Indian had earned his name from the other gunmen.

Sam kept his right hand on the grip of his holstered pistol as he walked several paces from the wagons. Jeremiah staggered after him with Pointer following closely behind.

When Sam finally came to a stop, he tossed a quick wave to Pointer. Jeremiah felt the Indian clamp both hands down upon his shoulders and roughly spin him around. It was only Pointer's excruciatingly tight grip that kept Jeremiah from falling over.

Something deep inside Jeremiah wanted to spit or bite the bigger man's hand since there wasn't much else he could do to strike back at him.

"Better watch yerself, Pointer," Sam said. "Looks like this one's found his second wind. Good thing I took his gun away, huh?"

Jeremiah had been so rattled that he barely even realized his gun wasn't in its holster. If his hands had been free, he probably would have just tried to strangle the gunmen's leader anyhow. "Take what you want and be on your way," he snarled. "Or untie me and I'll collect all the money I can for you. You're going to be pretty disappointed, though, because most of us spent most of what we had just to get this far."

"Is that a fact?"

"Yes, sir, it is."

"And how much did Emmett Natham pay to join up with your wagon train?"

"He came along to help us," Jeremiah said. "And he's more than earned his keep."

"Has he? That's a shame, because he could have paid a pretty penny for his spot with you folks." Looking over to Pointer, he mused, "How much did he rob from that bank up north? Three? Four thousand? Maybe double?"

Pointer shrugged.

"That was just his cut, mind you," Sam added. "And you'd have to double that because he killed one of his partners and probably took all his money as well. I suppose that'd be a safe bet, since I doubt he buried it with him."

"I don't know what you're talking about," Jeremiah said.

"I can see that, which is why I thought you'd like me to fill in some of the holes."

"All I'd like is for you to untie all of us and let us ride away from here. If you do that, nobody will say a word of this to the law and we can just part ways without any blood being spilled."

Sam stared at Jeremiah for a tense couple of seconds. In that time, Jeremiah wasn't sure if Sam was going to punch him in the mouth, laugh at him or start shooting. There was so much churning behind Sam's eyes that it was like trying to pick out a few individual clouds within a thunderstorm.

"One of my men was killed today," Sam said in a tone that cut through the air like a blade through tender meat. "And your friend Emmett Natham did the killing. By all rights, I should be the one who's fighting mad."

"Your men attacked us," Jeremiah said. "What would you expect us to do?"

The notion passed through Jeremiah's head that those might be the last words he would ever say. Sam's grip tightened around his gun, while Pointer stood by and watched.

Suddenly, Sam asked, "What's your name?"

The question wasn't too peculiar, but the time at which it had come struck Jeremiah as odd. He felt as if he'd braced for a kick in the stomach and got pinched on the cheek instead. In an uncertain voice, he replied, "Jeremiah Correy."

"How long have you known Natham, Jeremiah?"

Jeremiah kept his mouth shut. Since he hadn't had much luck in predicting where Sam was headed, he thought it best not to play along.

"I don't think you're a bank-robbing, thieving, murdering son of a bitch like he is, so it couldn't have been long. Pointer's got a good head for numbers. How long has Natham been keeping his head down?"

"Seventeen days," the Indian replied.

Nodding smugly, Sam said, "Seventeen

days would be about right. Have you known Natham for more than seventeen days?"

If he were being honest, Jeremiah couldn't have thought clearly enough to count up the number of days in which he'd known Emmett. Simply hearing him called by another last name was almost enough to make Jeremiah think of Emmett as a different person.

"If you knew him for longer than that," Sam continued, "you'd either be hiding him or in on one of his more recent jobs. And if that was the case, you'd have a price on your head just like Emmett Natham's got one on his."

There was the kick to the stomach that Jeremiah had been bracing for.

Jeremiah looked at Sam and Pointer as if he were seeing them for the first time. He then wheeled around to get a look at the line of wagons behind him. He could see Dave leaning against the wagon Noelle Inglebrecht had been driving while Charlie remained in his spot to guard the prisoners. There were a few items scattered on the ground, but not nearly as many as Jeremiah had expected.

"You didn't stop us to rob us?" Jeremiah asked.

Sam grinned once more, but that quickly

turned into a full-fledged belly laugh. "Rob you? You folks may be more of a danger to yourselves than we are. Do you know how long we've been on your trail?"

"A few days," Jeremiah replied meekly.

"And what the hell did you do about it?" After waiting for a few seconds without getting a reply, Sam shook his head. "Anyone hauling anything worth stealing would've been better armed than you folks. And you sure as hell wouldn't have just kept on rolling when you knew someone was following you. All you got that's worth anything is Natham."

"You've got him, so what are you going to do with him?"

"Haul his carcass into a town that's big enough to pay me what he's worth."

"You're bounty hunters."

Sam let out a sigh. Looking to the Indian, he said, "Take this smart fella back to the rest so they won't worry about him. Is one of those women yours, Jeremiah?"

Not knowing if he should answer, Jeremiah wasn't able to come up with a response before Sam barked at him again.

"If we wanted to rape them women it wouldn't matter much which one was your wife," Sam said. "I just figured you'd want to sit next to one more than another."

"My wife's on the end," Jeremiah said. "By the front wagon."

Sam looked in that direction and shrugged. "My guess would've put you with the blonde, but so be it. Pointer, take Jeremiah over to his wife."

The Indian spun Jeremiah around to face the wagons and then extended his arms to point toward Sara. He gave Jeremiah a nudge when they got to the wagons, made sure his ropes were tight and then shoved him to the ground so Jeremiah was leaning against the same wheel as Sara. After that, Pointer backed up and walked away.

Sara was anxious to see him. She started talking to Jeremiah as soon as he was brought over to her, but didn't get a response. She kept on trying to talk to him after Pointer had left, but with the same results. Finally, she put a harder edge into her voice that was normally reserved for when Jeremiah was trying to skip some of his chores or sneak off to the saloon.

"Jeremiah Correy, you better answer me."

Those words might as well have been cold water splashed into his face.

"What did they say to you?" she asked now that she could see she had his attention.

Jeremiah chewed on a reply, but kept the

words to himself. Since Emmett was moving and letting out a pained groan, Jeremiah wasn't about to take his eyes off him.

When Emmett opened his eyes and tried to rub his head, he discovered his own hands were tied just like all the other prisoners'. Slowly, his eyes brightened and he took notice of what was going on. "Jesus," he moaned. "They got us?"

"Yeah," Jeremiah said. "They did. Seems like they're only after someone by the name of Natham."

As much as he'd been hoping to see confusion on Emmett's face, Jeremiah didn't get his wish. Instead, he saw a flicker of anger followed by the subtle hint of shame.

"Emmet?" Sara asked.

Jeremiah looked at Emmett. "Yup. And Emmett Natham is a wanted man, to boot."

"What?" Sara said. "Wait a second. What did they tell you?"

"They told him the truth," Natham said. "That's my name and I'm a wanted man."

"Wanted for what?"

Natham lowered his eyes and clenched the muscles in his jaw.

"They told me it was for robbery and murder," Jeremiah said. "Is that the truth as well?"

Natham kept his head down.

Jeremiah nodded. "Perfect. Not only did I let a killer ride along with the folks I meant to protect, but I nearly got killed for him along the way. I hope they're not worried about us putting up a fuss when they drag you away, because I'd just as soon help them do it."

"You don't mean that," Sara snapped. "He saved your life. He did his best to save all of us."

"And look where it got us. We wouldn't be in this predicament if he wasn't along. Paul would still be alive and we'd be that much closer to Oregon."

Sara reflexively looked over to Natham as if to apologize for her husband's harsh words. When she saw his face, however, she had to stare at him especially hard. She kept staring as if she were trying to make out a detail through a frosted window. Then she slumped forward a little as if something vital had slipped away from her.

"Is that true?" Sara asked. "I mean . . . is all of that really true?"

Natham couldn't look at her. Either that, or he simply didn't want to look at her. Instead, he kept his eyes focused upon a patch of dirt in front of him and muttered, "I'm a wanted man. That's all you good folks need to know."

There were heavy impacts against the ground, which Jeremiah could feel all the way along his backbone. He took a quick glance around, but wasn't too interested in what was falling. Things were getting so far out of hand that it might as well have been the sky dropping.

Harold Inglebrecht had yet to make much of any noise. Jeremiah thought he could count on him for a bit of support, but the old man was hunkered down with his wife.

At that moment, Jeremiah couldn't think of a way for things to get much worse.

"Well, now!" Dave said as he crawled up into Anne's wagon. "What have we here? Looks like someone was tryin' to hide something from us."

Suddenly, things were worse.

CHAPTER 20

"Oh no," Anne said in a voice that sounded as tattered and frayed as an old dress. "Please, no. Get away from there!" As she screamed at the one-eyed gunman as he climbed into her wagon, Anne started to get up. She was stopped almost immediately by the ropes tying her hands together. It was only then that she realized those ropes had also been looped through the spokes of the wheel behind her.

Anne's arms were jerked back and pulled to a sickening angle before she was dropped right back down against the wheel and the ground. She didn't even twitch before struggling to get back to her feet.

"Someone hold that bitch down," Dave muttered as he climbed into the back of the wagon. "I got a little fishin' to do here."

"No!" Anne shouted. "Somebody, please!"

Sam walked right up to her and placed his hands upon her shoulders. From there, he managed to push her back forcefully enough to pin her against the wheel, but gently enough to keep her from getting knocked around any more than was necessary. "Unless you want this to be worse for everyone," Sam told her, "you'll just stay put and let my boys do what they gotta do."

"I won't let you take my —"

The last half of that sentence was lost when Natham lunged from where he'd been sitting to slam into Sam's side. Anne pressed herself even harder against the wagon wheel as her mouth dropped open in surprise.

She wasn't the only one to be surprised. Jeremiah hadn't even seen Natham coming and he was a lot closer to the man than Sam was. Besides that, Natham's hands had been tied just as tightly as everyone else's the last time Jeremiah had checked. Now Natham was wrapping one arm around Sam's midsection as his shoulder was driven into the gunman's ribs.

Sam let out a grunt as he was knocked away from Anne. He lost the wind from his lungs, but scrambled to draw his pistol.

Pointer moved like a mountain lion, keeping his head low and his limbs tucked in close to his body as he raced forward. By the time he got within arm's reach of Natham, he'd drawn a blade that had been sheathed at the small of his back.

Dave poked his head out from inside the wagon and nearly tripped over himself to jump out when he saw what was going on. He exploded from the wagon amid a shower of Anne's possessions and charged toward Sam from that side.

Natham let out a vicious snarl as he wrestled Sam away from the wagons. After taking a quick look over his shoulder, he wrapped his other arm around Sam to lock him in a powerful bear hug. He then shifted his momentum so Sam was between him and London Charlie.

The Englishman remained in his spot and was sighting along the top of his rifle. It looked as if he'd been close to pulling his trigger when Sam was forced into his sights. Letting out a silent curse, he lowered the rifle and scrambled to get a better angle.

Just as Pointer was closing in on him, Natham shifted his weight again and sent a mule kick straight into the Indian's lower body. His heel landed just shy of the Indian's groin and Pointer was quick enough to hop back while slashing quickly with his knife. The blade grazed Natham's shin, tore through his jeans and drew a little blood, but Nathan didn't even seem to notice.

By this time, Sam had begun thrashing

his feet and hitting Nathan with vicious elbows. Still wrapped up within Natham's grasp, Sam leaned his head forward and then sent it straight back again. The back of his head caught Natham in the face, finally allowing him to get free.

Natham blinked a few times as blood trickled from his nose. He paused to get Sam back in his sights, which allowed Pointer to snake an arm around his neck from behind and bring the knife up in preparation of driving it down into Natham's belly.

"Stop!" Sam shouted as he caught his breath and drew his own pistol.

Pointer kept his knife raised, but Natham wasn't so quick to follow orders. He slammed his elbow straight back into Pointer's ribs and then followed up with another powerful shot to the same place. The Indian took the first blow pretty well, but the second made him wince.

As Jeremiah watched the fight, he didn't want to blink. He would have let his eyes dry up and fall from their sockets before allowing himself to miss a crucial moment. Natham had broken free of everyone trying to restrain him and turned around to face Pointer. The Indian lashed out with a quick swipe of his blade, which Natham blocked using both of his forearms.

"Watch out!" Jeremiah shouted as he saw Dave raise his pistol and thumb the hammer back.

Natham took a quick look over his shoulder, started to turn away from Dave, then suddenly dropped to one knee.

A shot cracked through the air as Charlie fired his rifle. His bullet punched into the side of one of the Inglebrechts' wagons, causing the Englishman to swear and lever in another round.

Jumping back to his feet, Natham rushed to get close to Sam and grabbed the rope dangling from his right wrist so he could try and loop it around Sam's neck.

Sam was just quick enough to lean out of the way and deliver a vicious punch to Natham's gut. His other arm was bent at the elbow, keeping his pistol close to him as he aimed at Natham. "Stop it!" he shouted. "All of you!"

Once again, Pointer found himself pausing with his blade poised to carve a piece out of Natham. Letting out a frustrated grunt, he shoved his blade back into its sheath and turned to stalk back to the other prisoners. He walked straight over to Jeremiah, balled up his fist and sent it into his jaw.

Jeremiah's head slammed against the wagon wheel as his vision blurred. He wasn't able to pull in a full breath before Pointer was grabbing him under the chin with one hand and forcing him to look into his eyes.

"That was for interfering," Pointer snarled. "Do it again and you die."

Jeremiah couldn't have replied to that if he wanted to. Pointer's grip was so powerful that it seemed as if he could have squashed Jeremiah's skull like an over-ripe grape. He did manage to keep his eyes focused on the Indian, without flinching. All things considered, that was the biggest triumph Jeremiah could have hoped for.

After slamming Jeremiah against the wheel once more, Pointer turned to watch what was happening between Natham and the rest of the gunmen.

It was still a standoff.

Seeing that he was covered from three different angles, Natham stood with his arms dangling at his sides and his head slightly lowered. The rope that had held him to the wagon wheel still hung from his right wrist. His left wrist was bloody and streaks of crimson were smeared over most of that hand.

Oddly enough, Jeremiah felt as if his vision had cleared a bit after that second knock against the wheel. Then again, he couldn't be certain he was seeing everything perfectly since Natham's left hand appeared twisted and distorted. Blinking a few times, Jeremiah took another look and found that his first impression had been more or less accurate.

Natham's left hand seemed to be curled in on itself like a maple leaf that had been tossed onto a fire. Still dripping blood, that hand was much narrower than the right one due to the fact that Natham's thumb was bent in against his wrist at an unnatural angle. Just seeing it was enough to make Jeremiah queasy since it was so obviously a far cry from the way it should be.

But Natham raised that hand along with his other one as if nothing were amiss. He even spread his fingers a bit to show he wasn't holding anything. Even Sam winced at the sight of that.

"So that's what makes you so slippery, huh?" Sam asked as he stared at Natham's hand. "Guess that explains why lawmen can't keep hold of you."

Natham didn't say anything. He just kept his arms up and his hands open as Sam and Dave closed in on him.

"Put this one back with the others," Sam

said. "And don't do anything more than that. Make sure he snaps that thumb back into place before you tie him up again. Next time he slips free, I'll shoot whoever was responsible for tying him."

Dave grabbed Natham's elbow, stuck his pistol barrel into Natham's ribs and started shoving him toward the wagons. Wearing a cruel grin on his face, he grabbed Natham's curled thumb and jerked it straight down, sending a loud, wet snap through the air.

Sam walked alongside Dave so he could cover Natham as if he were simply accompanying him on a stroll through the woods. "You haven't lost your touch, I can give you that," Sam said. "I'd like to know why you got loyalty to these settlers instead of loyalty to your own men, though."

Natham's voice was scratchy and tired as he croaked, "They're not settlers."

"What was that?"

"I told you they're not settlers. They're just out to start a new life."

Sam shrugged while keeping his pistol aimed at Natham's head. "Settling here or settling there. It's all the same. Did you go soft on all of these folks or just one?" His eyes shifted toward Anne as a wicked smile crept onto his face. "I bet I know which one."

But Natham's expression didn't change. It remained the same even when Sam looked as if he were about to eat Anne alive. It remained the same when the ropes were cinched in tight around his elbows and forearms. It even remained the same when Dave made sure to slap Natham's bloodied hand after he was done tying the final knot.

"Maybe when me and my boys get to sowing our oats with them ladies," Dave said, "you can sit right there and watch."

"Shut up and tend to the ropes," Sam grunted. "Nobody's sowing a damn thing unless I say so."

Natham's expression remained the same.

At this point, Jeremiah was having a hard time keeping quiet. The only thing that allowed him to remain in check was the fact that Sam didn't seem overly anxious to get close to Natham, or any of the other prisoners.

Finally, Sam let out a single laugh and stepped back. "I'll let you settle in. What did you find, Dave?"

"Huh?"

"Before Natham got loose, you said you found something. What was it?"

Dave's eyes lit up and he snapped his fingers. Walking around to the back of Anne's wagon, he disappeared from sight.

Anne strained against her ropes frantically as sobs caused her chest to heave. Now that he was tied doubly tight, Natham could only stay where he was and turn to watch what happened with burning eyes.

When Dave reappeared, he wore a smile from ear to ear. He also carried something in his hands. He walked toward Sam, extended his arms and showed everyone what he'd found.

"That's what all the fuss was about?" Sam grunted.

Dave held the little box in his hands so everyone else could see the carvings on its lid. "It's a jewelry box," he said proudly. "Like the one my granny used to have. Take a look inside." With that, he opened the lid to reveal several thin silver chains, a few gold rings and a few brooches with specks of diamonds in them. "These should be worth something."

Sam nodded. "Maybe, but that's not why we're here. Put it back."

Reluctantly, Dave turned around to put the box where he'd found it. The sounds of greedy fingers scraping along the inside of that box rattled within the wagon until Dave stepped back out again. He patted his shirt pocket and grinned.

Jeremiah felt like he'd been through a

wringer. On one side of him, Anne was catching her breath. On the other side, Natham was closing his eyes and chuckling to himself. As much as Jeremiah wanted to show some relief of his own, there was still plenty more to be done.

CHAPTER 21

"Untie them," Sam ordered less than an hour later. "All but Natham, that is."

Since Natham had been retied to the wagon wheel to Jeremiah's left, the gunmen hadn't stopped moving. Jeremiah wasn't in much of a position to see what they were doing, but he could hear things being tossed to the ground and shattering on impact. The crash of breaking dishes was distinctive. Despite all the things that were being destroyed, Jeremiah held his breath for the moment when they would hear the surprised yelp of Claire finally being discovered.

But that dreaded sound never came.

None of the gunmen even spoke as if they'd stumbled across anything more interesting than household items and drawers full of folded clothes. Jeremiah was glad for that, but also confused. He was also so tired that he had to keep looking around to make certain Claire wasn't already tied up somewhere nearby.

Sara was quiet as ever, although she rarely broke eye contact with Jeremiah. There was the flicker of promise in her eyes that showed she was ready for whatever Jeremiah had in mind. All he needed to do was give a signal and she would be there. He didn't need to hear one word from her to know that much for certain.

What worried him the most was the Inglebrechts. Jeremiah watched as Pointer went to the elderly couple first to follow through on the order he'd been given. The Indian loosened the ropes on Harold's and Noelle's hands and then took a step back. Neither of them even made a move to take advantage of their newly granted freedom.

Shrugging, Pointer made his way down the line to loosen everyone else's ropes. He didn't take the ropes completely off, but he gave them just enough slack so they could free themselves. When Jeremiah removed his ropes and looked up, he found the Indian pointing toward Dave, who now watched over them with the rifle.

"You try to run," Pointer said, "and you'll die."

That was all the Indian needed to say. He walked back to what he'd been doing before.

Jeremiah was finally able to get a look at all of the wagons again. Even though he'd been listening the entire time, he was still surprised at the sight awaiting him.

The horses that had been shot were still crumpled within their harnesses at the front of the line. The rest of the horses had been gathered up and corralled nearby. All but two of the wagons had been completely emptied and stripped of anything that could be considered remotely useful. Those last two wagons were being reloaded by Charlie and Sam. What they couldn't load or didn't want was heaped into a large pile at the side of the trail.

"Any of you feel like running off had better think twice," Sam said. "Just sit tight and you'll be on your way soon enough."

It felt good for Jeremiah to straighten his legs and stretch his arms. He didn't realize how cramped up he was until he could once again enjoy his full range of motion. Even though he was still at gunpoint, Jeremiah let out a long, easy sigh. "Is everyone all right?" he asked in a voice that was just loud enough to be heard by the rest of the folks in his group.

Sara was still sitting down and massaging her wrists. "I'll be fine."

"What about you, Anne?"

She wouldn't answer. She'd lost all the color from her face and kept glancing around as if she was about to be shot for it. "Where is she?" Anne asked.

Jeremiah squatted down beside her so he could lower his voice even more. "I don't know," he said. "But it doesn't look like they've got her, so that's a good thing. Maybe she got away and went for help."

"If she just got away," Anne said, "that would be good enough for me."

Looking at the open country surrounding them, Jeremiah surveyed the miles of rugged terrain on either side of the trail. He could think of plenty that could go wrong to a grown man out there without provisions or a horse, but he figured it was best to keep from thinking of what could befall a nine-year-old girl.

"Just try not to mention her," Jeremiah said as he rubbed Anne's shoulder. "The best we can do for now is keep those men from knowing about her."

Anne nodded and rested her chin on her hands. Judging by the faraway look in her eyes, she wasn't going to be much good to anyone for a little while.

"What about you, Harold?" Jeremiah asked. "Are you and Mrs. Inglebrecht doing all right?"

Harold looked directly at Jeremiah for the first time since they'd been tied up. Until now, Jeremiah had figured that the old man was trying to distance himself so he could see to his wife or even come up with something on his own. There was also the possibility that he wanted to keep anyone from seeing the sweat that had covered his face. Now Jeremiah could see there was something else.

The old man wasn't just sweating; he was drenched. His skin was pale and it was plain to see the struggle he was going through to keep his hands from trembling too badly. Despite his best efforts, Harold was unable to look like anything more than death warmed over when he replied, "As good as can be expected."

Noelle was comforting her husband, even though she didn't seem much better than he was. Jeremiah walked over to them and offered each of them a hand. "Why don't you get up and stretch your legs?" he asked. "You'll feel better."

Harold seemed a bit confused, but he took the help Jeremiah was offering.

"Thank you so much," Noelle said. "This does feel better."

"Is Harold doing well?" Jeremiah asked.

"Oh, he's just not feeling his best. I daresay every last one of us has seen better times."

"Yeah, but . . ."

Noelle sighed and nodded as if she already knew what was on the tip of Jeremiah's tongue. "He hasn't had a drink for a long time. A bit too long."

"Hush up, Noelle," Harold snapped. "I'll be fine."

Jeremiah was glad to see that neither of them was hurt. He turned and walked toward his wife, but found Sara eyeing Natham anxiously. Once more, the look in her eyes told Jeremiah more than any number of words. The concern she was feeling wasn't exactly strange to Jeremiah. It was hard for him to stay on bad terms with the man after seeing what he'd done to divert attention from what they'd thought was Claire's hiding spot.

Sara moved aside as Jeremiah stepped in between her and Natham. Jeremiah then sat down and stretched his legs out. He felt a little bad for that since Natham was trussed up so tightly that he could hardly even breathe.

"That was quite a trick you pulled," Jeremiah said.

Natham glanced at him for a second and then looked away.

"How'd you manage it?" Jeremiah asked.

"Manage what?"

"Getting free of those ropes. I tried, but only dug them in deeper."

"I've got a trick thumb," Natham said. "Popped it out of joint when I tripped over a rock once and it comes out sometimes. If I try, I can pop it on purpose."

Jeremiah shuddered at the thought of that. "Bet it hurts like hell in the winter."

It took a moment for that to sink in, but when it did, the joke brought a grin to Natham's face. "Yeah, it does."

"Sounds like you've used that trick before."

The smile faded and was gone in a matter of seconds. "Yeah. I have."

"I wish there was something I could do to help you."

"Why would you help me?" Natham asked.

"Because you stepped up to help us. You've done it several times. I don't know what you might have done in the past, but —"

"That's right," Natham cut in. "You don't know. Let's just keep it that way."

Letting out a breath, Jeremiah glanced toward the gunmen and saw them joking back and forth like a bunch of ranch hands after finishing a day's work. Jeremiah looked back to Natham and asked, "You think you could get out of those ropes again?"

Natham shook his head. "Damn thumb's still out of joint. Besides, I'm cinched up too tight for a trick like that to work again."

"These men aim to bring you into the law," Jeremiah said.

"I know."

Jeremiah looked back toward the gunmen. This time, however, Sam was looking back at him.

"Do you know these men?" Jeremiah asked.

Natham was finished talking. His mouth was a hard line etched into stone and his eyes were cold bits of coal wedged into that same slab.

"You folks over there should get ready to go," Sam shouted. "We've been taking up this stretch of road for long enough."

There came the sound of something brushing against the ground, which was the only thing announcing Pointer's arrival. The Indian stepped up to within a few feet of Natham, locked eyes with Jeremiah and pointed toward the spot where Sara and Anne were standing.

Jeremiah looked at Natham and saw the tenseness in his eyes. Without bothering to ask for permission, Jeremiah dropped to one knee and reached for Natham's wounded hand. He grabbed hold of Natham's thumb and gave it one quick, powerful tug. The bones crunched beneath the skin and loudly snapped into place.

Every one of Natham's muscles contorted as he let out a stifled grunt. His eyes shot open, but the pain in them quickly faded. When he let out the breath he'd just taken, it turned into a relieved sigh.

"Whatever you thought you owed me," Natham said, "we're even now. Thanks."

Pointer grabbed Jeremiah by the arm and shoved him away from Natham. He then jabbed a finger to where he wanted Jeremiah to go. The look in the Indian's eyes made it clear that it was the last time he was going to ask so nicely.

Jeremiah walked to where the others were standing. Already, Sam was walking over there as well.

"I'd appreciate it if you folks came along with us for just a little while longer," Sam said.

"Do we have a choice?" Sara asked.

Sam looked at her and grinned. "I'll have to insist for the time being. You see, Emmett Natham is a dangerous man who's got plenty of friends. We just need to make certain none of you are in that group."

Anne was doing a good job of keeping her eyes on the wagons without making it too obvious. "Where are we going?" she asked.

"To collect the bounty for this murderer and then to go after the next deserving soul," Sam replied.

"What about our wagons?" Noelle asked in a voice that sounded equal parts dazed and frightened. "What about our things? Our horses."

"Once we straighten out whether or not any of you folks are dangerous or working with Natham, we'll take care of that. The ones of you that check out will be reimbursed for your losses. Sound fair?"

"How about we cut our losses and just part ways right now?" Jeremiah asked.

Dave and Charlie both raised their guns to cover the prisoners.

"Like I said before," Sam told him, "I'm gonna have to insist you come along."

CHAPTER 22

Jeremiah and the others were loaded onto one of the wagons like baggage. When Anne saw it was her own wagon that they were climbing into, she held her breath and tried not to make a sound. Despite her efforts, Jeremiah could still hear her. He didn't think that Dave was paying close enough attention to catch the trouble in Anne's face. He was kept busy enough with shoving everyone into the back of the wagon while keeping his pistol gripped in his other hand.

Natham was held back and away from everyone else. The Inglebrechts were shoved into the wagon first, followed by Sara, Anne and finally Jeremiah. He could hear Anne's worried sigh when it was clear that the prisoners were the only ones inside that wagon.

"Where is she?" Anne asked before she could stop herself from mentioning anything connected to her daughter. "Where did she go? Do you think they already have her?"

Jeremiah looked out from the back of the wagon and saw Dave walking away. The gunman was already tending to other business since all the prisoners were tied up so tightly that their hands and feet were going numb.

"I'm sure we'd know if they had her," Sara said. "There's not much else they could do with her besides throw her in here with us."

"I can think of plenty of other things they might do," Harold mumbled.

If her hands hadn't been tied, it was plain to see that Noelle would have smacked him. She flinched within her ropes, but came up very short so she snapped at him instead. "That's enough, Harold! For the love of God."

Those words seemed to have just as much of an impact on the old man as a backhand across the face. He twitched his head away and gritted his teeth but didn't speak again.

The women did their best to console one another, but Jeremiah didn't pay them any mind. His own thoughts were racing like a whitewater flow in his head. That rushing sound got even louder when he saw the gunmen walk out of sight as they moved ahead of the wagon.

As the wagon began to rumble and roll

forward, Jeremiah could hear the other horses riding ahead. Looking out the back of the wagon, he saw the wreckage left behind from the attack that already felt a week old.

Jeremiah rocked back and forth and then side to side. When he began to twist at his hips, he saw that he'd caught his wife's attention.

"What are you doing?" Sara asked.

Jeremiah felt his heart pounding like a hammer in his chest. "I don't think we're tied here."

"The hell we're not," Harold grunted. "I can't move my damn —"

"No," Jeremiah cut in. "I mean tied to the wagon. We're tied up, but not tied down."

After a bit of squirming on her own, Sara said, "That's true. We were just pushed in here and told to sit still or we'd be shot."

Jeremiah didn't recall anything being said to him when he'd been loaded into the wagon, but that didn't matter. All that mattered was the small window of opportunity that had been opened for him. "I think I can get out of here," he said.

Dropping her voice to a whisper, Sara asked, "Did you slip free of your ropes?"

"No, but I . . ." Jeremiah let his words trail off as the wagon was brought to a stop. The excitement he'd felt a moment ago was replaced by the cold grip of dread.

Harold started to say something, but Jeremiah shushed him immediately. After that, Jeremiah closed his eyes and cocked his head so he could concentrate on nothing else but what was happening outside and ahead of the wagon.

There were other horses approaching.

Lots of them.

The thunder of hooves enclosed the wagon on all sides, rolling in like a storm that died out as soon as the wagon was surrounded. Jeremiah opened his eyes to see a few horsemen coming to a stop about ten yards away from the rear gate. None of the riders looked at all familiar as they gazed into the wagon like curious children staring at a two-headed calf.

Jeremiah looked away from the riders, but concentrated on the voices he heard coming from outside and in front of the wagon.

"You see any more out there?"

That voice was definitely Sam's and it was so close that Sam was probably the one driving the wagon.

"Nope," replied someone who sounded vaguely familiar to Jeremiah. "There looks to be a pony coming along, but it's still a mile or so away."

"Just one?"

"From what I could tell. How many folks you expectin' to find along this beat-up stretch of road?"

"The way you're handing out the smart talk, I might start to forget that I'm the one that's paying you. And since you and your boys didn't do nothing but watch an empty stretch of beat-up road, I might also think that there's no need to pay you."

Even though he couldn't see the other man who was talking to Sam, Jeremiah had no trouble whatsoever picking up the anger in that one's tone.

"You pay what you owe or maybe you don't get free rein around here no more," the other man said. "Besides, I did plenty to keep Marshal Tanner off that killer's heels. I also told you what boat that killer was gonna catch. It ain't my fault if your boys don't know how to do the rest."

"There's plenty of crooked lawmen to be had, Art," Sam said with what sounded like a smile. "If you and yours think you're tough enough to butt heads with me and mine, then go on and try your luck."

Another quiet couple of seconds followed. Jeremiah could see the riders behind the wagon moving away so they could keep a close watch on what was happening. Those riders were moving their hands toward their holstered guns, but Jeremiah could only think about the deputy who'd been cut on the night that Emmett was chased out of that hotel.

Finally, Art broke the silence.

"We did our part, Madigan," he said. "Ain't no need for this to go bad. Especially when it looks like you made a pretty good haul. You catch that killer?"

"Yeah. I got him. He's still alive, so we should fetch full price."

"Because of me, you've been on that one's tail since the Sweetwater ferry. Don't tell me that bit of information didn't pan out because I had to do plenty of double-talking to clean up all them bodies you left at that trading post. That boat's captain threw a damn fit."

"I'll bet he did," Sam chuckled. "Of course, if Dave hadn't been so anxious, things might have turned out better all around."

"Go to hell, Sam," Dave muttered from somewhere to the left of the wagon.

"Fine," Sam said. "We'll pay you boys off right now and there's even a bonus coming to you from Dave's share."

"Bonus?" Art asked cautiously. "What's that for?"

"For a job well done. Actually, it's for a job that'll keep being well done. I'm fixing to cash in a little bonus myself and I don't want anyone getting wind of it just yet."

"Go see what he's talking about, Benny," Art said.

A silence fell just then that crushed Jeremiah and all the others in the wagon. He could feel his stomach clench as a horse slowly moved around toward the back of the wagon. Looking over to Sara, Jeremiah could see his wife's pale face looking at him as if she thought it might be for the last time.

The man who rode around to get a look into the wagon was a bit younger than Jeremiah had been expecting. In fact, if he didn't know any better, Jeremiah would have thought the man to be not much different than some of the young men who'd worked on his ranch over the years.

The rider's face was clean shaven, but that looked to be more through necessity than choice. Thick brown hair hung over his forehead, making him look even more like a big kid than a young man. He glanced at the prisoners without holding eye contact with any one of them and then nodded as he quickly rode back around the wagon.

"You selling them to slavers?" the rider asked. " 'Cause I know some Indians who'd be glad to take 'em off yer hands."

"Keep your speculations to yourself, boy," Sam replied. "All I need from you is to make sure nobody comes looking for them."

"I can't guarantee that," Art replied, "but I can make sure nobody hears about this mess you left behind."

"I'll want folks to hear about it, but on my schedule. Think you can handle that?"

Although the aggravation was clear enough in Art's voice, the deputy kept it in check. "Yeah. I can handle that."

"Then you just earned yourself a bonus."

"It better be at least three hundred," Art announced. "Anything less and it won't be worth it for us to stick our necks out."

"I see six of you, so why not make it a hundred for each? Does that make the split a little easier?"

"Sure it does," Art replied. Once again, there was more caution in his tone than anything else. "Why so generous?"

"Don't worry about that. Considering all you need to do is act dumb when the time comes, you're getting more than enough to keep your questions to yourself."

"All right. Fine. A hundred each. That's six hundred total on top of what you already agreed to pay."

Sam let out a haggard sigh, which was

clearly an act. Jeremiah could picture the gunman shaking his head while putting on the show. Finally, Sam ordered Dave to hand over the money. Jeremiah didn't need to see the deputy to know that Art was feeling more than a little pleased with himself right about then.

"Happy?" Sam asked.

"Yeah."

"And you'll forget about this mess we left behind?"

There was a slight pause before Art replied, "What mess? All I see is a pile of boxes that'll be picked through and scavenged by the next folks who pass by."

"That's the spirit."

Jeremiah heard the flick of reins, followed by the rumble of many more hooves than the ones needed to pull the wagon. When he took another look out the back of the wagon, all Jeremiah could see was the heap of crates, broken wagon parts and dead horses that was being left behind. As far as he could tell, the deputy and the men he'd brought with him were staying ahead of the wagon or keeping alongside it.

"All right," Jeremiah whispered. "I've got my chance."

"What are you —" Harold started to ask, but was cut short by a vicious glare from

Jeremiah. "What are you talking about?" the old man asked in a much quieter tone.

"I'm going to get off this wagon," Jeremiah replied. "I can fetch help. I can . . . I don't know what I can do, but I can do more out there than in here."

"Go on," Sara told him.

"Why don't we all go?" Harold asked.

When Jeremiah answered, he had to push his words out from the pit of his stomach. "Because I may be shot the second I jump from this wagon."

"Oh no," Sara said. "Maybe you shouldn't . . ."

That was the last thing Jeremiah heard from his wife before leaning over the wagon's rear gate and pushing off with both legs.

His ribs scraped along the top of the gate. When that same section of wood caught him in the gut, Jeremiah felt as if he'd been punched. His legs were the next to hit, but that wasn't much of a concern. Jeremiah was much more worried about the way his head had swung straight toward the ground with every ounce of his body's weight falling behind it.

Jeremiah instinctively tucked his chin against his chest and sucked in a breath to fill his lungs. His shoulders slammed against the ground and his legs flopped awkwardly on top of him.

For the next few seconds, he didn't know which way was up.

He couldn't even pull in a breath.

Jeremiah tried to straighten himself out as he felt all of his limbs contort at unnatural angles. First his shoulders seemed ready to snap loose; then a sharp jab of pain lanced through his back. Jeremiah's waist pinched in to squeeze his lungs empty and then his knees cracked him in the head.

When Jeremiah couldn't breathe, he thought he'd just made the last move of his life. He quickly realized he was having trouble breathing because his face was pressed against the ground. Jeremiah lifted his head and gasped for air. Although he worried about making too much noise, he couldn't keep himself from wheezing a few more times to replace the wind that had been knocked out of him.

Once his brain stopped rattling inside his skull, Jeremiah realized that it was too late to worry about making noise. His fall must have created enough of a ruckus to bring every last one of those riders around to see what had just happened. Lying in the mud with pain flowing through every inch of him, Jeremiah felt like the dumbest creature on God's green earth.

But none of the riders came to check on him.

Jeremiah could see two horses up toward the front of the wagon, or maybe a little ways ahead of it, but they weren't stopping.

In fact, the wagons seemed to be picking up speed.

Jeremiah lay on the ground craning his neck to keep his head out of the mud. His ears were filled with the rattle of wagon wheels knocking against the road. From his spot, he could see that Sam had elected to take all but two wagons along with him. Jeremiah could feel the rumble of the wheels against the ground along with the impact of all those hooves as the procession moved away.

As much as he wanted to get up and run away, Jeremiah still felt like a tangle of limbs that had been set on fire. All of his joints burned and, like insult heaped on top of injury, the ropes that kept him from running were digging into him so much that blood was seeping into his sleeves and jeans.

Despite all of that, Jeremiah kept his complaints to himself and his body close to the ground. If he couldn't get up and run, he figured the next best thing was to stay low and out of sight. If one of those gunmen did spot him right away, Jeremiah could just pretend to have fallen from the wagon by mistake. He sure wouldn't have to pretend to have been injured.

It took a few seconds, but Jeremiah soon began to think that he hadn't been heard after all. He felt that hope grow when he realized that the ruckus of the horses and wagons was more than enough to cover the sound of his less than graceful exit. Even so, he knew that one backward glance from the wrong man at the wrong time could bring Jeremiah's escape to a real abrupt halt.

He clenched his mouth shut and choked back every pained grunt as he hauled himself to a sitting position. Before he could come up with the quickest and least painful way to get off the road, Jeremiah saw something moving from the pile of crates that had been left behind.

It was more than just one box slipping from atop another. It was more like a few boxes being pushed to one side by something other than the wind. At that moment, Jeremiah wondered how he could be so foolish as to go through so much when the riders had simply left someone behind to watch that spot.

With no gun and no wind in his sails, Jeremiah held what little breath he had and prayed for some good bit of fortune to come his way.

CHAPTER 23

When Jeremiah saw the boxes shifting along the side of the road, he didn't know if he should try to hide from whomever was moving those boxes or if he should try to keep out of sight of those wagons. It would be only another few seconds before the wagons moved over the top of a slope, but Jeremiah knew that every second that passed could very well be his last.

Trusting his instincts, Jeremiah got his feet under him and struggled to stand up. Whatever happened, he decided it would be better to face it upright than lying in the dirt like a wounded animal waiting for the killing blow.

The boxes were still shifting, but the movement was very slight. Jeremiah watched until he could pick out the source of the movement, which was an old trunk beneath a pile of dresses and a bunch of hat boxes. One by one, those smaller things slid off the top of the trunk. Finally, the trunk let out a creak and it began to open.

The lid came up an inch or so, stayed there and then dropped shut.

Jeremiah took a quick look over his shoulder and saw the wagons rolling away without anyone seeming to notice they were short one prisoner. When he turned back around again, Jeremiah saw the trunk's lid had come up an inch or so, only to slam back down again.

Getting to his feet was a painful process, but Jeremiah did it quickly. He scrambled toward the boxes and things piled up alongside the trail, keeping his eyes open for anyone who might be waiting for him. As he got closer, the chest opened and shut once more.

"Claire?" he asked in the calmest voice he could manage. "Is that you in there?"

The lid came open again. This time, it opened less than an inch and stayed that way.

"It's all right, sweetie," Jeremiah said. "Can you see who it is? It's Mr. Correy."

Jeremiah took a few cautious steps toward the chest. "Are you all right? We've all been worried to death about you."

The lid lowered again.

"Nobody's angry at you," Jeremiah said.

"In fact, you did a real good thing by hiding the way you did."

The lid came open enough for some light to make it into the chest. Jeremiah couldn't see much, but he could just make out a pair of eyes and a few little fingertips.

"The bad men are gone, sweetie. You don't need to worry about them seeing you."

Those seemed to be the magic words. The lid was pushed open all the way this time and the little girl practically exploded from within the chest. She hopped out with the grace that only children possessed, landed on her feet and ran at full speed toward Jeremiah.

Jeremiah was thankful to see a smiling face. The only thing that would have made it better was if he could return the hug that she gave to him.

"I was so scared, Mr. Correy," Claire said in a rush. "I just ducked my head like I was told when all that shooting happened. I hid where I hoped nobody would find me, but was too scared to come back out again."

"Did anyone try to find you?" Jeremiah asked.

She nodded. "That's why I left my first hiding spot. All those men were so loud and I was afraid what would happen if they found me so I hid somewhere else. I hid under a pile of blankets, but then they came and took my ma and everyone else away so I got into that chest and tried to keep quiet."

Hearing the sobs building up under each one of the little girl's breaths, Jeremiah quickly tried to divert her from breaking into a crying fit. "You did real good," he said.

"What about my ma?"

"She's fine. She just wants to know what happened. You were so smart that nobody could find you and we were all worried."

Claire's trembling voice cleared up almost too quickly. A hint of a smile showed upon her face as she said, "A man went through some of our things, but he didn't look through all the blankets. Since he already looked in the chest where we keep all my skirts and bonnets, I climbed in there when nobody was around."

"I bet you're real good at hide-and-seek."

"I sure am. I use that same trick all the time."

"As long as it's working, you might as well use it," Jeremiah said.

"Mr. Correy? Why are you tied up like that?"

"Well, I'm not as good at hiding as you are, but I was also able to get away when

271

they weren't looking."

"It looked like you hurt yourself," Claire said gravely.

"Could have been worse. Do you think you can untie a knot for me?"

Her eyes widened and she nodded furiously. "I bet I can."

Jeremiah turned and extended his arms as best he could. "Great. See what you can do with those."

He could feel Claire pulling at the ropes and he could hear her straining to get the knots around Jeremiah's wrists to loosen. But even her thin little fingers couldn't get very far inside the knots. She tried for a couple of minutes as Jeremiah watched the trail. After a while, he heard a winded sigh and Claire's tired voice.

"They're tied real tight," she said.

"You're just going to have to try again, honey. You can do it."

"I can try something else, Mr. Correy."

"No. Keep trying the knots." He could hear her getting to her feet and walking away. Even as he spoke in a sterner voice, Jeremiah couldn't get her to come back to him. "Claire. You need to get back here. I have to have my hands free," he said. When he saw her disappear behind the crooked stacks of crates, he shouted, "Claire, come back here right now!"

She peeked over some of the crates to quickly look back at him, but ducked right down again as she rattled noisily through some of the discarded belongings.

Jeremiah got more and more anxious with every second that passed. He wanted to rush over and see what she was doing, but the way he was tied up made every movement awkward. Jeremiah still made it more than halfway to the crates before he saw Claire step around them again.

"They took our good silver," she said. "But there's still the ones we use every day." As she said that, the little girl held out her hand. Inside her fist, there was a short knife with a somewhat tarnished but sharpened blade.

"Good girl!" Jeremiah said. "Do you think you can cut these ropes?"

"Yes, sir, Mr. Correy."

Claire was all too anxious to run over to him with the knife gripped tightly in her hand.

"Be careful, now," he said as he felt the blade brush against the inside of his forearm.

She cut in a quick sawing motion as if she were slicing off a tough piece of steak. With Jeremiah pulling his arms apart, she didn't have to cut very long before the ropes finally gave way. Claire jumped back in surprise when his arms snapped out to the sides, but she laughed and walked in front of him.

"Here you go," she said while handing the kitchen knife over. "You'd better do the rest."

"Thanks, sweetie. You did a real good job." Jeremiah got busy cutting away the rest of the ropes dangling from his wrists and quickly shifted his efforts to free up his legs. Although he'd had enough slack to move, it felt awfully good to be able to get the full range of motion back in all of his limbs.

"Are there any more knives around?" he asked.

"I just know where ours are, but I can look through the rest. Those men left plenty around here."

"No time for that. What about any guns? Did you find any of those?"

She shook her head. "I think the men took all of those. Mr. Correy?"

"Yeah?"

"Where's my ma?"

Jeremiah looked into her face as he thought about how to answer that question. Despite the innocence in her tone, Claire was far from stupid. She'd been there when everything had happened. She'd been smart

274

enough to keep from getting captured. She'd even been smart enough to help him get free. The least Jeremiah could do to repay her was answer her question.

"Your mama is with my wife and the Inglebrechts," Jeremiah told her.

"Are they going to die?"

"Not if I can help it. I got away so I could help them."

"I want to help too."

More than anything, Jeremiah wanted to tell the little girl to find someplace safe and stay there. This was grown-up work and not something for a child to trouble herself with. It most certainly wasn't fair to ask a child to put her neck on the chopping block. But Jeremiah was quickly brought back to the unfortunate reality of the situation.

There was no safe place he could think of where he could just drop Claire off.

There was no place for her to hide where she could be safe from gunmen as well as the elements.

And there was no way for him to concern himself with just getting her to a warm bed while his wife, Claire's mother and everyone else simply rode off to parts unknown.

"You want to help?" Jeremiah asked. "Can you find any food or water that was left behind?"

She enthusiastically nodded and spun around to start digging through the crates.

Jeremiah spotted some of his own possessions and he dug through them as well. Even though the things were familiar and he'd taken part in packing up a good portion of it, that stuff seemed foreign to him. It was as if all those picture frames, dishes, books, shoes and countless other random belongings were no longer part of him anymore. They certainly weren't as important as when he and Sara had so carefully packed them away.

A week or so ago, the thought of leaving so much lying on the side of a road would have seemed unthinkable. Now all he wanted to find was his wife and take her someplace they could be safe and warm. All those things he'd spent so much time collecting no longer mattered.

He barely even knew Claire, but that little girl mattered more than all of his possessions combined.

Jeremiah went straight to a box full of clothing and started pulling out a few things he would need. He took a coat, some shirts and some wool socks, wrapped them into a bundle and tucked that bundle under his arm. He instructed Claire to find some clothes for herself and she immediately complied.

"What about this, Mr. Correy?" she asked as she held up a tattered doll. "Can I take this too?"

"Is that your friend?"

"No," she said. "It's a dog and his name is Patches."

"You can take him. Is there anything else?"

She looked over her small pile of things with a contemplative look in her eye that was similar to the one Jeremiah had had moments ago. Coming to a conclusion a bit quicker than he had, Claire shook her head and said, "No. This is all I need."

"You've got some warm clothes?"

"Yes."

"Then let's get moving."

"Where are we going?"

Jeremiah stopped and blinked a few times. Suddenly, he felt like a complete idiot. With the excitement of the escape and then finding Claire, he hadn't exactly had a lot of time to think about such details as what he was going to do next. Actually, Jeremiah wasn't expecting to make it this far.

"We're going that way," he said confidently while pointing up the trail. "That's the way the wagons went, so that's where we're going. We should be able to catch up with them, although it might take a while."

Going by the look on Claire's face, Jeremiah thought she might see right through to the fact that he was trying to convince himself of that plan as much as he was trying to convince her.

"We don't even have horses," she said. "How are we going to catch up?"

"We'll think of something. For right now, we'll just start moving." Before he could get moving more than a couple of steps, Jeremiah snapped his fingers and stood bolt upright. "Wait a second!"

Claire had run a few steps to get to his side, but she now stopped and ran back to the heap of crates to catch up to him once again. "What are you doing now?" she asked.

Jeremiah was digging through the crates and eventually started shoving them over so he could look under the next one. Eventually, he pulled a bundle of tattered canvas from the pile of his things and showed Claire a triumphant smile. "Found it!"

"Found what?"

"My maps!" Opening the bundle, Jeremiah sifted through some documents and finally pulled one out that was more creased and frayed at the edges than any of the others. "I plotted out where we were headed on this map. That doesn't mean those men will go the same way, but at least it's something to go by."

For a moment, Jeremiah had gotten so worked up that he'd forgotten he was talking to a little girl struggling to keep herself from being too frightened by all she'd seen and heard. He softened up his tone and put on a friendly smile, which caused her to smile warily back at him.

"I heard the men say they were going to a town," Jeremiah told her. "This map shows all the towns that are big enough to feed all those horses."

He also figured those towns were big enough to have an office where Sam could cash in a good-sized bounty, but there was no reason to explain all of that.

"One of these towns looks to be only a few miles or so from here. I wasn't planning on stopping there before, but we should be able to walk to it now."

"Do you think my ma will be there?"

"I honestly don't know, sweetie. But if she's not, we can at least get a horse. Things will go a lot easier once we can ride rather than walk, don't you agree?"

Eventually, a smile beamed from Claire's face. "Sounds like a good plan," she said.

"Let's hope so," Jeremiah said as he dug out a few more trinkets from his scattered possessions. "Now let's get going. Want to race me?"

Once she saw which way Jeremiah wanted to go, Claire darted past him like she'd been shot from a cannon.

CHAPTER 24

It was early evening before Jeremiah and Claire caught their first sight of that town. Although she'd started off running like her tail was on fire, the little girl quickly ran out of steam and slowed to a walk. There were times when she hadn't wanted to move at all, so Jeremiah carried her on his shoulders.

They walked into town hand in hand as the sun was just about to touch the western horizon. The sky was a brilliant gold, forcing Jeremiah to squint as he looked at the buildings spread out in front of them. It didn't look like a big place, but that was mostly because the streets were wide and spread out as if the town thought it had all of creation to make its own. Just as he realized it would be another half mile or so before they reached any of those buildings, Jeremiah received another bit of luck for the day.

"Headed into town?" a stout man asked

from the driver's seat of a small cart pulled by an old mule.

"Yes, sir," Claire replied before Jeremiah could form the words.

The man in the cart couldn't help but smile back at her as he said, "I can give you a ride there on one condition."

"What's that?" Jeremiah asked.

Although he leaned back after seeing the protective glare on Jeremiah's face, the man in the cart winked at Claire and said, "You need to sing me a song along the way."

"I know 'She'll Be Coming 'Round the Mountain,' " she offered.

"My favorite."

With that, the man waved toward the cart behind him and waited for Jeremiah and Claire to climb onto the back. He snapped the reins and got the old cart moving while Claire sang her song and swung her feet over the side.

"Sheeee'll beeeee comin' round the mountain when she comes!"

It was a short ride, but Jeremiah was grateful for the chance to move without walking. He also realized how distrustful he'd become of folks. While the stout man seemed friendly enough, Jeremiah was waiting for the time when that fellow would turn

282

around and threaten his life.

Perhaps Jeremiah would have to dive off the cart with Claire in his arms.

Maybe Jeremiah would need to fight the stout man before any harm could come to himself or the little girl.

But none of that came to pass. Instead, they were given a ride into town and dropped off at a place the stout man recommended for its thick steaks. After that, the man gave them a wave and moved along. Jeremiah still found himself standing outside the restaurant as if he was preparing to fend off an ambush.

"Come on," Claire said as she pulled Jeremiah toward the restaurant. "I'm hungry."

Everything seemed a whole lot better once Jeremiah's belly was full. He was still worn as thin as an old work shirt, but he wasn't as ready to take a swing at anyone who looked at him cross-eyed. That shift in his demeanor proved to be valuable when he tapped on the window of a little storefront connected to a stable.

The bald man inside the store shuffled from behind a small counter that took up most of the space within the shack. He waved impatiently toward the window and shouted, "We're closed," loud enough to be heard through the glass.

Jeremiah put on his most heartfelt smile and pointed toward the only sign posted in the window, which read HORSES FOR SALE OR TRADE.

But the man kept shaking his head. "Come back in the morning!"

Nodding, Jeremiah looked down the street and saw another small shack neighboring a corral. "Never mind," he shouted at the window. "I think the fellow down there will see me."

That caused the bald man's eyes to widen as he let out a flustered sigh and shuffled toward the door. "Hold on. I'll be right there."

Claire looked down the street and asked, "Is there another man that'll sell us a horse?"

"I don't know, but I suppose that doesn't matter now."

As the shop's door was pulled open, Jeremiah put on the face that was normally reserved for dealing with cattle buyers, hired hands or anyone else who was out to empty his pockets.

"What're you lookin' to buy?" the bald man asked.

Now that he was closer to the shopkeeper,

Jeremiah could see the deep wrinkles around the man's eyes, which looked like cracks in a slab of granite. His voice was just short of being shrill and his hands gripped the door as if he was about to slam it in Jeremiah's face.

"We need a horse," Jeremiah said. "I don't have any money, so it'll have to be for trade."

"What you got to trade?"

"Just this," Jeremiah said as he removed a few of the things from his pocket that he'd scavenged from the pile where Claire had been hiding.

The bald man looked down at a pair of pocket watches, a compass and some stickpins. Those things had been at the bottom of one of Jeremiah's trunks and were too small to be found when Dave had made his quick search.

"That won't get you much," the shopkeeper said.

"What can it get me?"

When he fished out the fanciest of Jeremiah's watches, it was obvious the shopkeeper was interested. He opened the watch, studied the face and spotted the silver and gold flecks embedded on the inside of the casing. Doing a fairly good job of appearing to be disinterested, he grunted, "I got a slope-backed mule that's still got some kick in her."

"We need to ride a ways," Jeremiah said. "And we don't have a saddle."

"I can toss in some secondhand gear."

But Jeremiah had danced this dance plenty of times before. He knew when he'd found a bargaining chip and what to do when that situation arose. Reluctantly, he peeled the watch from the shopkeeper's hands. "Sorry, I guess I'll need to try somewhere else."

"What else you got there?" the bald man asked quickly.

Jeremiah handed over the rest, but knew his silver and gold watch alone was valuable enough to trade for a decent horse and some used gear.

"Fine," the bald man said. "I got a spotted mare I'd be willing to part with, but I don't have much more than some reins and a blanket to toss over her back."

"Can I get a look at her?"

"Sure. Come on."

Jeremiah followed the bald man to the nearby stable and was shown the mare in question. Although he kept a sour look on his face, Jeremiah was expecting to find an animal in much worse condition. In fact, he would have been happy to get something a few years older. Jeremiah kept all that to himself, however, and only muttered every now and then while examining the mare.

"I don't have much option, but she looks good enough," Jeremiah said.

"Then we got a deal?" the bald man asked.

"Sure do." While handing over the watches, Jeremiah asked, "Do you get a good look at who comes and goes along this street?"

"Yep. That's why I set up shop here. I see most everyone that passes through town."

"What about a bunch of wagons accompanied by about two or three horses? Did you see anyone like that pass through today?"

Now that he had his payment in hand, the bald man was a bit more content to stand still and talk with Jeremiah. He took a few seconds to think the question over as he tapped his chin and mumbled to himself. Finally, he shrugged and said, "Could be. There's plenty of folks that pass through and plenty more of them are in wagons."

"This was a good-sized group. You sure you don't recall them being here today?"

"There was a few men who came through wanting to buy some feed, but they wasn't a part of no group."

"How much feed?"

"A couple sacks of oats."

"That's more than someone would need for a horse or two," Jeremiah pointed out.

"Depends on how long they wanted it to last. Do you want to take your horse with you now or wait until the morning? I got a dinner to get home to."

Digging into his other pocket, Jeremiah scrounged for anything he could find. All he was able to come up with was a set of pearl tie tacks that had been a wedding gift from his cousin Brad. "Are you willing to buy anything else from me or do you strictly trade?"

"That what you're offering?" the bald man asked as he eyed the tie tacks.

"Depends on how much you can pay for them."

The bald man grinned as if he were about to sink his teeth into his dinner right then and there.

After a bit of haggling, Jeremiah arrived at a price that was just short of fair. Although he knew the tie tacks were worth more, the bald man either didn't know any better or didn't want them so badly. Either way, it was plain to see the shopkeeper wasn't going to go any higher. Rather than part with them both on those terms, Jeremiah offered to sell only one. At least he could afford some food and a warm bed for the night with that amount.

Judging by the look on the shopkeeper's face, someone might have thought he was facing the possibility of losing his eye teeth. "That fellow buying the feed," he grumbled. "I might know where he went."

"I don't even know if that's the man I was thinking about or not," Jeremiah said, having become tired of the whole negotiation process.

"Was the man you're thinking about missing an eye?"

Jeremiah's head snapped up and he pulled in a quick breath. Even though that was the worst thing he could have done in the middle of haggling, he couldn't keep the interest from his eyes.

Like a shark swimming toward a patch of bloody water, the shopkeeper nodded and said, "Looks like he was favoring one arm over the other, but I couldn't tell you which one. Rough-looking customer, though."

"Was he heeled?" Jeremiah asked.

"A .45 by the looks of it, but firearms ain't exactly my specialty."

"Where did he go?"

"I'll tell you for that matching piece."

Jeremiah had to look down to remind himself that he was still holding on to the other tie tack. "It's yours if you can tell me where to find this man."

Suddenly, the bald man looked apprehensive. "I don't want him to know where you came by this information. He didn't look like the sort who'd welcome unwanted visitors."

"Do you even think he knows who you are?"

As he thought that over, the bald man looked back and forth between the street and what was in Jeremiah's hand. Finally, he shrugged and took the tie tack from him. "He's staying at Millie's. Go out the door, around the corner and down Fourth Street. You won't be able to miss it. The place is a cat—" He froze part of the way through his description once he got Claire back in his sights. Shrugging, he looked to Jeremiah and said, "You can't miss it."

"I understand. Thanks for the directions."

"Mind if I ask what business you got with that fellow?"

"Why? Do you think you could sell a warning to him?"

The bald man laughed under his breath and shook his head. "Not hardly. I was just wondering if I might be getting my horse back sooner rather than later."

"Assuming I make it through the night, I expect she'll be watered and ready to ride."

"Sure. I'll put her in the back stall. It opens to the lot behind my office, so you can come get her whenever you please. If you wait past noon, I'll have to charge you for the space."

Jeremiah sighed and headed for the door. "Quite a nice little business you've got here."

The bald man nodded once and replied, "Sometimes it even pays to stay a little past closing time. You have yourself a good night. You too, little girl."

Once the door closed, Claire turned to look at Jeremiah. "You got a lot of money from that man," she said.

"Not really."

"Are we going to rest soon?"

"Yes, we are," Jeremiah told her. "You're going to sleep in a warm bed tonight."

Claire was quiet as they walked down the street. Before reaching the corner, she asked, "Was he talking about the man with one eye who robbed us?"

"I don't know, but I intend to find out."

CHAPTER 25

Claire was tucked into a room rented under another name. The little girl had the window open and a ground-level view of an open field in case she needed to get out and run away in a hurry. She even had a plan as for where she needed to go and how long to hide before finding the law, which was only one street away.

That was the best Jeremiah could arrange considering what he had to work with. As much as he would have liked to stay and guard her every second, that simply wasn't possible. There was business that needed tending to and it was the sort of business a nine-year-old girl shouldn't see.

Jeremiah followed the bald shopkeeper's directions and found Millie's. If the bald man had been right about anything, it was that there was no way on earth for someone to miss that cathouse. Millie's was one of the largest buildings on Fourth Street and also one of the busiest. Even though the sign hanging near the front door advertised baths and spirits, the women hanging out the windows and sitting on the front porch didn't seem the sort to be serving up either of those things.

There were plenty of spirits to be found, however, and they were most definitely high. Jeremiah would even hazard a guess that he could get a bath in there as well, but it would most certainly require someone in there with him to scrub his back. One of the ladies who would fit that bill got up from her rocking chair and walked up to meet him before he could even climb the two steps leading to the front porch.

"Evening, mister," she said in a voice that had been soaked in whiskey. "What's your pleasure?"

Jeremiah looked her up and down. Although he wasn't interested in what she was selling, he was a man and couldn't help but notice that the clothes she wore did little to cover her up. A loose blouse was unbuttoned more than halfway, leaving next to nothing to the imagination from the waist up. Long, dark red hair flowed over her shoulders and covered more of her pale skin than the shawl that was hanging from her elbows.

"I'm looking for a man with one eye," Jeremiah said.

"Then you're in the wrong place. Only ladies here, my friend."

"It's not like that. He's one of your customers and I need to have a word with him."

Now it was her turn to look him up and down. When she did, it was obvious that she wasn't sizing up his build or the clothes he wore. For the most part, her eyes lingered on the empty holster that still hung around Jeremiah's waist.

"You better not be out for any trouble," she told him. "Because the men we've got in here don't carry no empty holsters."

Jeremiah shook his head. Putting on a tired smile, he said, "My friend was supposed to scout this place out for me and I want to see what he's got to say. If it's good, I might just be in the market to be one of your customers."

The redhead licked her upper lip and nodded as if she was still trying to decide what to make of him. Finally, she winked at Jeremiah and placed her hand upon his shoulder. "You're early. I think I know the man you're asking for, but he told us his friends wouldn't be showing up until after midnight."

"It's been a while," Jeremiah said. "I

couldn't wait."

"I just bet you couldn't. Come on. I'll take you to his room."

As Jeremiah was led inside, he felt cold beads of sweat push through his skin to trickle down his forehead. The redhead looked to be anything but dangerous, but he was still expecting her to call his bluff or see through the lies he'd been feeding her. From there, all she needed to do was scream loudly enough to draw Dave from his room.

But it wasn't doing Jeremiah any good to fret with that for too long. At the moment, he was being led by the hand through a house that smelled like perfume and burning candles. There was a dark blue carpet under his feet, making every step sound as if it had come from another room. A few women walked between rooms and every one of them looked Jeremiah directly in the eye, smiled and gave him a chance to change his mind about the companion he'd chosen.

"Don't be so nervous, darlin'," the redhead told Jeremiah as she squeezed his hand. "This can't be your first go-round."

"It's not."

"You look like you've been without comforts for a while. Maybe we should start you off with a bath. That is our specialty, you know."

"Maybe after I surprise my friend," Jeremiah said.

"This is a surprise, huh? Your friend seemed kind of rough. You sure you want to bust in on him?"

Jeremiah didn't have anything against the redhead or anyone in her line of work. Before meeting Sara, he'd visited a few soiled doves in a few different towns. Ladies in that profession were just like any other folks. Some were good and some weren't. What most of them had in common was a real sharp eye when it came to sizing a man up. Sometimes, their lives depended on being able to tell which were dangerous and which were simply blowing smoke. For that reason alone, Jeremiah was nervous being around that redhead.

Every step she took, she was taking stock of him. She listened intently to every word and was surely weighing them all in her head. When she stopped short of a hallway at the back of the house, the redhead caused every one of Jeremiah's muscles to tighten anxiously.

"He's in a room just down there," she said. "You sure you're a friend of his?"

"Yeah. It's just that . . ." Jeremiah looked

down at his hands and got inspiration from the last place he would expect. At least, that inspiration seemed odd when considering the spot he was in.

Allowing his nervousness to show through, Jeremiah didn't need to act in order to get his voice to tremble. "You see, I'm married."

"Yeah," the redhead replied as she tapped his ring with her finger. "I see that."

"I've been on the trail for a while and it's been a long time since I've been in a place like this."

She nodded and patted the back of his hand. "No need to go on about it. I can draw you a hot bath with a drink of whiskey to go along with it. You hurry up and say hello to your friend and I'll get you relaxed. After that . . . well . . . we'll see what happens."

Jeremiah also didn't have to act in order to seem relieved upon hearing the soothing tones of her voice. The redhead's touch was soft, gentle and reassuring. The promise in her eyes even stirred a few things inside Jeremiah that he wouldn't like to admit were there.

"What's your name?" he asked.

"You can call me Sadie. Your friend's in the third room on the left," she said while nodding down the hall. "Try not to take too long. Come find me when you're ready." With that, she turned and sauntered away. Sadie didn't need to look over her shoulder to check if Jeremiah was watching her swaying steps. She knew he was watching.

Any man worth his salt would have been watching her.

Jeremiah forced himself to look away from Sadie's intoxicating stride. All he had to do was set his sights upon the third door on the left side of the hallway to put himself back into a more suitable frame of mind. Unfortunately, that frame of mind came along with plenty of questions. The biggest of those rolled through his mind like thunder.

What the hell was he about to do?

Before he could ponder that question for more than a heartbeat, Jeremiah tried to open the door and found it locked. The rattle of the doorknob echoed through his ears like a gunshot, making him certain it was too late to back down. As he heard a few hesitant steps approach the other side of that door, Jeremiah stood to one side and knocked on it with his knuckles.

The person inside that room unlocked the door and pulled it open.

Jeremiah had his eyes focused on the opening so intently that he was able to recognize Dave's face from just the sliver he could see through that crack. There was a glint of recognition in Dave's eye as well, causing Jeremiah to grit his teeth and move forward.

Using his shoulder against the door, Jeremiah shoved his way into the room while knocking Dave back. He kicked the door shut and then delivered a vicious punch to Dave's stomach.

Dave stumbled back and crumpled around the punch to his gut. While letting out a grunting breath, he turned toward a nearby chair, which was one of the few pieces of furniture inside the cramped room.

Jeremiah looked in that direction and quickly spotted the gun belt hanging off the back of that chair. Since he was half a step closer to the chair, Jeremiah lunged for it with both arms outstretched. He was so intent on getting to the gun that he wasn't able to brace himself before Dave swung a quick jab to his ribs.

Dave's punch bounced off Jeremiah's side, robbing him of his next breath and sending a sharp stabbing pain through that entire half of his torso.

Running on pure desperation, Jeremiah kept reaching for the gun until his fingers closed around the handle. As soon as he got the weapon in his grasp, Jeremiah turned to aim it at Dave.

The one-eyed man charged toward Jeremiah like an angry bull. Jeremiah meant to get out of the way, but could only sidestep and knock his shoulder against another of the small room's walls.

Wheeling around with his teeth bared, Dave looked like something from a nightmare. There was no doubt he'd been caught unawares since he hadn't even gotten a chance to put on the patch that normally covered his bad eye. Jeremiah could see the clouded, shrunken remains of the eye wedged into Dave's scarred socket. Even so, that wasn't as disturbing as the viciousness reflected inside the eye Dave could actually use.

"You're a dead man!" Dave snarled. "I don't know how you got away, but you should've kept runnin'."

"Save your threats," Jeremiah said in the steadiest voice he could manage. "I'm the one with the gun."

Dave pulled in a few breaths and glanced at the gun in Jeremiah's possession. "Yeah? Well, you look like you'd sooner piss yourself than pull that trigger."

"You've got my wife held hostage. You really want to test me?"

Despite the arrogant grin on Dave's face, he lowered his arms and backed up a step. He straightened up to his regular height, which made him look less like an animal that was about to pounce. He didn't even flinch when someone knocked on the door.

"Hello?" someone asked from the hallway. "What's going on in there?"

"I tripped," Jeremiah said. "That's all."

There was a pause and then the woman on the other side of the door asked, "Are you sure that's it?"

"Yeah," Dave snapped. "Now git!"

Jeremiah could hear some muttering, but couldn't make out what the woman was saying. More importantly, he could hear footsteps moving away from the door and heading down the hall.

"There," Dave said. "You happy now?"

"Not hardly."

"Why don't you put that gun down before you hurt yourself?"

"Actually, I was just getting a feel for it," Jeremiah replied as he backed up until his heel touched the wall behind him. "Sit down."

"All I wanna do is talk like civilized folks."

"Right now, neither one of us is civilized. Now sit down."

There was a viciousness in Jeremiah's

301

voice that must have taken Dave off guard, because the one-eyed man lowered himself onto the edge of the bed without another question. He regained his composure quickly enough, but there was still plenty of caution in Dave's good eye.

"You surprised the hell out of us by disappearing the way you did," Dave said. "I didn't think you had that in you."

"You'd be surprised what else I'm capable of. Tell me who you are."

"You heard this story before."

"Sam told me you were bounty hunters," Jeremiah said. "That doesn't explain why you'd hold us all hostage. And don't tell me you're making sure we're not working with Emmett," he added sharply. "You and I both know that's a damn lie."

The grin on Dave's face twisted into another shape. Rather than looking smug, it made him look more like a kid who'd been caught in a fib. "Chasing wanted men ain't as profitable as you might think. There's men to buy off and expenses to pay. Especially when it comes to chasing down a murdering piece of trash like your friend Emmett Natham."

"Get to the part about taking prisoners. You could have ridden off with Natham without taking the rest of us along and leaving everything we own on the side of a road."

Dave shrugged as if he no longer saw the gun in Jeremiah's hand. "You don't even know who you're riding with, do you?"

"Sam told me about Natham."

"Not him. That asshole's stayed alive by being sneaky. I'm talking about them gray hairs you got in your group."

"The Inglebrechts?"

"Them's the ones," Dave said. "You don't know how surprised we were to find Noelle Inglebrecht riding along, pretty as you please, when we weren't even looking for her."

"Why would you be looking for her?"

"Because she comes from a family that can afford to pay a hell of a nice ransom without too much fuss," Dave grunted. "You didn't know she came from old money?"

"No. How would you know something like that?"

"How do you know where to find the best deals on buying cattle? Or where to take a herd to be sold off for the biggest profit? It's our business to know things like that. Besides, London Charlie got wind that Noelle Inglebrecht was moving along and was pestering Sam to snatch her up for weeks.

This just fell into our laps like it was meant to be."

"And what about the others?" Jeremiah asked. "What are you planning for them?"

Dave shrugged and narrowed his eyes as if he had the high ground instead of being the one caught at the wrong end of a pistol. "A good businessman knows how to take advantage of every opportunity."

Jeremiah shifted on his feet and felt his heart beating like a rabbit's. The more he tried to find the sense in what Dave was saying, the more his head swam. "You're just buying time for yourself," he said to the one-eyed man.

"I thought you wanted to know why you and your family's in such a bind. You pick bad company, mister, and that's a fact."

Hearing the way Dave laughed at those words was enough to ignite an angry fire in Jeremiah's belly. His grip tightened around the pistol and he spoke through clenched teeth. "You had your chance at Natham and you decided to take innocent folks prisoner instead. How's that make you any better than him?"

"It don't, I suppose," Dave admitted. "But at least we're up front with what we're doing. Natham's killed men in more ways than you'd care to know. He's double-crossed partners and he's burned through plenty more women than Sam or any of us have."

"Still sounds better than a bunch of damned kidnappers. What could you gain from holding me or my wife? The Inglebrechts didn't put up a fight. There was even a woman on her own. What's she worth to you?"

Although Dave didn't answer that right away, the look in his eyes spoke volumes. Rather than add any words to the wolfish glare, he said, "Don't try to pass yourself off as poor. Any fool knows a man's got to have some cash if he's gonna start up somewhere fresh. You got to buy up land, cattle and such as soon as you get to where you're going. Maybe you're to blame for doing such a piss-poor job of protecting what you got."

The longer Jeremiah tried to figure what could make a man like Dave tick, the more the room spun around him. That dizziness must have shown on Jeremiah's face, because Dave laughed at the sight of it.

"So, what now, rancher?" Dave asked. "I told you what you wanted to know."

"Tell me where the others are."

"I can do better than that. I can take you right back to them. Just hand over that gun and we can head out now. That is, unless you wanted to poke one of these fine ladies. Don't worry," Dave added with a smirk, "I won't tell your wife."

"Where are they?" When he saw another laugh start to bubble up from Dave like something working its way up from the back of his throat, Jeremiah straightened his arms and thumbed back the pistol's hammer.

Dave stopped laughing, but didn't take the smile from his face. "You shoot me and you won't ever know where to go. All that money will be split up among Sam and the rest of us while those pretty ladies will be sold off to Indians or whoever the hell else is in the market for them."

"Shut your mouth," Jeremiah said. "Don't say another word unless you're telling me what I want to know."

Dave kept his eyes locked on Jeremiah as he slowly moved toward him. "What if I told you I already had me a piece of that wife of yours?"

"I said shut your mouth."

"Soon as I saw you were gone, I kept that sweet little lady quiet myself," Dave said, following up on his previous taunts the way a hungry cougar jumped on wounded prey. "She was crying and carrying on."

"Where are they headed? Tell me or I'll shoot."

"She didn't shut up right away, though. I had to stick something in her mouth. You know what, though? She liked it. She liked every inch of it."

The gun in Jeremiah's hand barked once and bucked against his palm. Jeremiah jumped as well and watched Dave stagger back to fall onto the bed.

Dave locked his jaw shut and pulled in a haggard breath. His hand was clamped down over the fresh wound in his belly. Blood seeped out to soak into his shirt and cover his fingers in a matter of seconds. When he took his next breath, it was accompanied by a distinct wheezing sound.

"You . . . son of a . . ." Dave moaned.

Gathering himself up, Jeremiah stepped forward so he could stand directly over Dave and look down on him. "Tell me where they're going," he demanded in a voice that sounded so calm, it seemed to have come from someone else.

"I need a doctor, damn you!"

"After you talk."

After swearing a couple of times to himself, Dave opened his eyes and let his mouth hang open. He started to laugh when he heard the knocking on the door, but that hurt him too much to keep up for very long. "You hear that? You'll be . . . in jail before . . .

before the sun rises."

"And you'll be in a grave."

Every last bit of smugness left Dave's face. After looking at the thick coating of freshly spilled blood on his hand, he gasped, "Salt Lake City. They're headed to Salt Lake City. Now get me a doctor."

"How do I know you're telling the truth?"

"It's the truth, you bastard!" Dave snarled as he sat up and lunged with both hands for Jeremiah's throat.

Jeremiah pulled his trigger without hesitation.

His heart was beating so hard, he thought it might break out of his chest. His nose was filled with the scent of burned powder. Smoke from the pistol was curling up toward his face, but his eyes had already started to water.

Dave was finished.

When Jeremiah looked down, all he saw was a bloody body slumped against the wall. There was a final, forced sigh, which was followed by absolute quiet.

Jeremiah didn't even know exactly where that second bullet had hit. All that mattered now was for him to get out of that room as quickly as possible. While nobody was anxious to knock on the door, there were plenty of excited voices chattering elsewhere within the cathouse. There were bound to be other guns in there to protect the girls. Jeremiah figured it wouldn't take long before that door was knocked open and he was shown some of those guns firsthand.

For some reason, Jeremiah couldn't leave without taking another look at Dave. It wasn't any sort of morbid curiosity or even guilt. He just couldn't take a man's life and then turn his back on it so quickly. As he stared at that dead, unflinching face, Jeremiah knew he would never forget it no matter how much he wanted to.

That was the way it should be.

If Claire wasn't waiting for him nearby, Jeremiah might not have had the strength to climb out the window and get away from that cathouse in such a rush.

CHAPTER 26

Jeremiah wanted to toss the pistol he'd taken into the first hole he could find. And if he couldn't find one, he thought about digging a hole to bury the thing. But he knew he might need a weapon if he was going to stay on his chosen path. Actually, he knew if he was going to see Sara again, he would have to go heeled.

Every step of the way between Millie's and the hotel, Jeremiah expected to be stopped. He was certain he would be seen or dragged away before he could speak a word in his own defense. But he made it to the hotel without much trouble. When he got there, the only problem he faced was remembering the sequence of knocks he and Claire had agreed upon as their code for identifying each other.

Jeremiah knocked a few times and then swore under his breath. He tried to remember, knocked some more, knew it was wrong and swore again. When his fist was raised to try a third time, he saw the door come open and those familiar little eyes look at him through the opening.

"That wasn't the code," Claire said sternly.

"Then why did you open the door?"

"Because I could hear you saying bad things."

Jeremiah stepped into the room quickly, while trying his hardest not to push Claire in the process. "Yeah, well, that doesn't mean you should say bad things too."

"I didn't. You did."

"Yeah, well . . . maybe you should get some sleep." Jeremiah saw the dark circles under the little girl's eyes. Since he couldn't do much about them, he smoothed back her hair and lowered his voice to a more comforting tone. "Have you gotten any sleep?"

She shook her head.

"That looks like a soft bed," he told her. "How about you climb into it and try to sleep?"

"Aren't you tired?"

"Yes, but I'd rather sleep in the chair."

"You would?" she asked with a confused tilt of her head.

Jeremiah nodded. "Yep. I sleep better in a chair."

Either Claire was satisfied with that or she was too tired to argue with grown-up logic, because she shrugged and climbed under the covers. She curled into a tight ball and put her back to Jeremiah. Within moments, she was breathing loudly and deeply.

Jeremiah took the room's only chair and positioned it so that it faced the door. One quick look out the window was all he needed to see how little there was going on outside. That was both a welcome and a puzzling sight. He was most definitely glad that he wasn't being chased by anyone looking to make him answer for shooting Dave. Even so, Jeremiah had to wonder why gunshots and a dead body could be ignored so easily. Surely someone had to have discovered the mess in Dave's room by now and surely someone had to have seen Jeremiah jumping out the window or running down the street. At the very least, Sadie knew he was the last person to see Dave before those shots were fired.

Rather than stay up trying to second-guess other folks and their motives, Jeremiah settled into his chair and stretched out his legs. With his heels propped against the door, he knew he would awaken if someone managed to get through the lock and try to get into the room. Jeremiah rested his hand across the pistol he'd taken from Dave, so he could get the first shot at any intruders.

As sleep began to creep up on him, Jeremiah thought about everything that had happened that night. He thought about how he could get to Salt Lake City and what he should do with Claire in the meantime. He also wondered how he would pay for any other accommodations since he'd already sold off everything he had on him.

Part of him wondered if he should have gone through Dave's pockets or searched his room before running away.

The other part felt ashamed to have those thoughts rattling around within him.

Jeremiah woke up as if he'd been dropped from the ceiling.

His feet hit the floor, causing him to sit upright and pull in a quick breath. Although his instinct had been to turn and check on Claire, another instinct had caused him to tighten his grip on his gun as if to kill the first living thing in his sights.

Claire sat on her bed with her feet tucked in under the rest of her and looked at him with an easy smile. Without giving the gun in Jeremiah's hand a second thought, she said, "Good morning."

"It's morning?" Jeremiah asked as he looked toward the window. He could see sunlight coming through the glass, but could hardly believe so much time had passed.

"Yes, it's morning. I've been up for a while."

"You should have gotten me up."

"You were snoring," Claire said with a giggle.

"Was I?"

She nodded and hopped down from the bed. "Are we going to eat breakfast?"

"I'll see what I can do. It won't be much, though." As he stood up, Jeremiah was reminded in a dozen painful ways how awkwardly he'd slept in that chair. After tucking the gun into his holster, he pressed his hands against the small of his back and stretched some more. "I need to go and check on some things, so —"

"I won't open the door for anyone but you," Claire said.

"Actually, you might have to be ready to do more than that. Do you think you can jump out the window?"

"I could jump from the window of my old house, but Ma didn't . . . she didn't like it when I did that."

Jeremiah saw the change that came over the little girl's face when she mentioned her mother. Even if he was blind, he would have been able to hear the shift in her voice that was like day and night when compared to the giggle that had been there moments ago. Before he thought about anything else, Jeremiah was moving to the bedside and leaning down to look into the little girl's eyes.

"I'll do my best to get you back to your ma," he told her.

"I know," she replied with absolute faith. "Are you sad too?"

"Sad?"

"About Sara. She's nice, so you must miss her a lot. Just like Mr. and Mrs. Inglebrecht miss Paul."

Jeremiah winced a bit when he heard that, but knew that Claire didn't mean to make the morbid comparison. All he had to do was look at her face to know the little girl had only the best intentions. "I miss Sara a lot," he told her. "I want to get back to her too, just like I want to get you back to where you belong."

"Where are they? My ma and Sara and the Inglebrechts. Do you know where they are?"

Considering all he'd gone through to get

that information, Jeremiah wasn't quick to give it out again. That dark part of him that had taken root in the blood spilled within the last couple of weeks told him what could happen if anyone got to Claire and heard her repeat whatever she knew.

Jeremiah's next thought was the lengths he'd go to keep anything from happening to Claire.

"I think they're headed to Salt Lake City," he said. "So that's where we're going."

"That's far from here."

"I know, but we might not have to go all the way there."

Claire's face brightened a bit as she asked, "You mean if we catch up to them along the way?"

"That's exactly what I mean. Now, why don't you wait here and be careful like I told you?" Jeremiah went to the window and pointed down the street. "You see that stable there?"

After straining her eyes to look through the early morning glare, Claire nodded.

"If I'm not back in ten minutes," Jeremiah said, "then I want you to get out of here and run to that stable."

"Mr. Correy?"

"Yes?"

"How long is ten minutes? You sold your watch."

Jeremiah didn't have a quick answer for that. In fact, when he thought about it for a few seconds, he couldn't help but laugh. "How high can you count?"

Claire seemed absolutely perturbed by that question. "I went to school, you know."

"All right, then count to . . . six hundred. That should take ten minutes."

"It will if I count by Mississippis."

"Sounds like a good plan."

Nodding once more to settle the matter, Claire sat on the edge of the bed and counted quietly to herself. "One, Mississippi. Two, Mississippi. Three . . ."

Jeremiah left the room and shut the door behind him. It was a short walk to the front desk and he could smell biscuits and coffee long before he got there. A woman who looked to be in her late thirties was bustling about the front area, which contained the desk, a few chairs and a small table where the daily newspaper was kept.

"Good morning," the lady said cheerily. "How'd you sleep?"

"Just fine. Has there been anyone asking for me?"

She stopped what she was doing and walked behind the desk. Once there, she looked at a set of small square shelves built into the wall. Most of those shelves had nothing but keys on them, but a few had folded pieces of paper. The one she tapped had neither.

"No messages," she said.

"There was some trouble last night," Jeremiah said, doing his best to broach the subject carefully.

The woman's big blue eyes widened to become even bigger. "What happened? Are you all right?"

"I just . . . uh . . . heard there was a shooting down the street at a place called Millie's."

In the blink of an eye, the woman went from being alarmed to annoyed. "Oh, that's nothing to worry about. That is, unless you're a drunk or a whore."

"Pardon me?"

"There's always a couple shootings throughout the week down on Fourth Street," she told him. "Usually it's some drunk cowboy making noise or sometimes a man cheats at cards."

The more she talked about it, the more irritated the woman became. "Those whores who work down at Millie's bring nothing but trouble to this town. They've been put on notice so many times by the law that they've taken to cleaning up their own messes."

"Sounds like you know plenty about it."

"Everyone with a proper business knows. We're the ones trying to get them out of here. Since them whores run themselves and pay their taxes, the law lets them do whatever they please. Sometimes, there's shooting, but those whores just clean up the blood and go about their business. Terrible."

"Yeah," Jeremiah said in his best attempt to mimic the woman's tone of voice. "That's just terrible."

"Anyhow," the woman said as she shifted right back into the sunnier of her two dispositions, "can I get you and that delightful little girl of yours some breakfast?"

"Would it be possible to get it wrapped up? We need to get going."

"Sure." The woman ran her fingers along the edge of the desk as she walked around it and headed for the next room.

Jeremiah went down the hall and to his own room. Now that he'd had some sleep, he was able to knock out the code on the first try. Claire opened the door graciously. "Are you ready to leave?" he asked.

"Can't we eat here or do we have to take breakfast with us?"

"Were you eavesdropping?" Jeremiah

asked as he took another couple of glances between the door and the front desk to try and judge the distance between them.

Claire shrugged. "I just listened to what you were saying. That lady was awfully loud."

"Yes, she was."

"She doesn't like whores very much."

Jeremiah snapped his head back and tried to show her a stern glare instead of the surprised laugh that he almost let out. "That's not a nice thing to say."

"Well, she doesn't."

"She can like what she wants, but you shouldn't call a woman a whore. In fact, we should thank those women she was talking about because they probably saved us a whole lot of trouble." Even though Jeremiah knew those working girls might very well have saved his and Claire's lives, there was no need to remind the little girl of how grave things were.

Claire lowered her head. "I'm sorry." Suddenly, she snapped her head back up and spoke in an excited rush. "We can go see them and thank them ourselves! Maybe we can sit and have breakfast with them too!"

But Jeremiah had already taken her hand and was leading her down the hall. "That's a good idea, but we don't have time. Just try not to use that word anymore. It's not nice."

"Yes, sir."

They only had to wait another couple of minutes at the front desk before the woman who worked there reappeared with a small bundle in her hands. "If you have a canteen, I can fill it with coffee," she offered with a smile.

"That sounds great, but we don't have a canteen."

Before Jeremiah could say another word, the woman held up a finger, turned on her heels and dashed away. She came back quickly with a dented canteen in her hand. "Here you go."

"I couldn't. We don't have enough to —"

"Nonsense," she said while waving the rest of his protest away. "It was left here by some cowboy who was stirring up trouble the other week."

"Did he go to see the whores?" Claire asked.

Jeremiah might have looked surprised to hear that come from the little girl's mouth, but the woman who worked at the front desk seemed positively appalled.

"I don't know about that," the woman replied hesitantly. "But you shouldn't trouble yourself with such wicked women."

"They're not wicked and you shouldn't call them whores," Claire said sternly. With that, she took Jeremiah's hand and led him toward the front door.

Shrugging, Jeremiah allowed himself to be pulled away. "You sure I don't owe you anything for the coffee and canteen?"

She seemed a bit stunned, but not angry. "No, no. Take it with my blessing."

"Thank you so much," Jeremiah said as he reached out to hold the door open. "You've been very kind."

"Yes, thanks for breakfast!" Claire shouted before racing outside.

Counting out the money needed to pay his bill, Jeremiah handed it over and included enough to cover breakfast as well.

"Your daughter seems peculiar," the woman said.

"How so?"

"I'm sure she's just smart as a whip, but . . . I used to be a schoolteacher and a child shouldn't be saying those sorts of things."

Jeremiah nodded and headed for the door. "Well, she does have a point about one thing. It's not nice to call a lady a whore." With that, he tipped his hat and left the hotel. Once outside, Jeremiah found Claire standing at the edge of the boardwalk.

"Did I say something wrong?" she asked.

"Nope. Not a thing. I'll race you to that stable."

Claire's face beamed when she heard that and she took off like a shot. Jeremiah did a good job of keeping up for the first couple of yards. After that, the only thing left for him to do was choke on Claire's dust.

CHAPTER 27

True to his word, the shopkeeper kept the door of the stable's back stall unlocked. Jeremiah thought the store might be close to opening anyhow, but he got the mare he'd bought and checked her over without bothering anyone else. The mare was in fairly good condition and seemed to have been watered, fed and even brushed. A blanket and the secondhand rig were nearby, so Jeremiah got the mare ready to ride in no time at all.

Claire climbed onto the mare's back before Jeremiah had even led the animal all the way outside. She fussed and squirmed as though she were close to falling off. The girl was sitting awkwardly and winced as she kept trying to get comfortable.

"What's the matter?" Jeremiah asked.

Reluctantly, Claire lifted one arm to show the stuffed dog she'd been carrying. "I can't hold Patches and hang on to you at the same time, I just know it."

"Then we can put Patches away while we ride. Just hand him over and we can —"

But Jeremiah wasn't even able to finish his sentence before he saw Claire toss the doll away.

She pulled in a breath and resigned herself with a few words. "I don't want it anymore. I don't want to trip us up."

"There's room for Patches," Jeremiah said. "Once we get moving, it'll be fine."

"No," Claire said sternly as she patted the mare's neck. "Let's just go. I'm too old for dolls anyway."

Jeremiah had his doubts about that, but kept them to himself. In a way, he knew how the little girl felt by leaving something behind that had once been sacred. There were plenty of things that had once been close to him that were now lying in a ditch. After all that had happened, it seemed strangely appropriate.

The mare was a bit older than the shopkeeper had described; the animal barely put up a fuss as both Jeremiah and Claire got situated on her back. At the moment, all Jeremiah truly cared about was getting a move on.

If Dave had been in town the night before, that meant the others couldn't be too far away. And if Dave had rented a room with a bed, there was even a chance that he'd been expecting to stay there for a bit longer than the time it would have taken for him to tussle the sheets with a working girl.

Suddenly, Jeremiah pulled back on his reins.

"Wait right here," he said while climbing down from the horse's back.

Claire turned around to look at Jeremiah without even wobbling from her spot near the mare's neck. "Where are you going?"

"I want to see if we might be able to get ourselves a better horse."

"But I like this one."

Jeremiah motioned for her to stay put and Claire complied. He walked down the street as quickly as he could, weaving through the growing number of folks that were showing up to conduct their business. When he got close enough to see Millie's, Jeremiah grinned victoriously.

He thought he'd recognized the horse Dave had been riding when he'd first walked into the cathouse the night before. Sure enough, that horse was still hitched to a post outside. Jeremiah thought about the horses that had been gunned down when the wagons had been attacked and felt that taking Dave's horse was a way to get some measure of retribution.

Seeing as how the one-eyed man was dead, it wasn't as if Dave needed to horse any longer.

Before Jeremiah could take another step, he stopped and looked around. One man had caught his eye, simply because he stood like a single rock amid a flowing stream of people. That man stood across from Millie's to watch the cathouse's door from a distance.

Jeremiah turned and headed back to the stable as quickly as possible. So far, he'd had plenty of luck to get through everything that had been thrown at him and would need plenty more to keep going. There was no need to push it when someone could be waiting just to pounce upon whomever came to claim that horse. Jeremiah didn't know for certain if that was the case, but his gut told him to run. It also just felt right to take an older horse rather than steal another one and stoop even closer to the gunmen's level.

He didn't say a word when he got back to the stable. All Jeremiah did was jump into the saddle, make sure Claire was situated in front of him and then flick the reins.

"You didn't get another horse?" Claire asked.

"Nope."

She grinned and patted the mare affectionately. "I knew you wouldn't want another one. This Patches is just fine."

"This is Patches now?" Jeremiah asked.

"Yep." Shifting her eyes to Jeremiah, she asked, "What's wrong?"

"Nothing," he replied. "We're just getting the hell out of here."

"That's another bad word."

"I know. Hang on."

There were plenty of ways to get to Salt Lake City. Jeremiah could think of several trails used to drive cattle and a few others used by anyone who didn't have a herd to worry about. The one thing Jeremiah needed to be in his favor was that Sam and the others wouldn't be too quick to leave Dave behind.

That is, unless they already knew he was dead. If that was the case, the wagons could be long gone, headed for another destination or stowed somewhere until Sam and his remaining gunmen could bushwhack Jeremiah and tie him up even tighter than Emmett.

Jeremiah held on to his reins and gritted his teeth. Patches was keeping up a steady pace and had been galloping for about half an hour without complaint. Claire's head was wrapped up in a scarf that she'd worn around her shoulders and lowered against the rushing wind. It wasn't long before she was leaning back against Jeremiah as if she was simply resting in a comfortable chair.

Jeremiah brought his arms around to hold her in place, but didn't need to do much more than that. Claire had the balance of a cat and barely even shifted when Patches had to change her pace or jump to avoid a hole in the road. Because of that, Jeremiah was able to snap the reins again and push the mare to her limit.

Rather than try to guess which trail Sam had chosen, Jeremiah headed for higher ground on the off chance that he might be able to spot the wagons. The horse that had been tied in front of Millie's was from good stock and might have been missed more than Dave under the right circumstances. Those gunmen wouldn't have left them both behind so quickly.

At least, that was what Jeremiah hoped as he continued racing toward the top of a stony, tree-lined ridge. The higher the trail led him, the colder the wind became as it whipped around Jeremiah's head. Patches started to wheeze, but didn't slow down. Even so, Jeremiah pulled back on the reins a little before reaching the top of the ridge.

Once he had his higher ground, Jeremiah gazed down at the tapestry of trees, boulders and meandering streams laid out in front of him. He wasn't fortunate enough to see the wagons moving along somewhere in the distance. Jeremiah started to curse himself for wasting time in town when he could have been getting to this spot a little sooner. That bit of difference might have allowed him to catch a glimpse of the wagons where Sara and Anne were being held.

Jeremiah stared at the same bit of nothing for over a minute before Claire poked her head up to block his view.

"I can't see anything," she said.

Jeremiah didn't reply, even though he was in the same boat. Although he hated to admit it, he knew he was running more on instinct than anything else.

As slippery as that instinct was, it had a firm enough grip on him to keep Jeremiah rooted to that spot and his eyes searching the horizon.

"I still don't see anything," Claire said. "Do you see anything?"

"Not yet," Jeremiah replied.

"Which way is it to Salt Lake City?"

Jeremiah pointed toward the south. "That way as the crow flies, but all those wagons will probably have to come past us here before turning south."

"What if they stop somewhere else?" Claire asked, while also inadvertently giving a voice to Jeremiah's greatest fear. "Are there many towns between here and Salt Lake City?"

"Yes. Lots of them."

"Then why is this spot better than some other spot?"

"Something just tells me it is."

Claire looked in the same direction as Jeremiah and stared quietly for a few seconds. When those seconds were up, she asked, "Are you sure?"

"Something's seen us through this far. Sometimes you just need to have some faith that you'll make it a bit farther. Without that faith, there's no reason in stepping foot outside your own door."

The little girl nodded and kept watching the horizon.

Jeremiah wasn't sure how much sense he'd made to her, but most of his words had been for his own ears anyway. Even though he'd thought them up, put them together and spoken them out loud, a man sometimes still needed to hear something to see if it held up.

Those words held up just fine now that

Jeremiah had given them a voice. As if to show him just how solid the idea was, he spotted a cloud of dust forming about a mile or so in the distance.

His hand reflexively went to the spot where the saddlebag had been when he'd started off on this expedition, but only slapped against the mare's flank. Jeremiah looked down and swore under his breath while he was reminded that he was sitting on an old blanket rather than a proper saddle.

"Don't say those things to Patches," Claire scolded.

"Sorry," Jeremiah said to both of them.

"And don't hit her, either. She's doing her best."

"I know and I wasn't hitting her. I was looking for the spyglass I used to keep in my old saddlebag."

"Why?" Claire asked.

Since there were no saddlebags and no spyglass, Jeremiah pointed at the horizon and asked, "You see that dust cloud?"

Claire squinted in that direction and nodded. "Yes."

"I want to see what's kicking up all that dust."

"It's got to be a lot of horses."

"Maybe even a few wagons," Jeremiah added.

With excitement blossoming in her eyes, Claire twisted around to get a look at him. "You think those are our wagons?"

"I don't know. That's what I wanted to check. It could be other riders or maybe a train, you know."

But Claire shook her head. "I used to always watch for my ma to come home and I could tell when it was her horse riding up the road."

"Where did you used to live?" Jeremiah asked.

"Not too far from Cheyenne. Sometimes, there were wagons rolling into town and they made clouds like that. Trains were different too. That was smoke and that's a different color."

Jeremiah knew that Claire was right about smoke looking different than dust. He also knew she was right about spotting the difference between dust kicked up by one horse as opposed to that kicked up by many. And the longer he studied the dust cloud in the distance, the more he tended to agree with everything else she'd said.

"So, what do you think?" Jeremiah asked. "Should we head toward that cloud in case our wagons are kicking it up?"

Claire thought it over silently. She turned to study the cloud again and then turned back around to look at Jeremiah. "If it's not, we can still go to Salt Lake City, right?"

"Yes."

"Then let's try."

"All right." With that, Jeremiah snapped the reins and tapped his heels against the mare's sides. Patches responded with a few labored grunts, but got moving soon enough. Once the old girl crested the rise and was headed downhill, she built up speed without any trouble at all.

Jeremiah felt his spirits rise from the moment he left the top of that hill. There was no way for him to guarantee he was headed in the proper direction or that he was doing the right thing. All that mattered was that he'd chosen a path and was moving along it.

Claire curled herself up against him and did a fine job of keeping her balance without distracting Patches. Sometimes, it was hard enough for a horse to accept a rider without there being two in the mix. But Jeremiah quickly found that he had nothing to worry about where the mare was concerned. In fact, Patches caught up to that dust cloud in less time than Jeremiah had expected.

That dust cloud did nothing other than move in a southerly direction. It had even sprung up around the time that Jeremiah figured Dave would surely be missed by the others. All the pieces fit in his mind for that cloud to take him to his wagons. It wasn't much, but it was the best he had.

After a while, the dust cloud disappeared. Jeremiah knew that could mean that whatever had kicked up the dust had come to a stop or had simply rolled onto a patch of ground that wasn't so dusty. He coaxed a bit more speed out of Patches and headed toward the spot where he guessed he could catch sight of the source of that cloud.

It was a slow process that took an hour or two, but Jeremiah kept at it until he finally closed in enough to see what he'd been chasing after. The wagons were the first things he spotted. He had to count them several times just because he couldn't believe he could be so fortunate. There were three of them and those three wagons were flanked by other riders. Even so, Jeremiah choked back the victorious yell he so desperately wanted to let out.

"Are those the wagons?" Claire asked.

Jeremiah didn't answer at first because he was busy handling the reins and planning where he was to ride next. But Claire wasn't about to be ignored and she twisted around to get a look at the man behind her.

"Are those the wagons?" she repeated.

"I thought you were asleep."

Claire raised her voice to make certain she could be heard over the rumble of the mare's hooves. "Is that where Ma and Sara are? Did you find the wagons?"

"I don't know yet."

"Let's get closer! Let's find out for certain."

Jeremiah wrapped one arm around the little girl so he could hold on to her tightly as he pulled back on the reins. The old mare dug her hooves into the dirt and came to a stop. Even after she'd stopped moving, Patches sucked in one labored breath after another.

Leaning forward, Jeremiah made sure he was looking into Claire's eyes when he told her, "Whether those are our wagons or not, we need to be careful. Do you understand?"

"Yes."

"Those men who took our wagons are dangerous and they've all got guns."

"I know," Claire replied.

"Then you should also know something else. When we find them, I'm going to have to go after them on my own. I know you want to go see your mother, but you're going to have to stay behind for a little while until I know it's safe."

And just when Jeremiah was afraid he was frightening her with too many ugly details, Claire proved that she already had a firm grasp of them.

"What if you don't come back?" she asked. "What happens then?"

"Before I leave, I'll tell you the closest place for you to go if things go bad. You can go there or find someone along the way to take you there. Do you have anyone else you can contact? Someone you can write to or send a note to from a telegraph office?"

Jeremiah could see her face clouding over with fear and confusion. Although she was more than capable, Claire was still a child and was barely treading water at the moment.

"What about family or friends?" Jeremiah asked. "There's got to be someone."

"I have an uncle in Oregon. We were going to visit him."

"Good. If things go bad, you'll go to where I tell you to go and you'll send a letter to your uncle. Go to a church or a lawman. Do you think you can find one of those?"

She nodded. "Yes."

"Perfect. You'll find one of those, write

your letter and get it sent. You know how to get your way, so you can convince someone to get that message to your uncle. Isn't that right?"

She grinned and nodded, doing her best to shake off the tears that welled up in the corners of her eyes.

Jeremiah used the side of his finger to brush those tears away. "You're a strong girl and this doesn't mean things will go bad. You just need to have a plan in case they do. We need to get moving and catch up to those wagons. If they're the ones I think they are, I'm going to drop you off where you'll be safe and if I can't come for you, then someone else will. If it takes too long, you'll get somewhere to send your message."

"Someone else?"

"They'll use the signal. Two knocks, three knocks, then two knocks. Isn't that the signal?"

"You forgot it before," she said with a sniffle.

"I know I did, but I won't forget it again. I may have to whistle rather than knock, but I swear I won't forget it."

She nodded and sniffled a few more times. Claire was just able to swipe at her cheek before another tear rolled down it. "Do you think those are the wagons?"

"Yeah. I do."

"Do you think you can fight those men?"

"I'm going to try," Jeremiah told her. "We just need to have a little faith."

CHAPTER 28

Jeremiah did his best to stay levelheaded as he rode after the wagons. He was able to catch a good enough look at them to decide that they were indeed the ones he was after. As much as Jeremiah wanted to ride straight up to those wagons and wrangle them away from the killers, he had to keep those instincts in check.

For one thing, he didn't even have six shots to fire from the gun he'd taken from Dave. And even if he had all the ammunition in the world, there was still the matter of getting close enough to do some damage to those gunmen before he was shot from his saddle.

And so Jeremiah rode back and forth from the trail being used by those wagons so he could catch a glimpse of them to know they wouldn't get away from him. More than once, he felt peculiar to be the one spying on the wagons from afar when Sam had done that very same thing before starting his attack. Jeremiah wasn't just amused by this irony, however. He used it to his advantage.

Whenever he could, he mimicked the gunmen's own methods to keep an eye on the wagons without being spotted. He also used what he knew about them to guess how they might react if they did catch a glimpse of him. Jeremiah sometimes cut away from the trail and lay low so as not to be discovered when Pointer was sent ahead as a scout.

Seeing the Indian was both a blessing and a curse. As he knelt behind a patch of trees with Claire beside him, he watched the Indian ride along the top of the hill that Jeremiah had just left behind. It was only the second time all day that Jeremiah had been forced into hiding, but it drove home the fact that he was on the right trail.

Pointer brought his horse to a stop and looked around slowly. Even from a distance of at least sixty yards, Jeremiah swore he could see the intensity in Pointer's eyes. The Indian looked toward the trees where Jeremiah was hiding and then he seemed to look directly into Jeremiah's soul.

Claire must have felt the scrutiny as well, because she nestled in close to Jeremiah and spoke in a harsh whisper. "Do you think —" was all she got out before Jeremiah pressed a hand over her mouth.

As he eased his hand away, Jeremiah glanced over at Claire just quickly enough to make sure she saw the stern warning in his eyes. She nodded quickly and clamped her lips shut.

Jeremiah wanted to move so he was completely behind the tree instead of peeking around it. He wanted to lower himself onto his belly so the swaying grass might provide him and Claire some better cover. He also wanted to walk back to the spot where he'd tied Patches just to make certain the old mare didn't give them away by letting out a discontented whinny.

But Jeremiah didn't do any of those things.

Instead, he kept perfectly still and stayed in his spot. He knew that movement more than anything else would give away his position. Jeremiah might not have been experienced at being the predator or the prey, but he had the same instincts as any other animal. At that moment, those instincts told him to keep still no matter what else happened.

He had to keep still or be spotted.

Keep still or die.

After what seemed like an eternity of holding his breath, Jeremiah saw Pointer shift his eyes in another direction before finally walking away. Jeremiah didn't allow himself to relax until he saw the Indian climb into his saddle and ride back toward the wagons.

"All right," Jeremiah whispered to Claire. "He's gone."

The little girl let out a breath and pulled in another one, but didn't make another sound.

Glancing in every direction, Jeremiah surveyed the spot he'd chosen and discovered it was even better than he'd previously thought. There were about half a dozen trees clustered together around a few large rocks. The dirt was loose and there were plenty of spots for a nine-year-old girl to curl up and disappear within the tall grass.

Jeremiah turned around so he could face Claire directly and look straight into her eyes. He reached out with both hands to hold her by the shoulders as he spoke in a smooth, level tone. "You're going to have to stay here," he said.

"Are you going after the wagons now?"

"They've been rolling all day long. If they haven't stopped now, they'll have to stop real soon. Either way, I think this is the best place for you to stay."

She looked at him with a face that was

drawn into a tightly constricted mask. The harder she tried to maintain the facade, the weaker it became. When she spoke again, her voice was as brittle as cold glass.

"How long are you gonna leave me for?" she asked.

"Not long, I promise. But I'd rather leave you here than put you in danger with me."

"I want to come with you, Mr. Correy. I'm scared to stay."

"I know, but this is the best thing. They've already checked here, so there's no reason for them to check again."

Jeremiah also knew that Anne would have died before letting it slip that she had a daughter that hadn't been found during the first attack. That meant none of the gunmen knew Claire even existed. As much as Jeremiah liked that thought, it would have taken too long to explain it to the little girl. At that point, it probably wouldn't have made much difference anyhow.

"I can come with you," she pleaded. "I'll be quiet. I'll stay out of the way."

"No," Jeremiah snapped as he tightened his grip on her shoulders. "You've got to stay here. You'll stay right here until I come to get you."

"What if . . . what if things go bad?"

Closing his eyes for a moment, Jeremiah

pictured the area as if he were looking down at a map. It was an old trick that had shown him the way plenty of times when he'd been on trail drives, and it served him just as well now.

Jeremiah opened his eyes and said, "There were some telegraph lines less than a mile east of here. You know which way that is?"

She nodded and pointed in the proper direction.

"Good," Jeremiah said as he loosened his grip on her. "You just head for those lines and follow them to the closest town or telegraph office or whatever you can find just like we talked about before. At the very least, there should be someone riding to check those lines for damage every now and then. You'll find something, trust me."

"What if I don't?"

"You will. Besides, I don't plan on leaving you here. Understand?"

Claire stared deeply into Jeremiah's eyes as if she was looking for something important. Whatever she found there, it was good enough to bring a trembling smile to her face. "Yes, sir."

"Good."

Before he knew what he intended to do, Jeremiah wrapped his arms around Claire and gave the little girl a hug. She pressed herself against him, buried her face in his shirt and pulled in a deep breath.

"I'm leaving the canteen here in case you get thirsty," he said. "If you see any strangers coming, you hide real good. Dig a hole and crawl into it if you have to."

"Yes, sir."

Jeremiah didn't want to leave her there, but he knew it was the most prudent choice. All he had to do was think about where he was headed, and leaving Claire behind seemed like an act of mercy.

"If it gets too dark, you stay here," Jeremiah said. "Dig in and think about something nice."

"Just come back for me," Claire snapped in an unmistakably smart tone.

Knowing that it would only get harder to leave the longer he waited, Jeremiah turned and ran to Patches. He climbed onto the old mare's back, snapped the reins and rode to circle around and get behind the wagons.

As he rode, Jeremiah forced himself to think about everything but Claire. Focusing too much on keeping that girl safe was like concentrating too hard to stay upright when in the saddle. A man had to settle in and roll with the bumps. Forcing it was the quickest way to a hard fall. Fortunately, there was plenty more to think about.

In the short time it took to circle back onto the wagon's trail, Jeremiah looked for any other riders and listened for the rattle of wagon wheels. He thought about where the wagons were headed, what the gunmen had in mind once they got there and how much of an advantage surprising them would be.

Thinking about what could have happened to Sara, Anne or the Inglebrechts was almost too much for Jeremiah. The moment he felt his head start to spin, he forced those other things from his mind. Before the doubts in the back of his head could rattle around too loudly, Jeremiah caught sight of the wagons.

He'd managed to get behind them. The end of the last wagon was about forty yards in front of him, so Jeremiah pulled hard on the reins and steered Patches back off the trail. He brought the mare to a stop and reached forward to pat the old girl's head before she got too upset.

There wasn't much of anything for Jeremiah to hide behind, so he ducked as low as he could in the saddle and hoped for the best. Sure enough, the wagons kept rolling and none of the gunmen circled back around.

When he saw the wagons approach a fork

in the trail, Jeremiah looked back at the spot where Claire was hiding. He could still see the trees arranged in their tight little cluster, but was far enough away for them to start blending in with the other groups of trees in the area.

Jeremiah stared at that spot until he could still see it with his eyes closed. Even after that, he studied every line and every branch so he would be able to pick it out among a hundred other spots. Once those trees were engrained into his memory, Jeremiah flicked his reins and got Patches walking slowly along the side of the trail.

The sun was making its way toward the western horizon, and the trail was becoming rougher as smooth dirt and clay gave way to packed soil and gravel. Every step that Patches took made a sound like waves crashing against Jeremiah's ears. He winced at every one of them, expecting Pointer or one of the other gunmen to come rushing over to him so they could put a bullet through his skull.

But nobody came.

Even though Jeremiah could still hear the slow grinding of the wagon wheels, the wagons were clearly drawing to a stop. Once they had stopped completely, all that could be heard was a few horses moving about and the flow of shallow water.

Jeremiah wasn't familiar enough with the area to know which lake, stream or river it was, but he knew it must have been big enough to catch someone's eye. Since it would be dark soon, Jeremiah also figured the wagons were coming to a stop for the night.

There wasn't a town in sight. The wagons were keeping together and only a few horses were separated from the group.

Jeremiah most definitely felt as if an angel was looking over his shoulder. Considering how much work there was to be done, he would need all the help he could get, divine or otherwise.

After dropping down from the mare's back, Jeremiah led Patches to a spot even farther away from the trail. Before leaving the horse tied to her tree, he took Dave's gun from his holster and flipped it open to check how many live rounds were in the cylinder. It turned out that half the bullets were ready to be fired and the others were spent. Jeremiah snapped the pistol shut and then set the first live round under the hammer. Since he didn't need to check his pockets to know they were empty, he holstered the gun and started creeping along the side of the trail.

There were only some scrub bushes and a few rocks scattered about, none of which were much good for hiding a man. Fortunately, the sunlight was fading quickly and the gunmen were too busy squaring away the wagons to notice one more shadow slinking closer to the camp.

Jeremiah hunkered down low and scuttled toward the wagon at the end of the line. His eyes were focused upon a spot near the back corner of that wagon and he didn't see much of anything else. Whenever he tried to look at another spot, his nerves started to bunch up too much for him to keep moving. Jeremiah could only grit his teeth and take one step at a time before he lost his nerve.

Suddenly, Jeremiah heard footsteps crunching against the ground. Those crunches drew closer until there was no doubt they were headed straight for him. Jeremiah choked down a quick breath and dropped to the ground as quietly as he could between the wagon and a rock that was roughly half the size of a tombstone.

The steps were still coming, so Jeremiah hurried behind the rock. It wasn't big enough to cover him completely, but the sun was setting in front of him and put a long shadow upon the ground. The rock's shadow, combined with the one thrown by the wagon, was inky black and more than big enough to cover Jeremiah as he lay as flat as he could behind the rock.

Jeremiah clenched his teeth together so hard that he might have been able to crush stone between them. Now that the footsteps had rounded the wagons and were less than a dozen feet away, he knew the person making that noise could spot him if he looked toward the rock for more than a few seconds.

"You find him yet?" asked a voice that Jeremiah instantly recognized as Sam's.

The second one was Charlie. Jeremiah didn't have any trouble picking up on that one's English accent. "Not as such," he said. "Then again, Dave hasn't even come back yet."

Jeremiah couldn't believe he was fortunate enough to stay hidden this long. He looked over his shoulder and saw that the dark color of his jeans and boots was actually doing a hell of a job blending in with the shadows. Of course, the shadows were becoming so thick that anything standing still could have hidden in them.

"Since we're camping here for the night," Charlie said, "perhaps I should go and see if I can find him."

Sam grumbled for a moment but the words were lost amid the shifting of feet against the dirt. Every second that passed in silence made Jeremiah certain he was about to be shot through the back or in the legs.

"Nah," Sam finally replied. "He's probably drunk or at some whorehouse."

"Or both."

"Yeah," Sam laughed. "Or both. He knows where we're headed and where we are, so if he's not back in a few hours, I'll send you after him."

"Or perhaps Pointer should go. He's a much faster rider."

"Yeah, but he's also got the sharpest eyes around here. He can spot a black cat sneaking through a dark room, so I'll need him to keep watch. The last thing I need is for another of these damn prisoners to get away."

"He must have jumped while we were moving," Charlie said. "The foolish bugger probably broke his neck when he hit the ground."

"Could be."

Both men fell silent. Jeremiah imagined them staring at his boots or slowly sneaking up on him. As much as he wanted to peek around the rock to see what they were doing, Jeremiah also knew that any move he made would almost certainly give him away.

So Jeremiah waited.

He waited for one of them to pounce on him from above.

He waited for a gunshot followed by the pain of a bullet tearing through his spine.

He waited even though every second was torture.

"Damn!" Sam grunted. "I hate when Dave runs off like this. Let's just get the camp set up and a fire going. The quicker we do that, the sooner I can pay a visit to one of them ladies we got."

"I'll take second pick," Charlie said. "I've had my eye on that fair-haired beauty who's been so quiet."

"You'll have to fight Pointer for her. He's partial to ladies like her."

"Perhaps he won't be in the proper frame of mind for that sort of business. After all, he did bury one lady not too long ago."

Jeremiah pulled in a breath and felt his fist clench around a handful of dirt. Suddenly, it was next to impossible to keep still as the shadows grew colder around him.

"Pointer's buried plenty of ladies," Sam said. "It's never made him lose his appetite yet."

"Bloody savage," Charlie mumbled.

"Just try not to ruffle Pointer's feathers until after Art leaves. Him and some of his men will be coming to collect those women tonight, so we'd best get what we can before that blonde's too tired to walk."

With that, the footsteps crunched away and headed toward the wagons. Jeremiah pulled himself against the rock and leaned around it to get a look. He was expecting to see both men walking away, but instead saw one of them standing less than five feet in front of him.

Jeremiah was certain his luck had just run out. Not only did he feel every one of his muscles tense out of blind panic, but he also felt like a fool for allowing himself to be spotted so easily.

The figure in front of him stood still for a second before the sound of wood scraping against metal drifted through the air.

There was a flicker of light followed by the low hiss of a flame coming to life. Charlie's face was illuminated by the match he'd just lit as he brought the flame in close to light the cigarette clenched between his teeth.

Jeremiah watched from the ground, still waiting to be spotted.

But Charlie wasn't looking down. He wasn't even looking at the rock directly in front of him. Instead, his eyes were pointed out toward the open stretch of land to the east. His left hand was clenched around a small tin box that was the size of a deck of cards. When he shook the box idly, something rattled around inside it. Charlie held the match safe in his palm, looked down at it and dropped it into the inner pocket of his jacket.

Jeremiah wished he could take a moment to give silent thanks to whatever angel was looking out for him. Those thoughts were quickly pushed to the back of his mind when he saw Charlie take a step forward and place his boot on top of the rock.

Pressing himself against the ground as flat as he could, Jeremiah held his breath and stared upward at the toe of Charlie's boot. His hand found the pistol at his side, but he was reluctant to draw it. He didn't even want to pull his legs in closer to the rest of his body out of fear that the scraping might draw Charlie's attention.

"What in the . . . ?"

The moment he heard those words, Jeremiah knew he'd been spotted.

Slowly, Charlie walked around the rock. It wasn't long before Jeremiah saw the glowing end of the cigarette in Charlie's mouth. The instant he saw Charlie peek around the rock, Jeremiah pulled his legs under him and dug his heels into the ground so he could lunge for the Englishman like a rattler.

Jeremiah reached out with his left hand to grab hold of Charlie's shirt. As his fist closed around the material near Charlie's collar, Jeremiah's chest slammed against the top of the rock. When he came down, Jeremiah pulled Charlie along with him. Charlie started to let out a grunt, but was cut short when the top of the rock caught him in the chin.

As Jeremiah pulled Charlie to the ground, he drew his pistol. Stopping short of pulling his trigger, Jeremiah cracked the pistol's handle against Charlie's head. The Englishman was still squirming, so Jeremiah hit him with the pistol again. This time, Charlie went limp and fell to the ground in a heap.

Jeremiah dragged the Englishman behind the rock and watched to see if anyone had heard the commotion. Then he took Charlie's gun and tucked it under his belt. Since there wasn't anyone in sight and no footsteps rushing toward him, Jeremiah guessed he'd managed to put Charlie down without making a scene.

One down and a long way to go.

Chapter 29

Jeremiah hurried to the back of the wagon at the end of the line. As he got closer without hearing a peep from inside that wagon, Jeremiah began to imagine all sorts of bad sights he might find when he looked in there. Everyone he hoped to save could be dead or hurt or any combination of things.

When he leaned against the wagon and pulled open the flap of canvas covering the back, all he saw inside were several stacks of boxes and piles of burlap sacks.

Jeremiah leaned into the wagon a bit to make certain he was seeing everything he could. But there wasn't a living soul in that wagon. After taking a quick look at the wagon itself, he realized it was the one that had been in the middle of the line the last time he'd been there.

He knew his escape wouldn't go unnoticed, so Jeremiah wasn't too surprised by the fact that the men had moved the wagon with the prisoners in it toward the front of the line. Keeping his head low even though the wagon was more than big enough to keep him from being seen by anyone on the other side of it, Jeremiah ran to the next wagon so he could take a look inside it.

Before he got to the back of that one, he could hear muffled voices within the darkness. He peeled back the canvas flap and looked inside, which caused the voices to come to an abrupt stop. As Jeremiah leaned forward, however, he could hear Sara crying his name from behind whatever it was that covered her mouth.

Jeremiah could only make out a few shapes huddled toward the front of the wagon, but one of those shapes was crawling toward him. He could tell right away that it was his wife.

"Are you all right?" he whispered.

She nodded while scooting closer to him.

As much as he wanted to get her away from there before being spotted, Jeremiah couldn't resist peeling down the dirty bandanna that was tied around the lower portion of her face. As he exposed her mouth, Jeremiah covered it with his own hand and urged her to keep quiet.

Sara was close to panicking, but she managed to hold her voice down to a whisper. "You're all right," she said.

"Yes, and so is Claire."

"Where have you been?"

"Trying to get you out of here," Jeremiah replied. "I've got to go before I'm seen. They're almost done making the fire, so there's not a lot of time. Is everyone else all right?"

Sara kept her eyes on him even though it was plain to see she wanted to look away. In a trembling whisper, she said, "They killed Noelle."

"What?"

She nodded. "They took Harold and her away and talked to them. There was a shot and . . . she's dead."

Jeremiah wiped the tears from his wife's face as delicately as he could. "I'm going to get you out of there. All of you."

"Please get us out right now. They're going to sell us to some men."

Jeremiah knew there was much worse in store for them, but there was no need to tell her that. It was hard enough for him to start moving the bandanna up over Sara's mouth again. "I'm going to have to put this back. I need to stay hidden for as long as I can. I need to —"

The sound of footsteps came from the flickering light of the newly sparked fire. Now that all the wood was in place and the flames were going, there was less noise to cover the sounds Jeremiah was making. He was as aware of those changes as he was aware of the fear in Sara's eyes.

"Please, Sara," Jeremiah whispered. "Just trust me. Try to get the others to trust me too."

Jeremiah looked past his wife and saw Anne huddled in the dark. She watched him intently with eyes that were wide as supper plates.

"Don't worry, Anne. Claire's safe," Jeremiah told her.

He could see the relief on Anne's face as she started to tremble and cry.

For a moment, it seemed as if Sara were about to jump from the wagon just so she could be with him. At the last second, however, she backed away from him and lowered her head. Harold sat against the very back of the wagon with his legs splayed in front of him. From the look of him, the old man was practically dead.

Jeremiah couldn't stand the sight of them any longer. If he spent one more second looking into that wagon, he wouldn't be able to keep himself from standing up to the gunmen by himself. In fact, even as he ducked around the wagon to avoid being spotted, Jeremiah kicked around the idea of surprising the other two men.

Filling each of his hands with a pistol, Jeremiah knew he had enough bullets to kill two men. After what he'd seen and heard in that wagon, he knew he had it in him to send Sam and that Indian to hell. The only problem was that there were more than those two to worry about.

Jeremiah was suddenly aware of why he'd gotten to spend the last several seconds alone with Sara. Now that he was able to focus on something other than his wife's tear-streaked face, he could hear the sound of approaching horses. It sounded just as it had the last time Sam had met up with another group of riders. From what Jeremiah could tell, there was the same number of horses approaching from the northeast.

"Damn!" Sam shouted from nearby. "Looks like Art's already here. Where the hell are you, Charlie?"

Jeremiah brought his arms in close to his body, but kept the guns drawn as he hunched down and ran for the front wagon. The other horses were getting closer and Sam was walking toward the rear wagon.

As Jeremiah leaped back against the first

wagon, Sam turned and looked straight at him.

Jeremiah froze with his back pressed against the sideboard. Although someone in Sam's spot couldn't have seen more than a sliver of Jeremiah's leg, Jeremiah felt as if he were standing in the middle of an open field with the sun shining down on him. When he saw Sam move again, Jeremiah swore it was to draw his pistol and gun him down right then and there.

"Jesus, Pointer," Sam said as he shifted his eyes a few inches to the right. "You damn near scared the shit out of me."

As usual, the Indian didn't say much of anything. Instead, he pointed toward the rock where Charlie had been left in an unconscious heap.

"Something over there?" Sam asked.

Pointer lowered his arm and walked in that direction. He already had his hand on his holstered gun.

Knowing it was only a matter of seconds before Charlie was discovered, Jeremiah pulled open the canvas covering the back of the first wagon and looked inside. Natham was in there, tied up like a calf in a rodeo and wearing enough crusted blood upon his face to make him look like he'd been sleeping on a muddy riverbank.

"Jeremiah?" Natham asked.

Climbing into the wagon, Jeremiah asked, "They didn't gag you?"

"They'd prefer it if I talked. Where the hell have you been?"

"No time for all that. I need to know if you'd like to take a run at these men."

"I nearly chewed through my own arms to get out of these damn ropes," Natham snarled.

"Well, now's your chance," Jeremiah said as he set the pistols down and took Claire's kitchen knife from his pocket. "I just need you to swear you won't harm my wife or any of the others from our expedition."

Natham cracked a smile that also cracked the mask of dried blood on his face. "Still calling it that, huh?"

Suddenly, Sam's voice exploded from outside as the rumble of hooves approached the wagons.

"What the hell?" Sam shouted.

The only reaction Natham gave was to flick his eyes in that direction and then look back at Jeremiah. "I never would have hurt you or any of those good folks. No matter what else you heard about me, you gotta believe that."

"They say you're a killer and you never denied it," Jeremiah said, keeping the kitchen knife poised above the ropes tied around Natham's wrists.

"I done plenty of bad in my life, Jeremiah. That price on my head's genuine enough, but Sam Madigan ain't just out for the reward. He'll sell anything and anyone for a profit and he's killed more men than I ever have just so he could track me down."

"Where is he?" Sam shouted from outside.

Jeremiah looked over his shoulder, but the gunmen were enveloped in shadow and well hidden. The only trace he could see of the crooked deputy was a flickering shadow thrown off by the nearby campfire.

"I need to know I'm not doing more harm than good by setting you free," Jeremiah said.

"There's only one way to find out."

The other horses had arrived at the camp and men were dismounting.

Sam had stopped hollering and gotten too quiet for Jeremiah's liking.

Soon, there were whispers being passed back and forth between all the other men, and those whispers were beginning to surround the wagons.

Jeremiah placed the blade between Natham's wrists and sliced through the ropes binding them together. He freed Natham's feet with another swipe and then handed Charlie's pistol over to him.

"I'll take the knife as well," Natham said.

Jeremiah handed it over.

"There's some guns in the last wagon and one or two behind the driver's seat of this one," Natham told him. "See what you can do to get the next wagon away from here. That's where your wife and the others are."

"What about you?" Jeremiah asked.

But Natham was already gone. He'd hopped out the back of the wagon and rolled to the right without making more noise than a stiff breeze.

The wagon had a wooden barrier separating the back from the driver's seat. Therefore, Jeremiah had to climb out of the wagon and run around to get to the gun Natham had mentioned. The moment his boots hit the dirt, Jeremiah found himself in the line of fire.

Jeremiah spotted three men on horseback near the back of the farthest wagon. Sam was standing next to the tombstone rock and Charlie was using that rock to prop himself up. All of those men except for Charlie had their guns drawn and were pulling their triggers.

For a second, Jeremiah couldn't hear anything other than the blood pulsing through his veins and the panicked breaths he pulled into his lungs. He turned his back to the shooters and ran for the front of the wagon when his right foot skidded against a patch of loose gravel and his left one slid in the opposite direction. Although Jeremiah barely managed to catch himself with one outstretched arm, that stumble could very well have saved his life. Hot lead sliced through the air over his head and would have hit him if he'd been standing up straight. More gunshots blasted nearby, but those were coming from Natham as he knelt in a patch of bristly grass and fired from the hip.

Jeremiah turned to look at the gunmen and was just in time to see one of Art's men fall over as if he'd been hit in the head with a shovel. More shots filled the air, causing Jeremiah to vault up onto the driver's seat in one leap.

Once up there, Jeremiah looked around for the gun Natham had promised. Sure enough, a shotgun was tucked beneath the seat. Both of its barrels were loaded, so Jeremiah felt somewhat confident as he climbed back down again to land on the side of the wagons opposite of where Natham had gone.

Benny and another horseman were there to greet him and looked just as surprised to see Jeremiah as he was to spot them. Both of them raised their guns, but paused before pulling their triggers.

"Who the hell are you?" Benny asked.

Jeremiah blinked as his finger tensed against the shotgun's trigger. Before emptying both barrels at the others, Jeremiah said, "One of the prisoners got away. I think he went that way."

Looking at the direction Jeremiah had nodded, Benny waved and sent the second one in that direction. "Go on and see what you can find."

The second horseman made it about three steps before leaning forward and staring directly at Jeremiah's face. "You ain't one of Sam's men."

Jeremiah swung the shotgun toward that rider the moment he saw the man raise his pistol and take his shot. That round hissed past Jeremiah and tore a shred out of his shirt. Jeremiah kept the shotgun against his shoulder and squeezed his trigger. The shotgun let out a deafening roar and knocked the rider clean out of his saddle.

With all the other shooting going on nearby, Jeremiah didn't hear that rider hit the ground. He saw enough blood, however, to know that the man wasn't about to get back up. Keeping the shotgun raised, Jeremiah swung it toward Benny. He didn't get the luxury of aiming his shot, since Benny had taken aim first and was about to fire.

Jumping away from the wagon, Jeremiah meant to save his second barrel, but wound up pulling his trigger in haste. The shotgun spat out a plume of smoke and sparks, knocking Jeremiah to the ground. He didn't hear the rider's pistol and didn't feel a bullet rip through him, so he scrambled to his feet. At first, he thought Benny had been hit, but he was just leaning down low over his horse's neck. Benny rose again to send a shot in Jeremiah's direction.

The bullet drilled into the wagon behind Jeremiah, but he wasn't about to stand idly by and wait for him to fire again. Jeremiah knew his only hope was to run. Then again, if he'd only wanted to save himself, he would have started running away a long time ago.

Gritting his teeth, Jeremiah grabbed the shotgun like a club, swung it over his shoulder and then threw it at Benny. The weapon turned through the air and would have caught Benny in the face if he hadn't dropped down even lower to let the shotgun sail over his head.

When Benny straightened up, however, Jeremiah was charging toward him with a crazed look in his eyes.

A pistol barked once.

Lead punched through flesh and a man dropped to the ground.

CHAPTER 30

Jeremiah couldn't stop running, so he found himself at the horse after its rider had already fallen from the saddle. He turned around and saw Natham leaning from between the first and second wagons. The pistol in Natham's hand was still smoking.

"Come on," Natham said. "I need your help if I'm going to get this done."

Barely able to pull in a breath, Jeremiah wheezed, "But I don't even have a gun."

Natham extended an arm and slapped a pistol into Jeremiah's hand. "Here. I took this off one of them others. There's at least four shots left in it. Just cover my back."

Once that was said, Natham turned and pressed himself against the closest wagon. He didn't listen for Jeremiah to agree to the arrangement and didn't question if Jeremiah was capable of seeing the order through. He simply put his faith into another man's hands and got to the task at hand.

As terrified as Jeremiah was, he couldn't think of a way in hell he could do anything but what Natham had asked. The gun he'd been given was a newer model Colt than the one he'd brought with him from his ranch. It was warm in his hand and soon felt like a part of him as he tightened his grip around the handle. When Natham stepped away from the wagon and into the fray, Jeremiah stepped right out there with him.

Jeremiah was forced to take in the scene within a few blinks of an eye. There were two bodies lying sprawled in the dirt nearby. One of them was unfamiliar, so was probably one of the new arrivals; the other was Charlie. It seemed the Englishman had been awakened just in time for his own funeral.

Shots were still being fired, but Jeremiah couldn't see who was firing them. When a bullet whipped past his head, he reflexively looked toward the wagons and saw someone peeking out from behind the back corner. Another man leaned out from behind another wagon to sight along the top of a rifle.

Natham's arm moved in a fluid motion as he raised his gun and took a shot at the rifleman. His bullet sent a shower of splinters from the side of the wagon, which was enough to get the rifleman to pull himself back into cover.

"Toss those guns or I start shooting these women!" Sam shouted.

"You won't be able to shoot any of them before I get to you," Natham replied.

At that moment, Jeremiah realized that Sam had been the one peeking out from behind the second wagon. That was the wagon where he knew Sara and the others were being held. "He can do it, Emmett," he said urgently. "He's right there."

Without taking his eyes from his target, Natham snarled, "Just cover me, damn you. I won't see anyone else hurt."

Jeremiah didn't need to know anything about Emmett Natham or whatever sins he'd committed in his past. The ferocity in Natham's voice when he made that vow was more than enough to convince anyone of his intentions.

Leaning against the wagon so he was facing the area behind Natham, Jeremiah held his gun at the ready. Before he could settle into his spot, he saw a shadow move nearby that wasn't simply jumping because of the flickering campfire. Jeremiah squinted at the shadow and watched it circle around the horses and creep up toward the driver's seat.

As always, Pointer didn't say a word. The Indian hunkered down and rushed toward

Jeremiah with a long knife gripped in his hand. Thanks to the dark hair draped over his face, only Pointer's bared teeth could be seen clearly. By the time Jeremiah could see the Indian's eyes, he was already pulling his trigger.

The pistol bucked against Jeremiah's palm and illuminated Pointer's face in a brief flash of sparks. The Indian kept coming and swung his blade forward and up toward Jeremiah's belly.

Behind Jeremiah, Natham was firing round after round. Bullets scorched the air like a swarm of angry hornets as Natham and Sam exchanged barbed words amid the crackle of gunfire.

As Pointer dove toward him, Jeremiah pulled his trigger again. This time, he knew he hit the Indian because he saw blood spray from the bigger man's arm. But if Pointer even felt the bullet, he gave no indication. He kept coming and lashed out with his knife.

Jeremiah was focused so intently on that blade that he heard it whistle toward him and then shred his shirt as it sliced along his ribs. Pain lanced all the way through his body as a fresh flow of blood warmed his skin. Pulling his trigger out of sheer reflex, Jeremiah sent a shot past Pointer's left ear.

That bullet didn't draw the Indian's blood, but it caused Pointer to move in the opposite direction and give Jeremiah a little room to maneuver.

Even though Jeremiah was fighting for his own life, he could tell that Pointer was simply trying to get through him and to Natham. The Indian was already circling around like a mountain lion that gained speed with every step.

Jeremiah could feel more blood seeping into his shirt and the waistband of his jeans. His racing heart wasn't about to let him falter, so he brought up his arm, pulled in a breath and then pulled his trigger.

Pointer made it to Natham just as Jeremiah's pistol went off. The Indian had already shifted the knife in his grasp so the blade was angled downward. His arm was up by his ear and poised to drive the blade straight into Natham's back when Pointer was knocked to the ground.

Jeremiah's bullet caught the Indian between the shoulder blades and dropped him face-first to the dirt. Jeremiah still couldn't believe he'd stopped the Indian until he rushed over to where Pointer was lying and kicked the knife from his hand. Still straining to get to Natham, Pointer clawed at the ground and let out a strained breath.

When Natham turned around to take a quick look behind him, he found Jeremiah standing with Pointer's right wrist under his boot. "Thanks," Natham said. "Now keep him covered."

Now it was Jeremiah's turn to do some pointing. He aimed his pistol at the Indian's head, which was enough to finally get the bigger man to stop struggling. There wasn't enough wind in Jeremiah's lungs for him to form any words, so he simply nodded and kept the Indian pinned to the ground.

Natham ducked down low and ran away from the wagon. He'd already taken the guns from the closest body, so he ran past that and didn't stop until he got to the tombstone rock at the edge of the camp. Rather than hide behind it, Natham stood up so he could shoot over the rock. He sighted along his barrel, squeezed his trigger and sent a round into the man who had been using the last wagon for cover.

As Art staggered forward, he looked as if he couldn't believe he'd been hit. His eyes were wide and his mouth hung open, but no words came out. Instead, he simply dropped to his knees and flopped forward.

"There goes your crooked lawman," Natham said as he opened his pistol and checked to see how many rounds were left.

"What're you gonna do now, Sam?"

Jeremiah leaned so he could get a clearer look around the wagons. At that moment, he saw Sam step forward from where he'd been hiding. Unfortunately, Sam wasn't alone.

Keeping one arm wrapped around Sara's neck, he took a few steps and then turned to take a quick glance at Jeremiah. "There you are," Sam said. "I knew you couldn't have just fallen from the wagon. That would have been too easy."

Although Jeremiah wanted to raise his gun and take a shot at Sam, it wouldn't have been worth giving Pointer the chance to make a move of his own. A move like that wouldn't have done much good anyway, since Sam had already positioned himself with Sara shielding him from both Jeremiah and Natham.

"I suppose Dave won't be joining us?" Sam asked.

"He's dead," Jeremiah replied.

"You'll be dead too, Sam," Natham snarled, "unless you let that woman go."

Sam shook his head. "She's my angel. She's what's gonna set all this right again. You see, unless you give yourself up and come along with me, this lady dies. And if that don't get to you, I'll kill that blonde. I know you've got a sweet spot for that one."

Natham didn't twitch. When he shook his head, it was so subtle that the movement could barely be seen. "I already tried playing by your rules, Sam. I gave up easily the first time and would have gone along so you could collect your bounty. You had all those men on me and even had me tied up tighter than a Wells Fargo lockbox, but you still wanted more."

Shrugging as he dug his pistol's barrel against Sara's ear, Sam said, "I'll settle for your bounty now, seeing as how much trouble these ranchers turned out to be."

"You think I'm gonna believe you?" Nathan asked. "After what you did to Noelle?"

For a moment, Sam appeared to be confused. Finally, he nodded. "Oh, you mean the old woman? If her husband had told me where his money was stashed sooner, she'd still be alive. Surely, you carried out some business that way at one time or another."

Jeremiah wanted to run at Sam and tear him apart with his bare hands. He wanted to kill that bounty hunter no matter what might happen to himself along the way. It seemed as if Natham sensed this as well, because he showed Jeremiah a quick shake of his head to keep him in check.

If Pointer hadn't been continuing to

squirm on the ground as if he was still ready to fight, Jeremiah might have taken a run at Sam anyway. But, even wounded, the Indian still posed a threat. Jeremiah choked back every instinct inside him and stayed put.

"Let the woman go or I'll shoot you where you stand," Natham said. "I won't say it again."

Sam tightened his grip around Sara's neck, causing her to let out a hacking cough. "You're a devil with a pistol, Natham, but you been tied up too long. Your arms and legs still gotta be wobbly after all that time you were trussed up. Hell, I bet you're still numb in spots."

"Last chance," Natham growled.

But Sam's smile only widened and he shook his head. "You'd have to be at the top of your game to hit me and not this lady. There's no way you're up to full speed."

Natham let out a slow breath and lowered his gun.

"Good," Sam said. "Now step out here where I can see you."

Natham stepped around the rock and squared off so he was directly in front of Sam with less than ten yards between them.

Jeremiah didn't even see Natham bring up his gun. In the time it took for Jeremiah to blink, Natham had bent his elbow and fired.

Sam's head snapped back and both his arms swung outward as he dropped straight back. He hit the dirt with a solid thump, leaving Sara standing in her spot with her eyes locked shut.

Letting out a slow breath as he walked over to Jeremiah, Natham shook his head and grumbled, "He was right. I wasn't quite up to full speed." He then placed his boot against the back of the Indian's neck to keep him in place. "Why don't you go say hello to your wife, Jeremiah? I know she missed you."

Jeremiah couldn't rush to her fast enough. She went to him as best she could considering the ropes around her ankles and let out a joyful cry when she was scooped up into his arms.

The gun smoke was thick in the air, and Jeremiah's ears still rang from all that shooting. At that moment, however, the only thing he could smell was Sara's hair and the only thing he could hear was her whispering his name after the bandanna was pulled away from her mouth.

As much as he wanted to hold on to her, Jeremiah set her down again. "Emmett, do you think you can tend to Sara and the others?"

"Sure, but I thought you'd want the honors."

"I need to take one of these horses for a ride. There's one member of our expedition who's very anxious to join us."

Natham shrugged, put Pointer to sleep with a crack on the head from the butt of his pistol and then picked up the Indian's knife. Before Natham could start cutting the ropes around Sara's wrists, Jeremiah was on one of the horses and racing to the spot where he'd left Claire.

Once Claire was reunited with her mother, the wagons rolled on late into the night and even a ways into early morning. They weren't about to stop until the campsite was long behind them. Even after the flicker of that campfire was nowhere to be seen, the wagons kept rolling.

Jeremiah sat in the driver's seat at the front of the line, with the wagon carrying what remained of their supplies hitched behind him. Not so long ago, it would have seemed like a crying shame to leave those other wagons and all those other things behind in that pile so many miles back. Then again, a lot of things were different not so long ago.

Harold Inglebrecht had had a son and a wife.

Claire Mays was an innocent little girl who was happy to wave at strangers.

Emmett Natham had been nothing more than a good friend.

The more he thought about it, the more Jeremiah realized that not everything was as different as he'd thought.

One thing that did change was the fact that the expedition had picked up another passenger. This passenger, however, would accompany them only until they reached the next town that had a strong jail cell. Despite the messy wound in his shoulder, Pointer still put up a fight all the way; they had to bind his hands and legs in twice the amount of rope that had been used to keep Natham in line. Now that he was wrapped up tighter than a Christmas present, Pointer sat at the wrong end of Harold's rifle with his eyes closed.

"Not so tough now, are you?" Harold whispered. "You and the rest of you bastards will burn in hell for what you did to my family."

Jeremiah looked at the cramped space behind him where Harold and Pointer were wedged in between the seat and supplies.

The old man nodded solemnly and kept his shotgun in a steady hand. "You're the sort who likes to run free, ain't ya? It'll do you some good to stew in a cage for a few years. Or maybe the law'll hang you. Either way is fine with me."

Sara sat next to Jeremiah and was too content to speak. Instead, she simply laid her head on his shoulder and drifted in and out of sleep.

Looking over to the man riding alongside the wagon, Jeremiah asked, "How's Anne and Claire doing?"

Natham looked back and grinned. "That little one's still curled up and sleeping. I don't think Anne minds, though."

"Good. That's real good."

"I suppose this is it, then," Natham said.

Jeremiah frowned and asked, "This is what?"

"Good-bye. Unless you're fixing to become a bounty hunter, there's no reason to keep a man like me around."

"I've still got my own ranch to set up. I've even got a new investor or two. There'll be plenty of work for a capable man like yourself."

Reluctantly, Natham shook his head. "I'll just bring you trouble, Jeremiah. You folks have had more of that than you deserve already."

"It wasn't you who killed Paul and Noelle. It wasn't you who tied us up and dragged us along for this ride. It was them bounty hunters and they're not about to trouble anyone else."

"I've been running from men like Sam Madigan for most of my life," Natham said.

"Then you'll just have to start a new life. Isn't that why we were all headed to Oregon in the first place?"

"Yeah. I suppose it is."

"Take an honest job on my ranch and start over, Emmett. You've earned it."

Natham didn't say anything to that. Instead, he simply looked up at the dim streaks of orange and red spreading from the eastern sky and smiled. Letting out a breath, he nodded and settled back into his saddle.

CHAPTER 31

One year later

The Lazy Eight Ranch was everything Jeremiah had been hoping for when he'd left Wyoming. Of course, back then his intention had been to call it the Lazy Deuce. It was only supposed to be him and Sara along with a few hands running the place and making just enough money to keep their heads above water. Profit had never been his goal, but now that he'd added six to the two for which the ranch was originally named, Jeremiah couldn't help but turn a profit.

It had been a little while since they'd arrived in Oregon, but the house still smelled like freshly cut pine and Jeremiah couldn't help but grin as he walked through it. As always, Harold was in the office, working through the books and balancing the ranch's expenses.

"Supper's in a few minutes," Jeremiah said.

The old man looked to have aged a year for every month that had passed. Still, he smiled a lot more lately, even if those smiles didn't seem to go all the way down to his soul. "I'll be finished by then," he said.

Scents of baking bread, stewing meat and boiling potatoes filled Jeremiah's nose. Anne was a mighty fine cook and she only got happier when there was a full complement of workers that needed to be fed. Jeremiah waved to her as he walked through the kitchen, stepped through the back door and walked onto a porch that slanted a bit to one side.

"Emmett's not back yet?" Sara asked from her seat a bit farther along the porch.

Jeremiah walked over to her and ran his fingertips through her hair. As had become habit, he also reached down to rub the swelling of their first child within her belly. "He's driving the rest of the steers up from Kansas. If he doesn't get here tonight, he should be here tomorrow."

"You don't think that someday he'll just keep riding?"

Jeremiah shook his head. "Why would he want to leave all of this?"

She grinned and placed her hand on top

of his so she could rub a slow circle over her stomach with him. "You're a bit partial where that's concerned."

"Maybe. If he does move on someday, he won't leave us in a lurch."

"That's true." After a little pause, she asked, "Do you think it was all worth it? I mean, being here is great, but we all lost so much. And Harold . . ."

"The eight of us set out to cover some ground between one place and another. We wound up doing plenty more than that. Nothing this good comes for free. We fought for it. Some died for it and now we can sit back and savor it."

"Nothing this good comes for free, huh?" Sara nodded, closed her eyes and leaned back in her chair. "I like that."

Jeremiah straightened up and looked out at his land. From the moment he'd first arrived, that little patch of Oregon felt as if it had been waiting all this time just for them to arrive and fence it off.

Not too far away, Claire ran toward the house for supper. She had a beaming smile on her face and a black mutt nipping at her heels.

Jeremiah filled his lungs with clean Oregon air.

Nothing that good came for free. That was

for certain.

But this hadn't been free. Not by a flush. All eight of them had paid their way by treading a long, bloody trail.

Now they could reap the rewards.

Soon, Jeremiah thought with a sentimental grin, there would be one more.

ABOUT THE AUTHOR

Ralph Compton stood six foot eight without his boots. He worked as a musician, a radio announcer, a songwriter, and a newspaper columnist. His first novel, *The Goodnight Trail,* was a finalist for the Western Writers of American Medicine Pipe Bearer Award for Best Debut Novel. He was also the author of the *Sundown Riders* series and the *Border Empire* series.